AF413413

DISNEY

Tim Burton's
THE NIGHTMARE BEFORE CHRISTMAS

SHADOW OVER THE PUMPKIN QUEEN

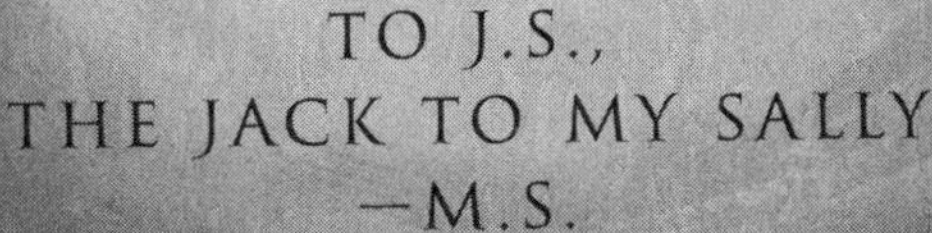

TO J.S.,
THE JACK TO MY SALLY
—M.S.

Random House Books for Young Readers
An imprint of Random House Children's Books
A division of Penguin Random House LLC
1745 Broadway, New York, NY 10019
penguinrandomhouse.com
rhcbooks.com/disney

Designed by Gegham Vardanyan

Library of Congress Cataloging-in-Publication Data is available upon request.
ISBN 978-0-7364-4725-6 (trade)—ISBN 978-0-7364-4726-3 (ebook)

The text of this book is set in 11.5-point Rameau Pro.

Manufactured in the United States of America
1st Printing

The authorized representative in the EU for product safety and compliance is
Penguin Random House Ireland, Morrison Chambers, 32 Nassau Street,
Dublin D02 YH68, Ireland. https://eu-contact.penguin.ie.

DISNEY

TIM BURTON'S
THE NIGHTMARE BEFORE CHRISTMAS

SHADOW OVER THE PUMPKIN QUEEN

MEGAN SHEPHERD

RANDOM HOUSE 🏠 NEW YORK

PROLOGUE

Ghosts & Ghouls
PUMPKIN QUEEN RESETS TIME
AND SAVES HALLOWEEN TOWN

In a harrowing series of events that nearly erased Halloween Town from existence, Pumpkin Queen Sally successfully restored our town's timeline to right where it belongs, perfectly in the present.

The time-bending incident began with an exchange program Queen Sally implemented to strengthen bonds among the holiday realms, with the assistance of Luna Slumberly, a rag doll from Dream Town. A potion mishap during the Halloween Exhibition opened a portal to the previously unknown Time Town—an ancient place that controls the flow of time in each realm.

There, Queen Sally and Luna discovered that Halloween Town's clock—a critical timepiece in the Hall of Time—had been sabotaged. When they returned home, they found a version of Halloween Town's past where the town did not yet exist—then a future where the town had been destroyed. To bring their town back to the present, Sally and Luna sought help across the realms, including in lovely Valentine's Town and the "fabled" Fable Town, home of the fire-wielding dragon Scorch, who joined their quest.

The trio's efforts led them to Tooth Town, where Sally accused the Tooth Fairy of stealing the Foreverglass, a mythical timepiece capable of resetting time. However, a shocking discovery revealed that Scorch himself had broken Halloween Town's clock, under the influence of a shadowy cloaked figure whose identity and motives remain unknown to this day. Scorch explained that, at the time, he was led to believe destroying a town full of monsters would prove him a hero, but he later expressed regret for his actions.

With the Foreverglass secured, Sally restored Halloween Town's timeline. The town's residents, who experienced the disruption as a strange sense of déjà vu, are now recovering. As part of his penance, Scorch was tasked with aiding in the cleanup efforts, which concluded with a community bonfire regularly described as "wonderfully festive."

Fortunately, the shadowy cloaked figure who manipulated Scorch has remained quiet since. There have been no further indications that this culprit is still targeting our town.

While we remain cautious about future threats, the Pumpkin Queen's leadership has once again proven instrumental in uniting the holiday realms and safeguarding Halloween Town. Long may she reign!

1

"Order, everyone! Order, please!" The Mayor bangs his gavel on the big oak table in Town Hall's council chamber, rattling the trophies and treasures on the shelves. The Mirror of Reverie—a gift from Fable Town's Lady Lore to Jack and me for our anniversary—knocks into a stack of spell books. A plaque that reads SCARIEST SHRIEK AWARD clatters to the floor, but the Mayor is too distracted to notice. "We have no time for pleasantries. This is a crisis!"

The tall witch takes an extra-long sip of squid ink tea. "Is it?" she chirps. "That's what you said about the time the candy corn shipment arrived a day late, too."

"This goes far beyond confections, I'm afraid." The Mayor, his face firmly turned to its ghost-white side, grimaces. He sinks into his chair with a groan. "Halloween as we know it is in grave danger!"

Out of the corner of my eye, I trade looks with Jack, seated at the opposite end of the table, and try to tame the smile tickling the stitched corners of my mouth. As rulers of Halloween Town, we take our holiday's future as seriously as we take vine borer bugs in the pumpkin patch. If I'm being honest, however, the Mayor *does* tend to get carried away with potential disasters.

"And what is this grave threat, Mayor?" Jack asks, drumming his long fingers on the table.

The Mayor throws his hands in the air and wails, *"Ladybugs!"*

The Wolfman rolls his amber eyes toward the ceiling with a groan that slides into a growl. The tall witch takes an exaggerated slurp of her tea, lips smacking with smug satisfaction. Jack sighs and props his sharp elbows on the table, rubbing the ridges of his brow.

"And what have these insects done?" Jack says, his patience pulling thin.

A few drops of rain plink against the window. Outside, dark clouds have rolled in to smother the midday sun, and I find myself absently tugging on a loose thread on my wrist that, lately, always seems in need of tightening no matter how often I pull it taut.

"Not the *insects*." The Mayor's voice is muffled by his hands clasped to his face. "The *costumes*. You all witnessed it too in last year's Halloween. Children dressed up as ladybugs. Fairies. Firefighters. *Bunnies!*"

"Ugh." The tall witch gags on the distasteful mental image. "How disgustingly adorable."

"And better suited for Easter, not Halloween!" cries the Wolfman.

"Precisely the problem!" The Mayor finally notices the fallen award and picks it up, brushing it off tenderly before replacing it on the shelf with the other best-fright awards. "Halloween used to be *scary*. Now, it's all about being cute. Silly. *Funny.* Last Halloween, I didn't see a single witch the entire night, except for our own!" He throws a hand in the tall witch's direction.

I drag my attention from the budding storm outside, tilting my head at an angle, considering this. "Is that such a grave problem? Nothing remains the same forever—people grow. Change always happens. Does it really threaten Halloween if children dress in cute costumes?"

All four faces—Jack's included—turn to me in horror. As one, the committee members shout, *"YES!"*

I blink my long lashes, tugging on my loose wrist thread, taking in their solemn stares.

For a few years now, I've served as Pumpkin Queen, ruling alongside Jack, striving to make the best decisions for our town and holiday. Halloween Town might not be my birthplace, but this is where my heart will forever reside. Jack is here. Zero. The Mayor. Lock, Shock, and Barrel, and so many other dear friends, including our most recent addition: Scorch. This monstrous town has become my home in every way that matters. I'm as rooted here as the elms.

And, most importantly, I've unearthed something I didn't know I had—my own inner scary self. Not the kind that screams, but the kind that creeps in on spiders' feet. The kind that doesn't need to raise its voice to be heard. The kind that *whispers.*

However, in moments like this, I'm met with a stark reminder that Halloween Town was not my first home. It's simple, really—I can't change the past. I'm a rag doll from Dream Town, daughter to Governors Albert and Greta. And as much as I love my adopted home with the ferocity of a blood-starved vampire, I still have more to learn.

I sigh. "I guess you have to be from here to truly understand."

"Nonsense!" Jack lays a hand on my shoulder, giving a bolstering squeeze. "Why, even the ghosts who have lived here longer than anyone have their own opinions on what makes up the true heart of Halloween. I'm glad you're questioning things. Keeps us on our toes! To me, it isn't about costumes. Or even candy! It's about *scares*. Without frights, Halloween is merely a twilight costume parade with an excellent candy buffet."

"Yes, I see that now." I rest my hands on the table, feeling the worn grooves beneath my cloth fingers like the etchings of an old map, tying me here, tying me to Jack and everything I'm fighting to protect. I sit up straighter, chin lifted. "So how do we make certain the world doesn't forget the heart of Halloween?"

The committee members bob their heads in thought, *hmm*ing and *aaahh*ing as they consider the predicament. The Wolfman scratches at his arm in a way that goes beyond deep thought—I think the poor fellow has fleas.

The tall witch stands up, tenting her gnarled fingers. "I propose a monster public relations campaign. Posters on every telephone pole!"

"No, no, that's far too tame," the Wolfman scoffs. "What about a frightening neighborhood watch? We'll patrol the streets in the lead-up to Halloween and smash any jack-o'-lanterns that don't make children quake in their sneakers!"

"All good ideas." The Mayor's head spins sharply back to his jovial pink face as he strokes his hefty chin. "But is it enough? We need something that no one has ever seen. Oh, if only Dr. Finkelstein were still at work in his laboratory—he could spark to life something truly terrifying! How long has he been banished to Dream Town for, now? Surely he's done his penance. What if we let him back into town?"

An invisible hand tightens around my throat, the stuffing inside closing up my windpipe. Jack must see the color leach from my fabric skin, because he pushes to his feet, pounding a bony fist on the table.

"Absolutely not! That egghead in a lab coat kidnapped Sally. He has over nine decades of community service left until he can call himself a Halloween Town resident again." Jack's eye sockets narrow into slits, the look he reserves for the field rats when they gnaw holes in the pumpkins.

"Agreed." I stand up opposite Jack, fighting to keep my voice firm with a queen's confidence, not a stolen little girl's. "There's no place for Dr. Finkelstein here. He was so quick to take me from my home that the last thing he deserves is his own."

"Sally, dear, of course," the Mayor purrs in a

rush, his warmer side swiveling to face me. "It was strictly a practical suggestion. No one is implying Dr. Finkelstein should be pardoned for his crimes, only that his irrefutable talents are wasted among lavender fields and pillow forts." He raises his eyebrows like question marks.

"No," I assert in a steady voice that leaves no room for debate.

We sit again, though Jack's gaze lingers on me from across the table, a twinkle in the dark caverns of his eyes. In a moment just between us, he winks. My heart pulls tight with the same deep love as when he first called me his queen.

The others continue to propose ideas, but their voices fade beneath the growing barrage of rain at the windows. As I gaze at the gray clouds outside, my mind rewinds back to those days I spent trapped in Dr. Finkelstein's cold stone house. Polishing the scalpels in his laboratory. Dusting cobwebs from his spare body part collection. Looking out the barred window at a town I so desperately wanted to be a part of–

My ears catch on something the witch says, pulling me from my thoughts, and I jerk upright like a marionette. "Sorry–what did you just say?"

"The Night Mare," the witch repeats, stirring her tea with one long warty finger. "Talk about having children quaking in their sneakers—that would make them run right out of their flip-flops!"

"I've heard of that before." It tickles some deep fold of my brain, reawakens a memory of traveling through a fairy-tale forest into a mysterious village with Luna and Scorch, seeing the statue of a ferocious black horse. "There's a statue of the Night Mare in Fable Town's Villain Village."

She nods, tapping her black fingernail on the teacup rim. "Long ago, before you came to Halloween Town, Cyclops claimed to have seen the horse with his own eye. Late one night while he was baking bat-wing cookies in the Cobweb Café. Said it looked a terror, yet he felt a strange sense of peace around it. Could feel its ancient magic." She dries her fingernail on her shirt sleeve, nodding sagely. "*Night Magic*—the strongest there is."

Goose bumps prickle up and down the fabric of my arms, and I fold them across my chest, hugging myself, instinctively protecting myself from a feeling that I can't put a name to but evokes both wonder and fear at once.

"Eh, the Night Mare is a myth." The Wolfman scratches his curved claws over tiny pink fleabites on his neck. "A story they tell pups to get them to settle down at night in their den. You know Cyclops. That one eye of his misses a lot." He raises a claw in the air. "But *nightmares*, now that could be something. Not the horse, but the dreams. If we could partner with Dream Town to increase the frequency of children's nightmares, we could restore terror!"

The Wolfman throws out his hairy fist in a sign of strength, but he accidentally knocks into the shelves. The Mirror of Reverie tumbles down.

I dive forward, catching it just in time. "Whew."

As the others debate, I sink back into my chair, cradling the mirror in my lap, its weight tethering me to the here and now, though my mind wants to be a million places at once.

I gaze into the mirror at the reflection of my big doll eyes—and feel transported.

Back when I first became Pumpkin Queen, I was a girl made of thread and stuffing, shy and unsure of myself, full of starry-eyed love for Jack. I was afraid I'd never stack up against the Pumpkin King in the townspeople's eyes. That I'd always have an eyelash out of place. A broken stitch. An awkward lump of stuffing. Even well into my tenure as queen, I still wondered: Would I fit in? Make the town proud? Rule as well as the other town leaders, like Santa Claus and Ruby Valentino, and even my own parents, Greta and Albert?

Now, I feel as if I've lived lifetimes since I was that timid girl marrying Jack atop Spiral Hill. I've traveled to wondrously new realms: towns where the rivers flow with melted chocolate and forests with sly foxes offering pie. I've even seen the ocean in all its beautiful, terrifying vastness.

And I've been tested.

I shiver to think of the mysterious figure who tried to sabotage Halloween Town. I saw a glimpse of our town's future destruction in this very mirror. Since then, this villain, whom Scorch calls the prince, hasn't shown so much as his shadow, but I can't shake the dark clouds that seem to hang over me.

Waiting. Worrying.

The air crackles at the edges of my vision, the council room warming as though a fire is roaring away in the cold, empty hearth. Rain pounds harder at the window, and a chill creeps over my ankles.

Spider feet crawl up the back of my neck as I gaze deeper into the mirror, trancelike. I haven't said the incantation to trigger its magic. Yet, as the other committee members debate around me, my reflection begins to stretch and shift like a fun house mirror, rippling until dark clouds crush in at the mirror's edges.

And . . . I'm suddenly gone. My reflection is now

replaced by a shadow-drenched specter of myself. Everything around me is coal dark. I can't see more than a few inches. Can't breathe. I don't know if I'm seeing a waking nightmare or a vision of the future or a slip of a memory. A whimper escapes my lips. My heart thrashes behind my ribs. I'm trapped in complete dark. Closed in. Claustrophobia burning through my veins until it erupts in a scream . . .

A shriek snakes out of my throat, and the mirror's silver handle slips from my grasp. I'm back in Town Hall. Not trapped at all. Before I can grab it, the Mirror of Reverie hits the sharp table corner.

The clatter of broken glass rings against my cloth ears.

"The mirror!" The witch gives a garbled gasp. The Mayor's face spins like a top. Jack jumps up, striding to my side, more concerned for me than the priceless treasure.

"Dear Sally," he says, "did you cut yourself?"

I shake my head numbly, dropping to my knees to cradle the precious artifact in the basket of my arms, but it's too late. A broken shard the size of my palm rests on the pumpkin-orange rug.

"I'm okay," I whisper, my voice sounding distant. "But the mirror is broken."

Jack helps me to my feet, cupping his smooth

palm around my pale cheek. "Why, I'm sure it can be mended. Out of dozens of realms, someone must know a good glassworker."

I gaze up at him, wanting to trust in the easy confidence in his smile. I wish my worst worry was a mirror in need of mending. Or a holiday that's grown too tame. But I can't shake the feeling that, somewhere beyond the borders of my town, something far more fragile than glass has shattered.

"Zero! Here, boy!"

As Jack and I walk home from the committee meeting, Jack calls Zero, who zips over from the town fountain to follow at our heels. We're headed for Spiral Hill, where we hold our weekly sword fighting practices. The morning's storm has come and gone, and it's brighter than normal outside, though something about the sickly-yellow sky makes the threads in my stomach curl. I'm left with an eerie feeling that the storm is only hiding behind the horizon, wolflike, waiting to jump back out with a growl.

With Zero trailing behind, we follow the cobblestone path through the pumpkin patch, where the creaky gates let out near an abandoned hospital, its stone walls now covered with heavy curtains of ivy. Old, dark burn marks lick along the western windows.

For most of my life, I was locked away in Dr. Finkelstein's cold laboratory. Separated from my town. Kept in the dark about my own neighbors, so even years after becoming Pumpkin Queen, I'm constantly still discovering things about my home.

I slide my hand into Jack's, smiling up at him, hoping to banish the warning tickle that crawls across my nape. "How did that old hospital burn, Jack?"

He gazes at the building wistfully. "For many years, it held a portal to another world in a basement closet. Oh, you should have seen the fun we had popping out at unsuspecting victims on their city streets! Talk about a fright!" He chuckles fondly, then sighs. "It was Oogie Boogie's doing. He tried to bring an electric pinball machine back through the portal. The thing shorted out and caused the fire. It burned the closet door. Most of the hospital, too. The portal broke."

My eyes sink to a long-forgotten croquet mallet in the front yard. "What about everyone who lived here?"

Jack tightens his stiff fingers around mine, looking thoughtful. "Oh, they're still here and there. After the fire, most of the hospital's ghosts resettled in the cemetery. Some of the others moved to the outskirts of town. In Recluse Woods. That's where the original Halloween settlement was, before our current town was built. There's still a handful of townspeople out there, you know. Wanderers. Outliers. Loners. By their own choice, I should note—I've invited them to town meetings, but they prefer their solitude."

The morose notes of the town band filter through the air, and when we turn the corner, we nod to the bandleader and his friends.

"Perfectly bone-tingling, boys," Jack says. "But you should be playing in town, not way out here, where your music is lost to the shadows."

The bandleader pauses his playing to chuckle. "Lost? Nothing's ever lost, Jack. There are echoes from every note ever played. You just have to close your eyes and listen." To prove his point, he pumps out a long wail on his saxophone that reverberates against the trees.

I reach into my pocket for a coin, rummaging through my spare needle and thread. The broken shard of the Mirror of Reverie presses into my fingertip, reminding me of my vision, and I quickly grab a coin instead.

I toss it into the bandleader's crooked hat on the sidewalk. The music slowly fades away behind us as we near the cemetery gates, which Jack swings open for me with a deep bow of his beanpole spine.

"After you, my patchwork princess."

I giggle behind my linen fingers as I bow back to him, tipping my head like a courtly maiden, and then watch as he reaches deep inside Zero's doghouse coffin and pulls out a hefty double-sided sword.

He admires his reflection briefly in the gleaming blade, and I know he's thinking back to that night a few months ago, when we were scavenging in Oogie Boogie's old lair for spare parts to fix the town's gate and Jack pried the sword free from the rusted-out wreckage. The pit was gray and still, so different from the kaleidoscope of neon colors it had been when Oogie Boogie lived there. The sword was one of many wielded by Oogie Boogie's playing card kings, part of his twisted oversized roulette wheel. Jack brought the blade home, polished its surface, and mended the nicks in the edge. It's been his weapon of choice ever since.

His long legs carry him to the top of Spiral Hill in

only three steps, where he swings his sword in slow, controlled circles, warming up.

I curl my fingers around the spare needle in my pocket, already speaking the enlargement spell's words as I pull it out. *"Expandere."*

The needle grows to be as long as my arm, the base the perfect thickness to fit comfortably in my palm. I twirl the sword in small arcs to warm up my wrists. The stuffing in my chest rustles, tickling me with excitement and anticipation.

We began sword fighting lessons after I discovered I could enlarge my needle into a weapon that could help defend Halloween Town. Since then, every Friday afternoon, we've sparred here on Spiral Hill, and my needle-sword has gone from feeling awkward in my hand to feeling like an extension of my will—sharp and deadly.

Jack rolls his shoulders, gripping the double-sided sword with both hands, testing its heft. His eye sockets gleam as he meets my gaze, a playful smirk tugging at his jaw.

I take my position opposite him, squaring my stance against the curving earth beneath my feet, holding the needle-sword at my side.

I toss him a wink.

"En garde!" I raise my sword for a jab to Jack's side, but he pivots and deflects my blade with an easy side swing, spinning back around with a flourish of his coattails. Before I can return to my stance, he taps the flat of his sword against my exposed back.

"Careful," he points out. "You left your back wide open."

I grin as I slash my needle-sword straight through his rib cage, now that he's close enough. "Maybe I was baiting you."

He gasps, theatrically clutching his chest, but then grins and steps backward to free himself from my blade. "You're getting faster, Sally. Bravo! But let's test those reflexes."

He lunges forward with a heavy diagonal strike, and my breath leaps to my throat as I raise my needle-sword to block, bracing myself with a wider stance. I catch his strike in a crouch and push off, thrusting our swords back his way, putting him on the defensive now.

"Good, good." His eye sockets are aglow with adrenaline. "I'll have to stop going easy on you."

I spin my grip on the sword as I scoff, "*You* go easy on *me*? We'll see about that!"

I circle him until I'm at the top of the hill, then use

the momentum of descending to push him backward, capturing the higher ground. I slice at his exposed side, but he dodges just shy of connecting. He doesn't give me even a moment to catch my breath before he lunges straight toward me, aiming high. I feel the kiss of the blade along my cheek, slicing off a single strand of long crimson hair.

I duck out of the way, reaching for the seams on my right shoulder as I tuck myself into a roll. I tug until the thread snaps, the whirl of movement hiding my actions from him, and then pop up behind him.

"Ah, there you are!" His voice dances as he twists toward me. He raises his sword for a swing, but his eye sockets tilt downward in surprise when he sees that my right arm is detached.

Before he can look for it, it creeps along behind him on its fingertips, grabs his anklebone, and tugs him swiftly and surely off balance.

With a garbled cry, he clatters over backward, dry bones clanking, landing squarely on his sharp seat bones at the base of Spiral Hill. His mouth parts in surprise as I press the tip of my needle-sword against the center of his skull.

"Still think you were going easy on me?" I ask, raising an eyebrow.

His bottomless black eyes crinkle, his jaw shifting into a dazzling smile. "Well played, Sally!"

I give a mock bow as my detached arm crawls over to me, tapping my leg to get my attention. I use the spell to shrink my needle back to normal size, then take a seat next to Jack at the base of Spiral Hill and pull out my thread to reattach my arm.

"Excellent progress," Jack congratulates me. "Soon you'll be ready to take on the Creature Under the Stairs himself–Halloween Town's most accomplished swordsman! When he wakes up from hibernation, that is."

I stitch my shoulder seam, and the bubbly feeling of triumph melts away as I gaze at the murky sun, remembering the morning's storm clouds. Moodily, I murmur, "It isn't Creature I worry about."

Jack follows my gaze to the remnants of dark clouds on the horizon, and his own smile falters. "You know, Sally, it's been quite some time with no sighting of this mysterious prince Scorch dealt with, who gave us such trouble last year. None of our searching or inquiring has amounted to anything. I'm starting to think Scorch might have mistaken what he saw in Time Town. Perhaps it was a trickster from Villain Village playing a joke on him."

I knot the thread and snap it, testing out my

newly mended shoulder by rolling it a few times. The joint moves fine, but the heaviness in my chest doesn't ease under Jack's assurance.

Jack rests his hand over mine, quieting my fidgeting. "We're the rulers of this town, Sally. We'll keep it safe. Together." A crow caws sharply, the sound bouncing off the gravestones, and Jack squeezes my hand.

He sighs. "And now, I'm afraid I must meet the vampires to tell them that they need to keep the midnight partying down—we keep getting complaints from the night-sleeping residents. Won't you come with me?"

He stands and helps me to my feet, and I run my palm over my mended shoulder seam, rubbing away the last soreness. "I'll meet you in town later—I want to deliver some flea potion to the Wolfman. Did you see him this morning? He'll scratch himself raw."

Jack nods, returning his sword to its hiding place in Zero's mausoleum. "Take Zero with you. He could use the exercise."

"Happily." I run my hand over the ghost dog's wispy-soft back.

The wind stirs, sending a shiver through the fallen leaves and casting long shadows across the graveyard, as we pull the heavy gate shut behind us.

The cobblestone path from Spiral Hill turns to dirt as Zero and I head beyond the cornfields into the barren landscape surrounding Lock, Shock, and Barrel's tree house. Ahead, spindly pines rise like needles on the horizon, but well before the tree line begins, a cozy cabin tucked between two spiral-topped hills pumps out a line of smoke from its chimney.

The Wolfman's house.

I thrust my hands into my pockets, running my finger over the jagged Mirror of Reverie shard, trying to tame the premonition prickling at my chest.

I knock on the door.

A gust of wind comes from the forest, skittering fallen leaves, and a shiver runs up my spine. I peer over my shoulder at the tree line. I can't help being curious about the people who call Recluse Woods their home. Are they lonely with only the trees for company? Do they ever stand on the edge of town, gazing at our parties as I once did, wishing they could join?

"Wolfman?" I cup my hands around my mouth to call through the door. "It's Sally. I've brought something to help with your itching. It's wild thyme and—"

My knee bumps against the door, which creaks open.

Zero and I trade curious looks—the Wolfman never leaves his door unlocked, on account of the squirrels determined to nest in his sofa cushions.

From inside come the sound of boiling water and the earthy scent of onion and sage. As the door swings open, I take in a fireplace stacked with freshly cut wood and a spick-and-span kitchen with a soup pot on the stove.

But . . . there's no one here.

My voice hitches as I call, "Wolfman?"

Zero whimpers, long ears raised and at attention. We enter cautiously. Zero sniffs around the living room while I go to the kitchen, where I peer inside the pot of bubbling stew.

It's boiled over, spilling broth everywhere.

I switch off the stove burner and frown as I muse aloud, "He wouldn't go anywhere and leave the stove on."

The leaves in my chest shift, poking and itching at me in a way that feels uncomfortably familiar.

Zero lets out a low warning growl as he noses around the Wolfman's welcome mat.

A chill takes hold of my cloth arms, and I hug

them around my patchwork dress, sliding a worried look out the window. "What is it, Zero? What did you find?"

I crouch next to where he's sniffing the mat. In the soft orange light coming from his nose, something on the floor glimmers.

With a trembling hand, I pick up three thumbnail-sized objects.

They're the size and shape of fat raindrops . . . but they're made of iron, heavy and cold in my palm, as if they're made to bruise, not dampen.

A sudden gust of wind blows through the open door, carrying the smell of a distant storm, and as the dry husks of leaves rustle against my ankles, my throat goes dry as sandpaper.

"Zero, we need to tell Jack about this," I murmur. "Now."

As I run back toward town, the wind threads through my hair, whipping the strands around my neck like scratchy dried snake skins. The skull-and-crossbones weather vane perched on the Haunted Bed and Breakfast spins out of control, as if the wind can't make up its mind. I've never seen a storm like this, one that comes from all directions at once.

Squeezing the iron raindrops in my fist, I check the vampire house, but their coffins are sealed tight, and there's no sign that Jack has been there. He isn't at our house, either. Nor is he anywhere else I look: the pumpkin patch, the Cobweb Café, Town Hall . . .

"Jack?" I cry, running through the town square, where Mummy Boy and Corpse Kid are kicking a jack-o'-lantern back and forth. A few raindrops fall on my scalp, cold and heavy. "Has anyone seen Jack?"

"He was looking for you." Corpse Kid gives the pumpkin a solid kick toward an overturned crate serving as a goal. "Saw him headed up there."

Mummy Boy jerks a bandaged thumb toward Dr. Finkelstein's former house, towering on a hill over town.

"Thank you, boys." My heart squeezes erratically as I climb the path up the hill, the rain falling harder now, soaking into my fabric skin. It isn't long before I crest the top, and the warm glow of candlelight spills out of the basement windows of Dr. Finkelstein's former house.

I pause, taking a moment to reassure my anxious mind. *Everything is okay—I'm sure of it.* As I blink up at the building, it's hard to believe the basement was once a spotless, sterile morgue. Since Scorch moved in, the basement has been full of quaint dragon signs instead: Platter-sized pawprints. Shiny shed scales. A few sneaky bites missing from the roast turkey in the icebox.

Through the cobweb-covered windows, I spot Scorch now curled on a rug by the fireplace, snoring softly. Luna's favorite book of bedtime stories rests beside him, waiting for her next visit.

Warmth spreads from my cotton heart at the sight. I'm thrilled that he has a home now—here, with us.

As I open the creaky front door, I brush my fingers against the words carved into the wood: *Hemlock Hall*.

Last Christmas, after we tore open spiderweb-wrapped presents and clinked mugs of toadstool nog while Zero gnawed on his new jackalope bone, Jack brought me to this very doorstep. He pressed his smooth alabaster hands over my eyes.

"I have one more present for you, Sally." His familiar voice poured into my ear like a melody. "You do so much for this town. We all wanted to do something for you. This building? It isn't Dr. Finkelstein's laboratory anymore. It's yours now. You've swept out the grave dirt. Brightened the lanterns. Planted hemlocks over the bog. Made it entirely your own—and so it needs a new name, don't you think?"

When he took away his hands, I gasped at the carefully carved letters, each lovingly etched with hemlock-leaf flourishes in Jack's elegant handwriting.

"Oh, Jack," I whispered. "A new start . . . Thank you."

Now, I climb the steps to my workroom on Dr. Finkelstein's—*no*, Hemlock Hall's—upper level.

"Jack?" I call, my voice strained and high.

There's a clatter of pots and pans, and then Jack appears at the laboratory door, his skull even paler than usual, his bones set tense and on edge. But they soften when he sees me.

"Sally! I went to the vampires' crypt, pulled all the curtains closed, and knocked on their coffins. Empty—all of them! All four of them are gone. I've looked everywhere. I asked around town—no one has seen wing nor whiff of them since last night."

The stuffing in my palms turns numb. A shiver creeps up my spine, each stitch pulling taut against a growing chill.

"Jack," I say in a trembling voice. "The Wolfman is missing, too. That's what I came to tell you. And look. I found these."

I unfold my fingers to show the strange iron raindrops.

A silence falls between us, broken only by the creak of wind high in the rafters. Jack takes one of the metal raindrops between his thin fingers, squinting and scrutinizing it in the gloomy light from the window. "What's this?"

"I don't know," I whisper, clasping my hands tightly against the chill threading through my seams. The wind shifts, rattling the ceiling joists harder, and I can't shake the growing feeling that something is out there, trying to wrestle its way inside.

A gentle voice rumbles behind me. "Scorch knows."

Jack and I both spin toward the door, where Scorch fills the threshold with his stocky, scaly build, his wings folded tense and tight at his sides. His massive curved claws tap anxiously against the floor, carving grooves into the wooden boards.

I swallow down a lump of stuffing. "Scorch? You—you know what these raindrops are?"

The dragon plucks anxiously at his tattered blue scarf with one paw as his eyes dart nervously toward the high windows. There, the rain paints a murky film over the glass, blurring the world outside until the trees twist into clawing shadows.

He draws a deep breath through his ruffled nostrils, shifting his weight as the floorboards creak below him. "Scorch has seen this before. The metal rain. The wind that doesn't know where to go. It's *him*. The prince. He summoned a similar storm when he first came to Scorch. Made Scorch lose his way in Villain Forest."

Jack tilts his head, eyes narrowed toward the windows. "You're saying this prince—whoever he is—can control the weather?"

Scorch's eyes dart to the windows, then back to Jack. "Not the weather. It's . . . it's like darkness follows him. Storm clouds roll off the edge of his cloak like he's dragging them behind him. Sometimes he makes them swirl around him."

I step forward, slipping my hand into Jack's, needing the grounding certainty of his unyielding bones. I think back on how there were no footprints at the Wolfman's house. No signs of a struggle. "If the prince could make storm clouds swirl, do you think he could make them carry someone away, lift them right into the air?"

Scorch considers this but shakes his head. "Scorch does not think so, or else the prince would not have needed Scorch to knock over the Halloween Clock in Time Town." He sighs deeply, his claws fidgeting with the frayed edge of his scarf. "Scorch thought the prince was gone for good. At least, Scorch had hoped so."

I whirl to Jack, my heart leaping into my throat, tugging so hard at the loose thread on my wrist that the ache spreads all the way to my chest. "I knew it,

Jack. That it was only a matter of time before we heard from the prince again. He's come back to finish what he started when he tried to sabotage our holiday clock—and if he's stealing away people without a trace, then he's grown a lot stronger!"

Jack's expression darkens. "Scorch, gather the townspeople. It appears our enemies aren't finished with us yet."

"Order, order, please!"

I bang my wooden gavel on the podium to no avail. Town Hall is packed to the gills, standing room only, every seat taken as people shuffle to make room for one another. Mr. Hyde sandwiches himself between hulking Behemoth and the Clown with the Tear-Away Face, who giggles nervously with every thunderclap outside. The graveyard ghosts perch on the windowsills. The Mummy family takes up the full front row. And *no one* is listening to me.

"Order—" I start again but am immediately interrupted.

"Sally!"

Two figures in the back wave frantically to get

my attention, looking completely out of place in their crisp silk pajamas, with nary a claw, hoof, or horn between them—only fabric and yarn, like me.

"Mom! Dad!" I abandon the podium as my parents hurry down the center aisle, meeting them on the stairs that lead up to the stage. "You were able to make it!"

Greta, my mom, pulls me into a hug so tight that it seems she might never let go. "We dropped everything when we received your delivery crow's message. If Halloween Town is in trouble, we'll be the first ones to come to its aid."

My dad, Albert, beams at me from behind his salt-and-pepper beard, though his eyes waver with worry. "Of course we came, moonbeam. You're our daughter."

Albert and Greta may not live in Halloween Town, but ever since their daughter became Pumpkin Queen, they've taken a keen interest in its future. Sure, there was a time when they begged me to give up my crown and take over leadership of Dream Town, but they ultimately accepted my decision to stay in my adopted town. And ever since then? They've been nothing but supportive, traveling to Halloween Town at the snap of a finger if I so much as hint at a thorny issue, falling over themselves to offer advice, showing up with warm milk and cookies, reorganizing my entire potion shelf "just to help."

Finally, my mother pulls back. "This is just awful. Is it true, what your summons said? People have gone missing from Halloween Town, and you suspect a foreign ruler?"

My father echoes her sentiments with a furrowed brow. "Why would anyone want to harm Halloween Town? Tell us everything, and I'm sure your mother and I can help sort this out. We've been solving town problems for fifty years. Why, when the Sandman was threatening to send everyone to sleep . . ."

As he launches into the familiar tale, I spy another rag doll over his shoulder, standing near the back with Scorch, scratching the base of the dragon's horns where she knows he likes best.

"You brought Luna with you?" My voice rises to a high pitch, my lips pursing tightly, eyebrows knitting together in concern. With people going missing, Halloween Town is the last place I'd want her to be. "Were her parents all right with that?"

"They're in Fable Town for an extended research project, collecting oral folk tales from deep-wood foxes. They're completely off the grid. They entrusted us with her care as she apprentices to be Dream Town's governor." My mother looks toward Luna with adoring eyes. "We've been keeping a close eye on her, keeping her safe and sound—but it's hardly a bother. Luna is nothing if not sensible."

"She really is," my father chimes in, his tone warm. "She's thoughtful. Thorough. You wouldn't believe how much her confidence has grown. She came up with a brilliant new slogan for our curfew campaign. *The safest way to keep nightmares away is to snuggle up in bed till the break of day.* Nighttime incidents are down fifty percent!"

They both look at Luna like she's a lantern in the dark. And maybe she is. Still, something about their praise stokes a hot, tight sting beneath my seams, and I force my stitched-on smile to remain in place.

Luna catches my eye and gives me a big full-hearted wave. I wave back. Sincerely. It's not her fault she's turned out to be the perfect leader my parents have always wanted . . . I didn't even *want* to be Dream Town Governor. I wholeheartedly recommended her for the role.

Still, I can't help twitching.

Jack reads my stiffened posture like tea leaves, because he immediately sweeps to my rescue with a hearty handshake for my parents. "Greta. Albert. It's always a joy to see you, even on such a troubling eve. Won't you take your seats?"

"Oh, we thought we'd help you and Sally with the announcement, here on stage," my mom begins, blinking her fishhook lashes in perfect willingness to help.

"A generous offer!" Jack lays his hands around my parents' shoulders, smoothly guiding them toward the steps. "But then who would keep those rascals Lock, Shock, and Barrel in order? We need your firm but gentle hand with them before they set off a smoke bomb in the middle of the assembly."

He squeezes a wink at me over his shoulder. I beam back at him, loving and grateful.

Alone, I spare a moment to take in the room, feeling the fearful energy hopping through the crowd like a plague of locusts. *You can do this*, I tell myself. *You're the Pumpkin Queen.* I take a deep breath before returning to the podium and pounding with the gavel. "Please, everyone! If you'll take your seats—time is of the essence! Jack? A little help?"

Jack extricates himself from my parents, who are peppering him with more unsolicited advice, and climbs up beside me. He grips both sides of the podium in his bony claws and gives a roar so powerful that it blows Shock's witch hat clean off and sends all the rafter bats scrambling.

"QUIEEEEET!"

The room falls so silent under his bellow that I can hear Cyclops's eye blink.

Satisfied, Jack straightens and adjusts his bat bow tie. "The floor is yours, my dear."

As the audience blinks up at me with nervous, expectant faces, I tuck a strand of stick-straight hair behind my ear and feel my cheeks warm. My chest feels tight, like the weight of every soul in this room is pressing down on my ribs, crushing my lungs, stilling my breath. But beneath the pressure, my cloth heart continues to beat steadily—encouraged by my love for each curious creature—driving me to stand tall no matter how much I want to crumple.

I clear the cobwebs from my throat. "I'm sorry we had to gather you all on such short notice. I know you have questions. Jack and I want to answer as many of those today as we can."

"I heard the Wolfman is missing!" the short witch croaks, clutching her cape.

"And no one's seen the vampires, either," the tall witch adds, raising a crooked finger in the air.

Jack leans into the microphone. "The rumors are true, I'm afraid. The Wolfman and the vampires are missing. Our efforts to locate them have failed." He loosens his shirt collar. "We have reason to believe they were abducted."

A chorus of gasps tears through the crowd.

Lock, Shock, and Barrel shoot to their feet in the front row. Lock raises his fists for a fight like the devil he's disguised as. He demands, "*Who* took them?"

Shock raises her witch mask to give a snarl. "*Where* did they take them?"

"*How soon* can we pummel this baddie black and blue?" Barrel pipes up.

I bang the gavel three more times. "Please, everyone! I know you are rightly concerned, but let us explain. When Halloween Town's timeline was mixed up, many of you helped bring our town back to its proper time, but we never fully explained the reason it was thrown into the past and the future."

Dozens of unblinking eyes swallow me up, and for a brief moment, I want to shrink into my boots. Sensing my worry, Jack leans in to speak—but I stop him with a hand over the microphone.

"It's okay," I whisper. "It was my decision not to say anything at the time. I owe them the truth now."

He straightens, giving me the podium.

I lift my chin and announce into the microphone, "The truth is, it was no mistaken spell. Someone—a ruler whose identity is unknown—sabotaged us with the intention of destroying Halloween Town. Once we set time back to the present, we carefully prepared for his return, but he appeared to have vanished. However, given these new disappearances, Jack and I have reason to believe he might be back."

A low murmur ripples through the crowd—sharp whispers, furrowed brows, a few crossed arms.

The Undersea Gal moans, "So you knew all along and didn't tell us?"

"We would have brought this to your attention sooner," I insist, "but Jack and I wanted to try to handle things ourselves first. There was no reason to spread fear until we had more information."

A small voice from the back rings out, clear and bright, "What can you tell us about the mystery ruler? That's what truly matters now—how to get the missing people back."

All eyes turn to Luna in the back row, whose black yarn hair is combed and straight, the red patches on her cheeks freshly washed. A different type of murmur spreads through the crowd as the debate shifts away from the fact that I chose to hide this information and toward solving it.

I give a soft nod in Luna's direction to thank her.

I take a deep breath and announce, "Some time

ago, a cloaked figure known only as 'the prince' manipulated Scorch into breaking the Halloween Clock. This wasn't just some trick-or-treat prank. The prince preyed on Scorch's insecurity of being a kindly, gentle dragon in a realm of villains. He told Scorch that if he destroyed Halloween Town—a land of monsters—he'd be accepted as a hero. But the prince lied. He only wanted the clock destroyed to decimate our town. And it nearly worked." I pause, shuddering at the vision of Halloween Town in ruins I saw in Lady Lore's mirror.

"We want to hear from the dragon!" the Undersea Gal pipes up, slime bubbles popping from her lips.

"Yes, yes, yes," Igor moans. "Scorch is the only one who has seen this villain. What does he have to say?"

The crowd slowly parts to reveal Scorch, crammed in the back corner beside Luna. His ears flatten timidly, but Luna whispers something to him, and slowly, he lifts them. His tail fire burns brighter, casting a warm glow over his sunset-colored scales.

Scorch hesitantly lifts his voice. "Scorch didn't know what he was planning. He called himself a prince and said he ruled a faraway realm. He never showed his face, only his cloak with a high collar, made of smoke and storm clouds. He promised Scorch would be welcomed in Hero Haven if Scorch stole the clock. Celebrated, even. He said Scorch would finally belong, finally have a home and friends. . . . Scorch was foolish for believing him. Scorch knew it the moment he met Sally and learned she was a friend, not foe. But it was too late. The clock was already broken. The prince just laughed and vanished into the fog. Scorch tried to find him. But he was gone."

Murmurs spread like wildfire as people swap speculations. With their words buzzing in my ears, I don't realize that I'm tugging on my loose wrist thread until Jack quietly takes my hand in his behind the podium and gives it a comforting squeeze.

I steady my nerves and speak again into the microphone. "Does anyone have any information about this prince's identity?"

Barrel jumps on the bench, slides his skeleton mask back, and says, "There are plenty of princes in Fable Town! I've seen 'em!"

I press my lips together to keep from asking how and when he snuck off to Fable Town. Instead, I say, "I've also been to Fable Town. Those are only *storybook* princes. Despite their titles, they are merely townspeople, not rulers."

Attendees jostle against one another as they throw out other theories, each more implausible than the last. The Clown with the Tear-Away Face honks his joke horn once, twice, thrice, setting my nerves on edge. Amid the melee, I notice a gloved hand rise calmly from the back row.

Shading my eyes against the bright spotlight, I strain to see. The lights catch on a glistening titanium skullcap, and the leaves in my stomach frost over until they're curled tight as pill bugs.

"I believe I may offer unique insight into this situation," an all-too-familiar droning voice rings out.

Sweet, wicked spirits . . . *what is Dr. Finkelstein doing here?*

4

Reflexively, I squeeze Jack's hand tighter behind the podium. My head reels, spinning like a bat in a hurricane, and I whisper to Jack with a strained voice, "Didn't you tell the Mayor we wouldn't let Dr. Finkelstein back here?"

Jack looks as surprised as I am by the doctor's presence, his browbones lifted nearly as high as the rafters. "I most certainly did."

His eyes then narrow with a predator's glare, and his jaw pulls back to show small pointed teeth, and I know my impulsive husband is about to do something rash.

Dr. Finkelstein will be lucky to keep his head bolted to his body.

I swiftly rest a hand on Jack's forearm, my heart still thrashing, but manage to keep my voice steady. "Let me handle this. Dr. Finkelstein is my father . . . er, my kidnapper."

My face goes hot at the slip of the tongue, and I glance sidelong at Greta and Albert in the front row. My true parents. I've spent so many years calling Dr. Finkelstein my father that it's still buried somewhere deep in my core, as much a part of my stuffing as cotton tufts and oak leaves.

"Dr. Finkelstein," I call, loud and clear, though my hands are clasped so tightly behind the podium that my knuckles turn bone white. "You do not have permission to be in Halloween Town. Behemoth, arrest the doctor for escaping his probation and prepare him to be sent back to Dream Town—"

Albert, in the front row, quickly stands, his jaw stitches pulled tight, his big hands plucking at the folds of his robe. "Ah, Sally, as a matter of fact, Dr. Finkelstein accompanied us from Dream Town with our permission. We granted his temporary parole request—it seems his companion, Jewel, knocked her brain loose after tripping on a cobblestone, and only he can bolt it back in place."

I'm so stunned that all I can do is blink my big fishhook eyelashes and stare as though my father is speaking in an ancient tongue. Barely aware of what I'm doing, I snatch up the gavel and bang it on the podium.

"Recess!" I call into the microphone, my voice squeaking. "We'll . . . we'll call this meeting to a close for today and . . . and reconvene tomorrow, everyone, while we continue to consider our next moves to protect the town." A bead of sweat soaks into my temple. "Mom. Dad. *Dr. Finkelstein.* Please meet Jack and me backstage. *Now.*"

My stitches are set so tight that when Jack rests a gentle hand on the small of my back, I nearly snap. Now it's his turn to calm the beast inside me as he guides me into the stage wings while the townspeople anxiously turn to one another, eager for the opportunity to discuss this new threat.

I hear the drone of Dr. Finkelstein's wheelchair motor as he climbs the backstage ramp, and then his beady black lenses are peering up at me in the shadows, mirrorlike and chilling, waiting for me to speak first.

Suddenly, I'm a little girl again, wooden spoon in hand, serving him worm's wort soup with bated breath, desperately hoping he—my father—approves.

Stuffing pokes out from where I've bitten through my bottom lip. For some time now, I've carried this awful truth like a secret shame inside me: Dr. Finkelstein was never my father. He was my jailer. I've tried to smile through the pain. Tried to be dignified, following Albert and Greta's example of how a perfect leader should look. But right now, I'm just a rag doll twisted by anger and heartbreak.

Without thinking, I blurt out, "Soup every day, hours over a boiling cauldron, and you never once said thank you!"

Jack jolts upright beside me, blinking rapidly. Even Dr. Finkelstein hesitates, his fingers fumbling at his spectacles like they might shield him.

"Sally," he says in a thin voice. "Your realm is in danger—do you really wish to discuss soup?"

Something snaps loose inside me. I fling my hands toward the rafters and give a banshee scream. "It isn't about the soup, and you know it!" I'm like a live wire as I pace, fabric skin twitching and prickling, chest so tight I tug anxiously at my breastbone stitches.

Jack opens his mouth to speak, always ready to defend me, but this time his words falter. His jaw hinges open and closed like a fish, dark eyes searching for the right way to help. But there's nothing he can do, not when all the hurt is in the past.

Dr. Finkelstein folds his gloved hands tightly in his lap. "I've admitted to my mistakes and accepted my punishment."

"Mistakes?" I bark a harsh laugh. "Like forgetting to set the oven? Leaving the laboratory door unlocked? You stole me from my home and made me believe I was your daughter!"

He flinches but doesn't look away. "I never intended to deceive you. I only wanted a child who would brighten the house. Who lived and breathed and sang and . . . and *smiled.* Who had been loved, so she knew *how* to love. Not like the others."

My feet drift to a stop, a tickle worming up my back. "Others?"

He pauses, his lips folding tight as though he's said the wrong thing, before he breezily continues with a dismissive wave of his hand, "Earlier experiments. Companions that didn't work out. I didn't want automatons; I wanted a daughter to make my laboratory into a home. Who would bring warmth, nurturing, sustenance."

My mind turns back to his laboratory's collection of skulls and the miscellaneous body parts that Igor salvaged from the cemetery–I've always known him to tinker around with creations, but Jewel is the only one I know of that he's brought to life.

Were there others before her?

I ball my fists, working the hinges of my jaw, and shake my head. "Warmth, nurturing, sustenance? Sounds a lot like *soup*, not love."

Before he can respond, Albert rushes up the backstage steps, followed by Greta. Their faces are pinched, gaunt. My mother twists her fingers in knots. "Sally, we didn't have time to consult you earlier about Dr. Finkelstein's parole request. It was a last minute decision to allow him to come, and we assumed you'd want to be compassionate, to take the higher road—"

"You're a ruler now," Albert adds. "And a good ruler knows when to set personal grievances aside for the sake of her town. Jewel is a Halloween Town resident, and for better or worse, so is Dr. Finkelstein. He was terrible to you, absolutely, and should continue to be held accountable—but Jewel shouldn't suffer for his crimes. Compassion isn't just for the easy cases."

A pit opens inside me, a yawning grave that I fear will long sit empty. From the corner of my eye, I spot Luna heading our direction, Scorch padding along loyally behind her, and something curls tight in my core. Luna, who is everything my parents want in a ruler. Patient. Prudent. Who is the daughter they *should* have had.

But Luna, oblivious to our discussion, comes to stand at my side, not theirs, her bright button eyes shining up at me in admiration, and I realize in that moment that my disagreement with my parents has nothing at all to do with her.

I won't let my parents come between me and Luna.

"Sally, your townspeople are talking about invading Fable Town," Luna whispers in a rush. "They're threatening to capture every storybook prince in the realm and drag them back here for questioning."

"I told them the Fable Town princes aren't the culprit!" I curse under my breath, pacing in a tight circle into the backstage shadows, needing a moment of solitude to close my eyes and think.

But even that, it seems, is asking too much.

Dr. Finkelstein comes to rest beside me, clearing his throat. "Sally, don't be so stubborn that you'd harm your own people just to spite me. Let me help. While I do not know the prince's identity, I may know someone who does. At the All Realms Gatherings, we scientists from across the towns compare notes and help one another with experiments. Professor Cirrus in Weather Town is a brilliant meteorologist. That dragon mentioned a storm cloud cape—if anyone would know about unusual garments turning into storm clouds, it's him."

"Weather Town?" I repeat, eyeing him warily.

The town name floats through the air like a stray snowflake. When Jack and I discovered the secret doorways in the Hinterlands, Weather Town was one of the first new realms we identified. The lightning-bolt door was our first clue. Later, my parents explained that it is a land where every neighborhood has a different weather pattern: Windblown West, The Big Snow, The Rain Streets, and Sunshine Alley. But—

"We were told Weather Town was too dangerous to travel to," I say measuredly. "Step through the Weather Town door and you might end up directly in a lightning storm."

Dr. Finkelstein rests his hand on his chair's controller as he wheels himself back around toward my parents. "That, my dear *queen*, isn't my problem to solve. It's yours."

My stomach pulls tight as a button, like every stitch in me is drawn too hard, ready to rip me apart from the inside. A gristly ache rises in my throat. I swallow it down, fighting to stay composed when the wild part of me inside only wants to scream.

I step out from backstage to look at the agitated crowd milling among the benches, riling one another up with monstrous boasts, and my eyes fall on the witches. They're bickering loudly with each other, their shrill voices screeching against my ears.

Jack comes to stand beside me, his browbone raised in a silent question, and I tip my head in the direction of the witches.

"Can those two still scry using their cauldron?" I ask.

"Now, now, watch your feet. Er, claws. Hooves. Whatever you stomp around on, be careful!"

An hour has passed since the town meeting. The short witch nudges through the small group of us gathered in the back room of the apothecary shop she and the tall witch share. It's a much smaller space than Town Hall, with room for only the witches, Jack and me, my parents, Scorch and Luna, and a handful of town residents. The rest cluster in the open doorway and press their faces against the windows. The short witch tosses a handful of stinkhorn fungi into a heavy cast-iron cauldron that's bubbling away atop a lime-green flame, then stirs it with an enormous wooden spoon nearly the same size as herself.

The tall witch sweeps in with a basket overflowing with ingredients that she sprinkles into the cauldron with a flourish. "Crow's feet. Dried maggots. Rotten flowers from a grave. Oh—and a pinch of cinnamon." She winks at Jack. "That's just for the *ambiance*."

Impatient, Jack taps his shoe on the stone floor.

The short witch stirs the concoction counter-clockwise, humming a strange, off-key melody that prickles the threads on the back of my neck. The cauldron's contents begin spinning faster, until I have to steady myself with one hand on its rim.

She continues to stir until the potion blurs. Pin-prick bubbles form and pop in quick, colorful bursts.

Faintly at first, an image appears on the swirling surface like a grainy old television set. The bubbles' pops and fizz transform into a staticky voice.

"Hello? Hello, is someone there?" An image of a scientist with cottony tufts of white hair squints out from the cauldron. He shakes his head and mutters to himself as he turns away, "Strangest thing. I go to crank up the windmaker machine and hear voices coming from the water basin! Might be time to hang up the umbrella, old boy. . . ."

I quickly lean over the cauldron's rim. "Professor Cirrus? We're here!"

Blinking hard, he doubles back with his bushy white eyebrows sky high. "Well! What's this? A rag doll in my water basin!"

He removes a pair of eyeglasses from his lab coat pocket and puts them on to see better. As the image sharpens, I realize he isn't close to my height–rather, he's seated on a tall stool. If he were to stand, I doubt he'd even come up to my waist.

"Professor, I'm Queen Sally from Halloween Town, and we've contacted you on the advice of our resident scientist, Dr. Finkelstein, because we need your help."

Nodding gravely, the professor leans forward on the stool. "Well, well, the Pumpkin Queen herself! I've studied your town's meteorological patterns, particularly the unusual movement of your sun, which never rises above eventide height, even at the pinnacle of noon. Oh! And your easterly winds have a very strange pattern of . . . erm . . . one moment."

A glass beaker behind him erupts in a tiny bolt of lightning, and he garbles as he turns to adjust a setting. "Apologies . . . my town is counting on me quite urgently at the moment, you see . . . if I don't get this wind shield set correctly, we're afraid we'll lose more residents. . . ."

Jack and I exchange quick, meaningful looks. My fingers curl around the cauldron's edge until my knuckles blanch, a caterpillar of premonition inching up the back of my neck. "Did you say . . . you're losing residents?"

The professor sighs deeply. "Our lead umbrella maker and two windmill technicians disappeared yesterday. They were blown into the sky right off Sunshine Alley. A third technician managed to get indoors in time—it seems whatever dark force is behind the strange storms is only strong enough to function outdoors. Weather Town has been in a panic. I'm designing a wind shield that I hope might create such strong gusts as to protect us, but it's highly experimental—"

My stuffing turns to jelly as I brace myself on the cauldron to keep from toppling over. The prince is targeting other towns besides ours? It doesn't make sense—he only went after *our* clock.

Jack addresses the professor. "Here in Halloween Town, several of our people have gone missing, as well. All under strange weather phenomena, I should add. They were taken during a storm that came from no one direction. And these were left behind."

He holds out the iron raindrops in his palm, mindful not to drop them in the swirling cauldron waters.

Professor Cirrus's face crumples as he takes in our anxious expressions. "So, it's happening to you, too," he murmurs, his voice barely audible above the cauldron's hiss. "I had hoped it was just us. We've found the same iron raindrops, and I wish I had better news for you. There are only a few conditions which could result in iron rain. All of them are theoretical, to the best of my knowledge. If a realm's magnetic field were to reverse, it could pull iron ions from the soil into the atmosphere, where they would cluster and fall as rain. Alternatively, in regions where trolls reside, their belches seed the clouds with iron-rich minerals that could form ferric raindrops. Likewise, volcanoes might spew gaseous iron from deep underground into the upper atmosphere, resulting in iron rain. And there's always witchcraft."

Jack cranks his head around to look at the witches, whose chins wobble beneath his ferocious countenance.

"Not us!" The tall witch sputters. "We can cast the odd spell here and there, yes, but if we had enough power to reverse magnetic poles–"

"Would we live in this shambling old hut?" the short witch finishes, jerking her chin up toward the cobweb-covered rafters.

"I should add," Professor Cirrus jumps in, "that witchcraft is unlikely to be the cause. Just as each town has its own time zone, it also has a unique, self-contained weather zone; for example, it may be sunny in St. Patrick's Day Town and pouring in Easter Town. There are certain rare weather phenomena, however, with the ability to move between realms. You've heard of currents in some places that carry warm air to colder regions? We have similar currents, though not composed of water or air. They run on magic. Tap into one, and it can transport weather conditions from one realm to another. I believe that is what we're looking at—someone capable of creating their own weather zone to move between realms. Storms, wind, rain, sun. They could wield it all."

"Not sun," Scorch pipes up from the far side of the cauldron, blinking his heavy dragon eyelids. "The prince does not like sun."

"Excuse me? What did you say, young dragon?" The glass-encased storm behind the professor begins to tremble as a miniature tornado builds in its center. Professor Cirrus turns down the wind dial and adjusts a few switches so he can hear better.

"When Scorch met the prince," Scorch explains, "the prince kept his collar pulled high even in the dark. Said sunlight hurt his eyes. Burned them, even."

Professor Cirrus freezes, his hand still on a lever. "You say that sunlight hurts his eyes?"

Scorch nods. "He moved like he didn't need it. Like he could see through shadow even better than daylight."

The apothecary shop falls into silence, broken

only by the babble of the cauldron. Professor Cirrus whispers, almost to himself, "That sounds like . . . no. It can't be."

I squeeze Jack's hand and lean forward, the tips of my hair dragging in the bubbling potion, and ask urgently, "What does it sound like?"

"If what this dragon says is true, then it's the missing clue I've been searching for. Listen carefully." Professor Cirrus pushes his spectacles up his button nose and whispers in a low, tremulous voice, "Have you heard of *Shadow Town*?"

My nerves pop and crackle against my fabric skin.

"Shadow Town?" I repeat, and look around at the blank faces of my friends and family. "No, I haven't."

"Few have," the professor replies. "It's a place of the forgotten. Of the lost. Most pressingly, it's *entirely underground*."

"The dark," I murmur softly. "That's why the prince doesn't like sunlight—his eyes are used to shadows underground!"

Professor Cirrus nods gravely. "Evidence would suggest Shadow Town's ruler has a powerful brand of magic unlike anything we've seen before. Shadow Magic, you might call it."

A deep wrinkle buries itself between my brows. "Wait, but what did you mean by 'the forgotten'?

The Wolfman isn't forgotten! The vampires aren't forgotten!"

Professor Cirrus holds out his hands helplessly. "As I said, outside of my own weather pattern research, I only have hearsay. Regardless, all evidence indicates this is where our missing people have most likely gone."

My stomach sinks, heavy with the feel of water-logged stuffing. It's hardly the definitive answer I wanted, but still, it's a step in the right direction. "We're grateful that you solved this part of the puzzle, Professor. We'll see what we can do from here to crack the next part. We'll be in touch if we learn anything."

"Thanks to that dragon of yours." He offers a small but warm smile at Scorch, who dips his head shyly. A crack of thunder goes off inside his weather experiment, and he nearly topples off his stool as he spins around to adjust the controls, muttering over his shoulder, "Good luck, Pumpkin Queen. To all of us."

As he attends to his machinery, I signal to the short witch to stop stirring. As the potion stills, our window into Weather Town gradually fades.

Slowly, all eyes turn to me. It feels like every brick in town is resting on my shoulders. I can barely keep my head high. If I were wearing my crown, surely it would slide right off.

Shadow Town? Lost people? An underground realm?

My chest feels pulled taut. I wasn't made for this. I was stitched together in Dream Town—a place of lullabies and lavender, not midnight forests and sharp-toothed snarls. I was never meant to carry the weight of an entire town on my patchwork shoulders.

But none of that matters now, does it?

Stitch by stitch, I'll remake myself into whatever this town needs me to be.

Jack squeezes my shoulder, giving me a little extra of his backbone at a time when I feel the intense lack of my own.

"I'll write letters to the other realms right away to see if any of their townspeople have gone missing," I volunteer. "With luck, the prince is only targeting Halloween Town and Weather Town. I'll mail them in today's crow post, with a spell to expedite the delivery."

Jack turns to the other residents gathered in the apothecary shop. "I'll head up a task force to strengthen the town's defenses. We might not be able to make a wind shield, but you heard what the professor said about staying indoors. We can seal off exposed windows. Fasten a weather vane to Town

Hall's roof so we can track the wind's direction, too. Who's with me?"

Monstrous hands shoot into the air, both from the group in the back room and those clustered in the doorway.

I clasp my hands together. "We should try to find any information we can on Shadow Town. Old legends. Mentions in spell books. Inscriptions carved into gravestones."

"The Lullaby Library," my mother chirps, her fingers working anxiously at her satin pajamas' uppermost button. "There are more books there than stars in the sky. Stories about every place beneath the sun. If Shadow Town has ever been written about, an account will be there."

I give her a smile. "Thanks for the advice, Mom. It's as good a place to start as any. I'll come with you."

The worry lines etched on my mother's face ease as she takes a deep breath, calmer now that she has a purpose.

"Count me in, too!" Luna raises her pale hand high. "The more eyes, the better. Besides, I know the library nearly as well as the archivists themselves."

"Scorch will help!" The dragon lifts his tail.

I can't help grinning and scratching his horn bumps, so touched that tears push at my eyes.

"You'll need my help spotting things!" Cyclops lumbers forward, tugging his baker's apron over his pointed ears.

The witches nod at each other in silent agreement before piping up in unison, "We'll join you, too!"

More hands rise among the crowd gathered in the shop and just outside, tentatively at first and then faster as enthusiasm spreads. My stomach draws taut, afraid to hope, but it's spreading like an infection. Excited eyes. Energetic nods.

After some debate, we divide the crowd into two groups. Half will come to Dream Town with me, and half will stay with Jack to reinforce our own town. The poor mayor keeps swiveling his head from one group to another, wanting to join both missions, worried about being left out.

Jack pats him on his topsy-turvy back. "Naturally, you must stay here, Mayor—we'll need your hearse to carry supplies!"

The Mayor settles on his grinning face, adjusting his black widow bow tie.

Work begins on boarding up windows. Meanwhile, I pen the letters to the other rulers, seal them with a magical stamp to speed the delivery crow's wings, and tuck them into his mail bag.

"Fly true," I whisper as he takes off.

Once everyone is ready to depart, I spare a moment to pull Jack aside and take the Mirror of Reverie shard out of my pocket. I press it into his palm.

"I kept this when the mirror broke," I say quietly, folding his finger bones over the shard. "Take it. The rest of the mirror is back in Town Hall. I'll carry it with me to Dream Town. Do you remember when Lady Lore gave it to us? She said it could be used for communication with other magic mirrors. So, when it broke, it occurred to me we might be able to use the pieces as a kind of telephone. I tested it, and it works. We can use this to talk while I'm in Dream Town and you're here."

He tucks the shard into his suit pocket. Then he threads his long fingers through the loose strands of my hair, gazing at my patchwork face as if it's as bright and beautiful as the moon. His eyes deepen. "We're going to save this town, Sally. And when we do, no vengeance-bent prince or cutesy trick-or-treater will ever doubt what we are again—ghoulishly scary. Just as Halloween is meant to be."

He kisses me softly, short and sweet like a sip of garden mint tea, and it fills me up with love and hope and certainty that we'll get through this—that this quiet of the storm won't be our last moment of peace.

5

The moment I step into Dream Town's Lullaby Library, I'm greeted by an oversized teddy bear clutching an open storybook. Its plush fur is worn thin in places, rubbed nearly bald by generations of sleepy children who've curled up beside it. The scent of warm vanilla lingers in the air—like sugar cookies fresh from the oven—and it tugs at something tender in my chest.

From somewhere above, I catch the gentle rustle of turning pages. I glance up at the spiral staircase that winds through the center of the building, rising all six floors, with wrought iron bridges branching off like the spokes of a spider's web. In the past, this sight has always made me feel like I've stepped straight into a dream.

Now I think only of the nightmares snapping at my heels.

Zero breezes up to me, nuzzling my palm. I scratch his ghost head.

Luna pushes through the throng of Halloween Town residents, as well as a handful of Dream Town residents who joined in. She's hidden behind the towering Behemoth and the Clown with the Tear-Away Face, so she climbs onto the teddy bear's shoulder and lifts her hands to get everyone's attention. "We'll split up among the floors. Any two-footed Halloween Town residents can start in the basement—that's where we keep the stuff of nightmares. Those who slither or fly, take the mezzanine. Dream Town residents, take the ground floor—Greta and Albert, you can show everyone the reading alcoves."

When she finishes assigning levels, people pluck up candlesticks from the wall sconces and divide into groups heading toward the spiral stairs.

Soon, it's only Luna, Scorch, Zero, and me left in the cavernous foyer—along with the head librarian at the circulation desk, who flicks us stern looks whenever we raise our voices.

I clutch a pewter candlestick shaped like a

mouse, its tail the curled handle, and whisper, "What about us?"

Luna's eyes sparkle. "We're taking the attic. That's where the rarest books are kept."

A chill brushes my ankles from some unseen corner, but I clutch the candlestick tighter. "Lead the way."

Luna bounds up the stairs, but I follow more slowly, each step echoing into the vast library. Zero flutters along at my heels. Somewhere above, a child giggles—reading a joke book, maybe. On every floor, the ceilings are painted with whimsical, dreamy murals, which grow more fanciful as we climb: a starlit sky on the third floor, a spring-green tree canopy on the fourth, a flock of griffins on the fifth. On the sixth, everything changes—no paint, no murals, just mirrors on every surface, reflecting never-ending versions of ourselves.

I pause on the next step to brush my fingers over my bone-white wedding ring, briefly closing my eyes, and a flash of my nightmare returns.

Trapped in a blackness darker than death. My breathing cut off. I'm swallowed by total darkness without so much as a glimmer of light.

A soft tap draws me back. Scorch gently pats my back again with one of his wings. "Sally okay?"

"Y-yes, Scorch. Thank you. It's a vision I had, still haunting me. Of Halloween Town's destruction, and I couldn't stop it from happening."

Luna stops on the stairs, pivoting back toward me. "You had a vision?"

I nod, still toying with my ring. "At least, I think that's what it was."

She taps her finger thoughtfully on her chin. "I've been studying a book from your parents' library. There's a chapter about visions, calling them cousins to dreams. It says that like dreams, they're just stories created to make sense of the world." She sweeps out her silken hand to point to the vast shelves of books. "They aren't real like you and me."

I glance up at her, the mirrored ceiling reflecting soft folds of hesitation on my face. "So if my vision is just a story, then why did it feel so real?"

"Because . . ." Luna pauses, searching for the words. "Because they aren't just stories meant to entertain. Or help children fall asleep. They're stories meant to teach us something about ourselves. Maybe the version of you in your vision was your fear speaking. And . . . maybe you could tell yourself a different story. One where you're the Sally who never gives up."

I watch Luna for a moment, my hand tight on

the rail, and in the soft certainty of her gaze I see so clearly what my parents admire about her.

With a touch of awe, I say, "You've changed a lot from the shy girl I met at last year's exhibition, do you know that? The one always hiding behind her bangs." I affectionately reach out to ruffle her hair. "I'm glad apprenticing with my parents is helping you so much."

Her red-patch cheeks brighten. "Oh, goodness. I adore working in the governors' office, but it was our adventure that changed how I see the world!" Her eyes take on a faraway look as she clutches the banister like she's leaning over a ship's rail. "Mermaids. Dragons. Tooth pixies. I realized life was meant to be lived, not just read about!"

Her shining face kindles a grin on my lips and a little bit more strength in my heart.

We finish the climb, reaching a turreted attic packed with floor-to-ceiling shelves. It's a hushed place. Colder than the levels below, with their large fireplaces. The scent of mint hangs in the air, mixing with the old-book smell of ink and leather. The only light source is an enormous stained glass window in the shape of a crescent moon, its clouded panes soft shades of blue and gold and starlight yellow. Over-sized cushions and blankets are piled in the attic's center to form a giant cozy reading nook.

"Well." Luna points to the first shelf on our right. "Why don't you start at the beginning, and I'll start at the end?"

"Deal. Scorch, can you brighten the light in here so we can see better? And, Zero, check the floors."

Zero dives toward the floorboards, sniffing at spilled crumbs. Scorch nestles down into the cushioned nook, holding his tail fire high to give us ample reading light, but I'm still grateful for my candlestick, if only for the small flame's warmth.

Keeping the light close to the books' spines, I run my padded finger over each title.

Tales of Stars and Silence
The Sleeper's Almanac
Chants and Charms from the Hinterlands
The Silk Weaver's Storybook
Ramble Tales for the Longest Nights

I fall into a rhythm, finger bobbing over the hills and valleys of book spines, and as the ocean of words pulls me into its lull, the question behind Luna's advice returns: *What story do you tell yourself?*

From some deep place within me, words rise to the surface. *Once upon a time, a rag doll girl was locked in a scientist's tower . . .*

The story I tell myself is an old one, as familiar to me as my painted nails. It begins with a girl stolen away from where she belonged, raised among monsters, who fell in love with the Pumpkin King. His love mended her broken soul, piece by jagged piece, until she was someone new—someone stronger than before.

I tell myself that story, I think, because I *need* to believe it's true.

But love? Love isn't always gentle in real life. It's more than butterfly kisses and pumpkin pancakes. Sometimes, love is sharp-edged and terrifying, standing on the edge of a thousand-foot fall. I think about that night I nearly lost Jack, deep in the depths of Oogie Boogie's lair, the sounds of their confrontation echoing in my cloth ears. I remember how my hands shook. How helpless I felt, bound and trapped. That fear could have paralyzed me. Instead, it stoked my determination. Made me strong enough to endure.

Not because I was fearless—because I was *afraid*. Just like I was on our adventure to Fable Town, Time Town, and Tooth Town. I can use this fear again to make me strong.

We search for what feels like forever. Dust clings to my fingers, and the wick of my candle burns low. The silence of the library presses in around us like a goose-down blanket, broken only by our footsteps creaking on the attic floor.

I'm about to reach the end of the bookcase when Zero lifts his ears and pumpkin nose at attention. A low whine escapes his snout as he floats over to a crooked shelf near the back—one of the few we haven't yet searched.

He noses insistently at a thick volume wedged between two crumbling atlases.

Luna tugs the book free, and something thin and shimmering slips from between the pages.

She picks it up cautiously, holding it to the light of Scorch's tail fire. "It's a feather," she says in surprise. She frowns before sliding a book off another shelf, a birding guide. She flips through it until she locates the feather's match. "It belongs to a burrowing hemlock owl. It says here they nest deep underground, creatures of silence and shadows. Look, the feather is singed." She gives it a tentative sniff. "It still smells of smoke."

"Smoke," I echo. "Underground burrows. Shadows. That's the right direction. Good job, Zero!" I pat the ghost dog between his floaty ears, and he barks, pleased with himself.

Luna wipes a thick crust of dust off the old book, then tilts the cover this way and that to try to read its faded gold title lettering. "*Old Worlds & Other Forgotten Places*," she says aloud, eyes glittering. "If any book holds information about Shadow Town, it has to be this one!"

We head to the reading nook, where we flop on tufted cushions and open the book beneath Scorch's flickering tail flame. He rests his chin on my shoulder as he listens to me read the table of contents.

The Unicorn and the Lily Pad
A Tower to the Sun
Night Magic's Impossible Riddle
The Last Song of the Moon Child

Luna scratches her chin. "Which story should we start with?"

I tuck a strand of hair behind my ear, trying not to let the fragile hope in my heart bubble over and scald. "You pick."

Luna flips to a story halfway through the book. Her lips tremble as she reads aloud, her words an anxious tumble.

"'Thorna of the Wild.'" She looks up. "I've never heard of this one, and I've read more bedtime stories than anyone I know." She clears her throat and starts, "'In the never nowhere, a herd of centaurs dwelt happily in the deep of the Ever Woods, baking cattail-flour bread and singing songs of the old winds. One day, a headstrong girl named Thorna went picking wild daisies, wandering too close to the Lake of Sunken Things, where her mother had warned her never to tread. Her hooves stuck fast in the mud. From out of the watery depths, a carp cackled. . . .'"

We have our heads buried in the book, the rest of the world falling away until the library's ever-present vanilla scent is overshadowed by the rich aroma of pine forests. A twinkle catches the corner of my eye, and for a moment, I wonder if someone has come up to the attic with a lantern.

I don't want to tear myself away from the story to look—

Until *hoofbeats* clatter on the wooden floor.

A girl has suddenly appeared in the attic, and she's not among the group we entered with. She has tangly tawny brown curls. A crown of wild daisies circles her soft fur-tipped ears. Below her simple cotton tunic stretches the body of a shaggy-haired pony with muddy hooves.

"Sally!" Luna grips my hand, quivering with incredulity as she stares at the girl. "What's happening?"

The centaur girl's eyes widen in equal confusion

as she touches her flower crown, then her tunic, as if to confirm she's real, her gaze full of wonder as it sweeps across the library attic.

"Who . . . who are you?" she whispers.

"Who," I say back, my own wide eyes a mirror of hers, "are *you*?"

But the answer, I realize, is right in the book Luna's holding in her lap.

My head pivots sharply up and down, between the book and the girl. Her warm sable-colored tail is woven with tiny white wildflowers that match the flower crown on her head. Impish freckles form a con-stellation across her nose, and her hooves are muddy.

"Th . . . Thorna?" My voice wavers like I'm speaking to a ghost as I rest my palm flat on the open page—on *her* page.

Her horse ears swivel forward eagerly. "Yes, that's me, but who are you? What realm is this?" Her elvish upturned nose twitches as she takes in the shelves of books. "Rag dolls and a dragon . . . so you aren't just children who love stories?"

A note of disappointment lingers in her words,

though her eyes still sparkle with a curiosity that can't be snuffed out.

"You're in Dream Town." I motion to the crescent moon-shaped window. "This is the Lullaby Library. We were reading a story about you, and now, somehow, here you are."

Her eyes widen. "Ah! That book must be a Grimoriel!"

Luna blinks, her face wide and open. "A Grimoriel?"

Thorna explains, "A Grimoriel is no mere storybook. It's a magical artifact. When you read my story, you summon me. Well, not *me*, exactly—more like my shadow self, or a projection. See?" She waves her stubby fingers in front of the lantern, and the flame flickers behind her semi-transparent skin. "Think of me as a friendly ghost who can visit as long as you're reading my story."

"I know everything there is to know about ghosts, but I've never heard of a shadow self," I say with a glance at Luna. "Do shadow selves come from . . . Shadow Town, by chance?"

Thorna's eyes go so round that the whites flash with a fearful, haunted look. "You know about Shadow Town?"

Luna's and my eyes meet again, unspoken

questions buzzing between us, as a pit opens deep in my insides.

"In fact," I say slowly, "we've been searching for information about it. Here, in the library. We know almost nothing about it—or its ruler."

The sparkle snuffs out in Thorna's eyes until her irises are black as coal. "Shadow Town is not a place you find. It finds you. It's buried underground, deeper than the oldest bones from the oldest creatures. So dark you can't see beyond your own hands. The only light comes from glowworms, or wasp-wax candles, if you're lucky enough to have one in your cell. But few are." She wraps her arms around herself as if the memory chills her.

"What do you mean, cell?" My voice is hollow. All I can think of is the Wolfman's cozy cottage. And the vampires' spick-and-span castle, so lovingly decorated in bat motifs. "You're . . . imprisoned?"

She shudders. "We all are. Everyone who's been forgotten and dared to try to do something about it." At our blank stares, she sighs deeply and looks down at the warm plush cushions longingly. "I was born in a realm so wild that it's nameless. We just *were*. My herd of centaurs. A family of fauns. Every spring, a flock of white swans would arrive and change into towheaded children with the most incredible tales of their journeys."

A tear slips down her freckled cheek, her wide eyes glimmering like pools on the verge of spilling over.

I swallow down a lump of cotton in my throat. There's something beautifully tragic in the way Thorna speaks about her home. And yet, here she stands, nothing more than a projection—transparent, ephemeral, clinging to a place everyone else has forgotten.

"What happened?" I ask softly.

She wipes away the tear, sniffling. "Our lives were simple but happy. Brambleberry stew roasting over campfires. Children galloping after one another, playing chase. Dancing to the notes of my mother's wooden flute. One day, everything changed. My father began to fade. It started with his hooves. The next day, his tail was gone. Within a week, only his ears remained, and then those faded, too. One by one, I watched my entire herd disappear. I was the only one left. Alone, I went in search of the faun family, but their village was abandoned. No white swans came that spring. Everything in our world had faded away. And then I, too, faded."

Her sadness stabs somewhere deep inside me, sharp as a needle. I know what it feels like to lose a place that was everything to you—a home, parents—and to wake up in a foreign, cold place.

"What a nightmare." Luna's bottom lip wobbles with overflowing heartbreak.

As more tears spill out of Thorna's eyes, Luna tugs a handkerchief out of her pajama pocket and offers it to her.

Thorna sadly shakes her head as she waves away the handkerchief. "That's kind of you, but I can't touch anything, remember? I'm not actually *here*."

Thorna's gaze travels to the specks of dust in the air like sparks traveling up into a night sky. "When I faded from our forest, I woke in the dark—in a realm where there was no sky, no sun, no stars. At first, all I could see was a blackness so thick I was afraid I had died. But then my eyes adjusted to the glowworms' light, and I was able to make out figures. My family was there, too, waiting for me with eyes filled with bittersweet tears. We were together again but trapped in an earthen cell that had been clawed out by badger guards. Over time, I met the inhabitants of the neighboring cells. The Yule Goat. Dodo birds. A kindly old warlock named the Stone Man. All characters that, like us, had been forgotten by souls from across all the realms."

A shiver runs down my spine at the word *forgotten.* The bandleader's words of wisdom drift back into my head. *Nothing's ever lost. There are echoes from every note ever played.*

Yet, at the same time, the core elements of my *holiday* are being forgotten by many. Year by year, Halloween is changing. Softening. If we can't bring back the scare, at what point will we all fade away to Shadow Town, too?

I plunge my hand into my dress pocket and squeeze the iron raindrops to root me back in the present. "Did you try to escape? To return to your realm?"

The last hint of rosy pink in Thorna's cheeks bleeds away. I've seen this look before, on Halloween night. It's the same wide-eyed fear I see in trick-or-treaters when my sinister cackle tears through the night.

"Oh, no," she whispers. "Once you're in Shadow Town, there's no leaving, even if you're remembered by someone. Prince Dorian forbids it. And if you try, like my parents did at first, you get locked away."

I sit lightning-rod straight, pulling so hard on the loose thread at my wrist that it hurts. Cold fear drips thickly down my spine. "Prince Dorian? That's the ruler?"

Thorna looks away. "Yes. Prince Dorian Dark."

Luna squeezes my shoulder, her small hand quaking. Her eyes are impossibly big. This is the information we've been searching for, but it doesn't feel like victory. The tremor in Thorna's voice leaves an ache gnawing through my stomach.

"I'm told that Shadow Town wasn't always so bleak," Thorna says, her gaze distant as she looks out the stained glass window. "There used to be cozy lights everywhere—lanterns and candles and bonfires. There were twilight markets bustling with merchants peddling crystals and powdered roots. They lived hand in hand with burrowing owls and badgers and foxes. And there was a door to the Hinterlands." She looks sharply down at the floor. "But something changed. When residents were remembered and tried to return to their realms, Prince Dorian suddenly built a golden gate and locked it. He wanted them to stay. Anyone who resisted him, like my herd, was thrown into the earthen cells."

My chest tightens, ribs pressing inward until it feels impossible to breathe. Prince Dorian had a responsibility to help Shadow Town's forgotten souls return to their realms, yet he chose to trap them.

As a ruler, I find the thought incomprehensible.

Thorna continues, "A fierce argument broke out between him and his twin sister, Princess Dahlia. She unlocked the gate to set everyone free, then stole the key so it couldn't be locked again. After that, she disappeared. Prince Dorian searched for her everywhere—always muttering about his sister and her terrible betrayal, but something had twisted in his mind. He was confused or . . . or out of sorts."

"Why do you say that?" I ask.

"He kept referring to his sister as a queen—but Dahlia is a princess." Thorna shrugs, then looks wistfully toward Scorch's softly roaring tail fire. "Anyway, in the end, Dahlia's brave efforts were useless. When he couldn't lock the gate, Prince Dorian created beasts made of storm clouds to guard it, preventing anyone from crossing."

I scrub my fingers against my temples, wearing the fabric thin. "When we encountered him before, he needed help just to break a clock. Now he can summon storm beasts?"

"His powers grow with every person he takes," Thorna explains quietly. "At first, everyone arrived in Shadow Town on their own—forgotten and faded away, like me. But then Prince Dorian discovered something. As the town's population grew, so did his power. So, he stopped waiting. He began taking people by force from other realms, forgotten or not. And it wasn't just their presence that empowered him. He found a way to siphon off the very qualities that made them who they were. When he captured my centaur herd, he absorbed our brute strength. When he imprisoned the Yule Goat, he drained centuries of ancient wisdom. When he set his sights on Weather Town, it was for their knowledge. Their science. Their understanding of the skies, so he could command the storms themselves."

I think of the Wolfman, with his fierce canine cunning, and the vampires, with their night flight ability. What powers did Dorian siphon off them?

I swallow down a lump of stuffing so thick it sinks into my stomach like a boulder.

"How can we help *you*?" I ask softly.

Thorna looks sadly at the book in my lap. "I don't know that you can. Once you close that Grimoriel, my projection will end, and I'll be back in my cell in Shadow Town."

My cloth fingers curl tightly over the book's corners. "I promise you, Thorna, we'll do everything we can. We'll find a way to get you out of Shadow Town and back to your home. As a ruler, I have a responsibility to keep other rulers in line. I promise that this won't be the last time we talk."

She offers a small smile that shows a flicker of hope—then nods.

Reluctantly, I shut Thorna's storybook before I lose the strength to do so. The book closes, the pages nothing but a soft rustle, but it hits my lap with the weight of a cinderblock.

Thorna immediately disappears, leaving only floating dust in her wake.

My heart raps in an unsteady melody.

I came into this fearing for Halloween Town's fate—but now, I can't stand by and let the residents of Shadow Town suffer under the same threat. The weight of it all keeps growing, unraveling and twisting into a much bigger mystery than I ever imagined, like a knit scarf that simply keeps going and going. Every time I think I've found the edge, it slips farther from my grasp.

"I need to tell Jack about this," I say.

I pass the book to Luna, then take the broken Mirror of Reverie out of my satchel, sparing a moment to gently run my finger over its cracked surface. My stomach tightens with worry about what could be happening back in Halloween Town in my absence.

"Eye of silver, wisdom's gleam, show me the truth unseen," I murmur. "Show me Jack Skellington."

The mirror hums in my hands, its surface beginning to pool into liquid quicksilver. But then it starts rattling in a way it never has before, the pane clattering violently in its silver frame.

Jack doesn't appear. Neither does Town Hall, or our home, or any glimmer of life at all in Halloween Town.

The mirror shows only liquid black.

I bite my lip, curl my toes, try not to panic.

When I'm on the point of putting it away, the rippling surface smooths just enough for me to detect a faint glow in the darkness. I squint, holding the mirror closer, trying to make sense of what I'm looking at.

"Jack?" I call. "Jack, are you there? Can you hear me?"

A groan answers me—one I recognize by heart. That slight, specific creak of a hinged jawbone, the sigh of air through a hollowed-out windpipe.

"Jack!"

It's so dark that Jack might as well be in a coffin six feet under. As my eyes adjust, I make out the faintest shape of his bones—normally bleached white as snow, but now glowing a soft neon green. At once,

I think of the garish lights from Oogie Boogie's lair—but Oogie Boogie is long gone.

"Jack, please, answer me!"

All I get is another groan, as though he's been knocked out cold. As my head spins with fears, I shove the mirror back in my satchel and, shaking, push to my feet.

"Sally?" Luna asks. "What was that? Where's Jack?"

"I have to get back to Halloween Town," I say in a voice that sounds too high, too distant, unlike myself. "Right now. Stay here, Luna—you stay with her, Scorch. Find my parents and tell them where I've gone. Zero, go with them in case they get lost. You know the way. And send the rest of the Halloween Town residents home and tell them to lock the town gates behind them."

"Sally—"

Her words fade. The world is a blur as I tumble out of the Lullaby Library, stumbling through the lavender fields until I find the Hinterland grove with the jack-o'-lantern tree.

I tear open the door, throwing myself through the opening and falling, falling, falling. I crash down in the cornfield like a jumble of old laundry—and straight into the middle of a vicious storm.

Rain soaks into my fabric skin, immediately weighing me down. My hair is plastered against the back of my neck. But I pick myself up and start running. With my waterlogged limbs, I move in slow motion like I'm in a dream—no, a nightmare.

The wind howls as I bolt through an empty town square, straight to the house I share with Jack, my dress twisting around my knees like it's trying to hold me back. The storm continues to rage—branches claw the air, rain lashes sideways, and our weather vane spins around and around like it can't make up its mind where to point.

"Jack!" I shout, my voice snatched clean away by the wind.

The front door hangs ajar.

I push open the door and enter, feeling like everything is strangely off-kilter. Moonlight enters at a slant, painting the stark stone floor in a cool wash of blue. Wind blusters at the windows, rattling the panes until I feel the echo of my own teeth chattering.

"Jack?" My voice is strained, high-pitched. "Jack, are you here? Please, Jack, answer me!"

The door slams shut behind me with a thunderous clap, blown closed by the wind.

I jump and clutch a hand to my chest. I look up

at the clock hanging high in the foyer—it's ten past midnight.

Jack should be here.

For the first time, my eyes catch on envelopes that are scattered on the foyer floor among the wind-blown leaves, fanned out like a losing hand of cards. I fall to my knees, hardly feeling the cold tile beneath me, and snatch up the nearest envelope.

It's addressed to me, sealed in pine-sap wax stamped with a conifer. I recognize the emblem of Christmas Town immediately.

I rip open the letter with fingers stiff from cold rain.

Dearest Sally,

Forgive the brevity of this letter—I have no time for pleasantries. I received your letter and am dismayed to inform you that we are also under attack here in Christmas Town. Two of my gift-wrapping elves disappeared overnight. Only iron raindrops were left behind. As much as I want to come to your aid, I'm afraid I'm needed to protect my own town.

As Captain of the Joint Towns' Council on Safety, I am implementing a travel restriction among the realms. No unauthorized travel is permitted, for residents' safety. Rulers may travel only in cases of extreme need.

Your friend forever,
Santa Claus

With bloodless fingers, I open the next letter, then the next. They're all the same. The Easter Bunny. The Tooth Fairy. Father Time. They're all missing residents, all boarding up their towns against this vicious new threat, all preparing for the travel restrictions.

Every town is on its own.

I put out the order for Halloween Town residents to return to the shelter of our town gates—so I must trust they're safe. Then I think of my parents, whom I left behind in the Lullaby Library in Dream Town with Luna.

Will Prince Dorian set his sights on them next?

The door creaks, and I push to my feet with a gasp, throwing it open as wind splashes rain against my face.

"Jack?"

There's no one there, but I step onto the walkway, my pulse battering my cotton veins.

A small, hard object nearly trips me, and I wince.

When I look down, the dull shine of metal catches my eye.

I stoop, panic wriggling through my leafy stuffing like maggots, and reach out a shaking hand to touch the tiny iron raindrops resting next to what I overlooked in my rush earlier—Jack's skeletal footprints in the dust.

And the knowing fills me with dread.

It's too late.

I'm too late.

Jack's been taken to Shadow Town.

6

I don't know how long I sit on the checkerboard tile floor of our foyer amid the letters from our fellow rulers while the storm runs out of steam beyond the windows.

All I can think is *Jack is gone.*

Dimly, I'm aware of soft footsteps in the foyer, followed by a soft hand on my shoulder.

"Sally?"

I jump back into the present, staring up at my mother's worried face. My father stands behind her, his wooly eyebrows knit together with concern as he shrugs out of his thick velvet robe and lays it over me, tucking in the edges tenderly.

"You ran out of the Lullaby Library so quickly—Luna told us a little of what happened." He tips his head back toward the front door. "Everyone's outside. We tried to come straight away, but the fog outside of town stopped us. Luckily, Zero showed us the way. Everyone wants to know if you're all right."

Right on cue, a pumpkin glow fills the doorway, where Zero floats in with ears billowing. But not even the sight of him can warm my heart.

"It's Jack." My voice squeaks like rusted hinges. A sheen of sweat breaks out on my brow, dampening my fabric skin, as something deep within me hardens. "He's gone."

My mother gasps, pressing a stitched hand to the folds of her robe.

"You think Prince Dorian took him?" my father asks, squeezing my knee beneath his robe.

Weakly, I hold up the broken Mirror of Reverie. "Jack has the missing shard of this mirror—we can use it to communicate with each other. But when I tried to reach him, there was only darkness."

"Try again," my mother urges.

A whimper rolls off my tongue—I'm afraid of what I'll see. Afraid of only more darkness.

Still, I steel my nerves, digging deep into my stuffing for an extra ounce of strength. I extend the mirror in front of me with the same straight, confident stance that Jack taught me for holding my needle-sword. *Hold it like you mean it, Sally.*

In a shaky voice, I say, *"Eye of silver, wisdom's gleam, show me the truth unseen.* Show me Jack Skellington . . . again."

This time, my parents lean in, too, silently peering into the mirror. Its silver surface ripples like a boulder dropped into a lake, rattling again in its frame, causing waves that distort the reflection of my big pearl-button eyes.

For a moment, I hold my breath.

But then—only darkness. No glimmer. No bones. No Jack.

A wail crawls up my throat. I clamp a hand over my velvet lips, as if I can keep it in. My arm drops, my grasp on the mirror slackening. I'm so devastated that I barely notice when Zero swoops in to hover over my left shoulder, his nose pulsing its orange light.

He barks insistently.

A faint thrum of hope flutters in my veins.

I widen my eyes as I look between Zero and the dark mirror, at whatever has him so excited. "You see something, don't you, Zero?"

He barks again.

I peer closer into the darkened mirror, and the realization hits me. "It's the lights in here!" I look up at the bright flickering foyer lantern. "They're too bright."

"Go outside," my mother eagerly suggests. "It's a moonless night. Pitch-black."

I stumble outside and down the front steps into my overgrown herb garden. The town residents press against the gate, eager and curious—they're all here, even the ones who came to Dream Town, just like Mom said.

"Put out all the lights, everyone!" I call.

The Clown with the Tear-Away Face wheels over to blow out the nearest streetlamp. The Mummy family snuffs out their lantern. Even Scorch extinguishes his tail fire.

It takes my eyes a moment to adjust to the hazy night, but as I hold up the mirror, a gasp brushes across my lips.

"I can see something now—I see lights!"

A lime-green haze casts an eerie glow over what first appears to be a dark sky dotted with twinkling stars. But as my eyes adjust, the shapes of jagged stalactites and stalagmites emerge, like the massive teeth of some colossal beast—and I realize I'm not looking at the night sky at all.

"It's a cave," I say. "Larger than an entire town. Those lights must be glowworms."

I start to turn in a circle, taking in the surroundings. In the distance, I can make out a cluster of lights that looks like a village, though from what I can see, it's a gloomy kind of place, all tired, squat cottages and darkness so thick they might as well have painted the streets black. Perched above the village are four tall shadowy spires with low lights flickering in the windows—a castle.

As I continue to slowly turn, I'm able to make out a dirt path that runs between the stalagmites, with what looks like enormous ferns rising on either side— but in the darkness, they're ghostlike and frightful.

My feet continue to turn, and then . . .

"Jack!"

Tree roots come into view, thick and straight enough to form bars over a dug-out cell. I rush forward, squinting into the mirror.

The light is even dimmer here, but I hear a familiar rasp of dry bones as someone moves. In the next moment, I'm staring right at Jack's shadowy face as he peers into his broken mirror shard.

I swallow down a gasp. My husband has always been gaunt, but now he looks *withered.*

Jack plucks two glowworms from his cell's low

ceiling and tucks them into his empty eye sockets, and I can finally see his face more clearly.

"Sally?" His voice is a dry rasp. "Is it—is it really you?"

"It is, Jack. I'm here in Halloween Town." My words spill out in a rush as the townspeople press in behind me to see. "What happened to you? Are you okay? Are the Wolfman and the vampires there?"

His bones creak, frail and stiff, as he leans against the root bars to support himself. "They're here. Locked in a cell not unlike this one. Sally, there are so many of us prisoners. Leprechauns. Elves. Tooth pixies. Even Lady Lore's own mirror maker. The prince has been busy."

I squeeze the mirror's silver handle, wishing it were Jack's hand.

"I'll let myself be taken," I volunteer, choking back a hiccup. "The next time he comes with his storms. I'll sneak in your sword so we can cut through those tree roots and free you. Then, together, we'll figure out a way to escape—"

"*Sally, no.*" His glowworm eyes widen as he thrusts his face closer to the mirror shard. Long haunting shadows spill over his brows. "Promise me you won't get yourself captured. The ruler here is immensely powerful, and his Shadow Magic grows with every person he takes. Since he abducted the Wolfman and the vampires, he can summon dangerous creatures out of his storm. I have no idea what new powers he gained from me, but it's too dangerous for you to come."

I cry out, "I can't leave you there!"

His head swivels as he looks both ways, then fixes his glowing pinprick eyes on me and drops his voice to a barely-there murmur. "Listen carefully. The other prisoners have been exchanging as much information as we can. The prince's name is Dorian, and he has a twin sister, Dahlia. She ran away years ago—rumor has it she went to Halloween Town."

That's exactly what Thorna told us, too. But I cock my head, blinking hard. "We'd know if a foreign princess was in our realm."

"Perhaps not." Jack's whisper is urgent, his eyes shifting like he expects to be caught at any moment. "It's easy to lose oneself in Recluse Woods. Plenty of souls out there don't want to be found. Search for her there—Zero knows the paths. He can guide you. As Dorian's twin, she's the only person who knows how to defeat his Shadow Magic."

"But how will I know it's her?" I ask, trying to move the mirror closer to see better, but a strange fog has begun to cloud its surface. I frown, wiping my linen palm against the glass, but it doesn't clear it.

Jack says something else, but his voice is distorted this time, crackling like static. *Or thunder.*

I tap the mirror's side a few times, trying to jolt it back into working. "Jack, something's wrong with the mirror."

Scorch suddenly thrusts his big dragon head next to mine, his eyes wide and round.

"Look," he says. "That is not fog. Those are storm clouds. They're *in* the mirror. The prince's cloak . . ."

Before Scorch can finish, the mirror shard is wrestled away from Jack. For a moment, there's nothing but a smear of black . . . and then a gaunt face suddenly fills the mirror.

I cry out, stumbling backward.

I first notice the man's mismatched eyes. One gray. One blue. There's something mesmerizing about them that's hard to describe, like a kaleidoscope's ever-shifting colors. In the shadow-drenched light, his face is all prickly sharp angles; he's tall and thin like a skeleton, but lacking Jack's grace. His skin is a light violet color that reminds me more of a bruise than Dream Town's lavender fields. A tangle of wind-swept, reaper-black hair sticks up at odd angles, with a streak of white hair like a scar across his hairline.

Storm clouds swirl around him. It's hard to

describe the feeling the man exudes. His stormy magic makes me think of a carnival magician, yet his air of melancholy has nothing to do with fun house amusement.

In his mismatched eyes, I see only bottomless pits of anger.

"Well, well. Sally the rag doll." His voice rumbles, his eyes sparking like lightning might crack from his blue and gray irises at any moment. "Or should I call you Pumpkin Queen? You've certainly come a long way from scrubbing floors."

My limbs stiffen. Before I can ask how he knows about my past, he leans in closer to the mirror. "Did I hear you say you want to come to Shadow Town to be with your husband? Very well. *Wish granted.*"

His mouth contorts into a sneer as he reaches toward me.

Impossibly, with a burst of silvery light, his gloved fingers reach *through* the mirror. Wisps of storm clouds bleed through the mirror's surface like candle smoke.

My heart ices over.

I freeze, as immobile as a headstone, as Prince Dorian Dark fastens his iron grip on my shoulder.

"Let me go!" I shout, bursting out of my frozen state.

Anger cuts through my voice like broken glass, tearing out of me as I fight against the prince's hold.

His long bruise-purple fingers dig into my nearly weightless skin, pinching the leaf-and-cotton stuffing inside.

The startled townspeople shout behind me. Zero growls at the hand reaching out of the mirror, snapping his ghostly jaw, but his teeth are nothing but air and dreams.

A wail climbs out of my throat, my body pinwheeling backward, yet no matter how hard I try, I can't escape the prince's grip. I'm too soft and lightweight. With a sudden, vicious yank, Dorian pulls me forward toward the mirror's frame.

Panic spikes through me as gasps ring out from the crowd.

"Let her go!" Behemoth, stout and steady as a boulder, takes hold of my elbow. The Undersea Gal winds her webbed hands around my opposite shoulder. My parents rush forward and wrap their arms firmly around my waist.

Beside me, Luna's face slackens, her voice breaking as she stammers, "How . . . how can he come through the mirror? It's a visual portal, not a physical one!"

"It's his Shadow Magic!" I cry, straining against the prince's hold. One of the people he abducted—Lady

Lore's mirror maker, I realize—must have transferred their magic to him.

"Scorch will help Sally!" With a bellow, Scorch ignites his tail flame, lifting it toward the mirror, but Luna suddenly throws herself between his tail and me.

She gasps, "You can't, Scorch—you might set Sally on fire, too!"

While everyone urgently debates behind me, I brace my hands against the mirror's metal frame, locking my elbows to resist Prince Dorian's strength. He shoves his other hand through the mirror's quicksilver pool and latches on to my left wrist, then tugs hard enough that I lose my grip. I yelp as my arm plunges into the mirror as far as my elbow.

I feel like I'm about to be squeezed through a keyhole. My body is much too large to fit through the mirror's width, and yet I'm all soft, pliable fabric. Meant to be hugged and squeezed.

There's a chance he *can* pull me through into Shadow Town.

With the prince holding my arm and my townspeople gripping the rest of my body, I cry out like a toy fought over by two quarreling children. The seams across my rib cage groan and strain. I'm not made of bone or steel like so many of my friends—if I'm pulled too hard, I'll tear apart.

"Why . . . are . . . you . . . doing . . . this?" I gasp, each word forced out of my stretched, threadbare lungs.

"You and I are overdue for a long talk," Prince Dorian spits. "Dahlia and I created Shadow Town as a refuge for everyone abandoned and forgotten. Like *we* were. But you couldn't resist meddling, could you? Couldn't let us be happy at last?"

"I didn't *do* anything!" I sputter. "I've never met you before!"

Prince Dorian's face twists into an angry sneer, his lavender teeth flashing.

"This is a disaster!" the Mayor wails behind me. "Sally will be stolen just like Jack! Someone, close the portal!"

"We can't," my mother gasps, still tugging at my shoulder. "If we do, Sally will be severed."

Being pulled apart at the seams is a fear that haunts every rag doll. Our limbs can easily be detached and resewn, but what if they're separated between *worlds*?

My captured hand, in the Shadow Town side of the mirror, flutters its fingers urgently at me, trying to get my attention. My index finger points insistently at my shoulder seam.

It wants me to detach the limb, I realize.

Tears prickle behind my linen eyelids, but I blink

them away and, determinedly, grab the thread that holds my left arm on to my shoulder.

I tug.

With a *pop*, it breaks.

My left arm falls away into Dorian's grip–into Shadow Town, while the rest of me is in Halloween Town. Momentarily, I'm free. I stumble back into a jumble of protective arms–Behemoth's, the Undersea Gal's, my parents'–and in the chaos, the mirror tumbles out of my hand and lands with a clatter on a dried patch of forget-me-nots.

Through the mirror's surface, Prince Dorian appears caught off guard, falling backward, my detached left arm tumbling down beside him. The momentary shock on his face soon twists into anger.

Before he can push to his feet, however, I signal to my detached left hand, and it clenches into a tight fist, swings around, and pops him on the nose.

He shrieks, clutching his face, and my hand starts clawing him like an annoyed house cat.

While my left arm distracts Prince Dorian, putting up a valiant fight, I bend down to scoop the mirror back up with my right hand. I might be free of his grasp, but I can't abandon my poor arm in Shadow Town.

My fingers have barely brushed the handle when

the prince reaches his hand through the mirror again. I shriek, trying to kick the mirror away, but he manages to grab on to my ankle. He tugs hard enough to make me crash down onto the ground, then drags my leg through the mirror up to mid-thigh.

Panicked, I reach for the thread at my hip, not knowing what else to do.

Pop.

My left leg detaches. It falls through the mirror into Shadow Town, where it kicks against Dorian's shin again and again.

"Arm!" I call. "Leg! Come back to me."

Swiftly, I plunge my remaining hand through the mirror, grab my detached arm, and pull it through the liquid quicksilver. My leg hops anxiously on the other side of the mirror, and I reach through and pull it out, hugging it close with my free hand.

I'm okay, I think. *I'm whole. All parts accounted for.*

Prince Dorian's hand rises through the mirror as he tries to fit himself through—but he's all bone, too thick and stiff to pass through.

"Break the mirror!" someone shouts.

"Challenge accepted!" Lock, Shock, and Barrel shout in unison, rushing up with a wheelbarrow piled high with sparking fireworks they must have stolen from Fourth of July Town. Lock's grin is wild, and his devil mask looms like a specter in the moonlight. "Step back, everyone—no treats now, only a trick!"

The night suddenly explodes in a symphony of light and sound. Fireworks blast into the air, scattering golden sparks and thick plumes of colorful smoke.

The mirror shatters in a cascade of silver shards.

There's no more sign of the prince.

My parents rush over and wrap their arms tightly around me as tears soak into my soot-streaked dress. I cling to my detached limbs as though I might drift apart entirely. As I look around at the faces of my friends who risked everything to save me, my stomach pulls tight as a spindle.

With a shaking hand, I stow one of the broken mirror shards in my pocket.

I want to feel safe. And maybe I am, now. But I'm shaken to my very core—because I might have been spared, but Jack is still trapped in the world beyond the mirror.

7

Back at home, I sit at the kitchen table, hands splayed on the wooden tabletop to ground myself. I'm dazed. Shell shocked. In fact, the only thing that manages to pull me out of my stupor is the scrumptious smell of the troll cookies that Luna pulls out of the oven.

"Here. You need food." My mother takes the seat next to me, sliding over the piping hot cookies. When I don't move, she gently rubs my knee. "It's okay, Sally. You're safe now. Prince Dorian didn't pull you through to Shadow Town."

She rests her palm on my face, tenderly stroking

my cheek seam with her thumb, still her little lost girl even now that I'm grown.

Moving like a puppet, I take a cookie, but it tastes like sand in my mouth. I push away the tray. All I can think of is Dorian's grip on my shoulder. His harsh, angry words.

You had to meddle, didn't you?

Ever since Dorian pulled me through the mirror, that phrase has battered my mind again and again, like shovelfuls of dirt thrown on a coffin. At the time, I was so frantic to escape that I didn't pay close attention. Now, though, as I'm slowly growing more clearheaded, his words burn through my mind.

What in the world was he talking about?

I swallow a dry bite of cookie, then clasp my trembling hands in my lap, hiding them under the table so no one will see, and glance at the dark clouds beyond the windows.

"You should go back to Dream Town," I tell them in a thin voice. "Make sure your people are safe. You heard what Jack said—the prince is abducting people from all towns."

My mother nudges the cookie tray my direction again. "We've been in communication with Santa Claus. Since it's a while before his holiday, Christmas Town is slow, and the polar bears are guarding its gates. He's agreed to watch over Dream Town in our absence. We couldn't leave you now."

"But Luna—"

"Her parents are unreachable, deep in a remote section of Fable Town woods while they pursue their research project. They couldn't return even if they did know the dangers, because of the travel restrictions. They entrusted her care to us, so Luna is safest wherever we are."

I look up through my lashes at their determined faces. My father's chin tips high. My mother squares her shoulders. "You *need* us."

A shout comes from outside, followed by the sound of hammering. I rush to the window, pressing my hand against the glass.

In the town square, the Mayor is emphatically calling out directions through his megaphone to everyone. They're carrying on Jack's plan. Boarding up windows. Erecting more weather vanes.

My heart hammers against my ribs, loud and hollow, each beat echoing like funeral bells. The weight of what lies ahead presses down on me, relentless and cold, but then I catch sight of Jack's latest book on the kitchen counter—bookmarked, just waiting for Jack to pick it back up. The cozy sight fills me to the brim with renewed determination. I won't stop until Jack is here with me, the book in hand, ready to regale me with stories of his grand adventures.

"Well, if I can't convince you to return home, then I suppose we could use the extra hands," I admit. "See what you can do to help the townspeople put up reinforcements."

I bend over to tug on my boots, pulling the laces taut.

"What are you going to do?" My mother asks with eyes wide open.

I call to Zero and rest my hand on his ghostly head. "Zero and I have a mission of our own—we're headed to Recluse Woods."

Zero and I travel along the dirt path that hugs the cemetery wall, the same path Jack and I took when we passed the abandoned old hospital. When there was a working portal to another realm here, this must have been such a bustling place. Now, the building's burned-out windows stare like unblinking eyes, giving me shivers as my footsteps crunch through a thick layer of fallen leaves.

Ahead, the path forks; the cobblestone road to the left will eventually lead to the Hinterlands, I know—Jack and I have taken it many times on our adventures. The path to the right, however, is barely more than a foot trail through cornfields that disappears into Recluse Woods.

I hesitate at the fork, drawing my cloak tighter against the fog that looms knee-high, feeling the leaf-and-cotton stuffing in my chest rustle anxiously. The crows caw sharply overhead, a warning. I've only come this far a handful of times, to gather wild feverfew by the woodland stream.

Swallowing down my fear, I step onto the right-hand path.

As the trees grow denser, the air turns cooler and the fog thickens. The trees' silence, which I might enjoy if the situation were different, feels unsettling now. After a few hundred feet, Zero and I reach the stream bank where the feverfew's tiny white blossoms grow. I hesitate only a moment before crossing a fallen log—a makeshift footbridge—over the stream.

This is the farthest I've ever traveled into these woods.

The overgrown trail follows the winding stream to a beaver pond that is ringed with cattails and marked by a rickety old fishing dock that I don't dare to tread on, certain even my light weight will make it collapse.

Something small and black darts across the path, making me stop short.

"Zero! Did you see—"

Another one of the creatures pops out of the tall dried grass ahead, blinking its sly green eyes at me.

A black cat.

Two more black cats emerge from the grass, their curious tails twitching in the fog. A fourth one catches my eye, perched in the crook of a winter-bare tree.

"Here, little friends." I crouch down and click my tongue, which always brings Halloween Town's stray black cat to me for a chin scratch. But as soon as I address this wild herd, they dart off deeper into the forest.

"Wait!" I cry, one hand extended.

But the cats are gone.

As Zero and I venture deeper, we come across old wooden fences and shriveled pumpkin vines choking the ground—a sign someone once farmed here, but whoever they were, they're long gone. I shiver and walk faster, passing a small forgotten cemetery nestled beneath hemlocks. The headstones are worn and cracked, barely legible, with ivy creeping over them like greedy fingers.

A smokehouse looms in the distance, its roof

sagging under years of neglect. Beside it, a few broken-down stalls mark the remains of what was once a market square.

"This must be the old settlement Jack told me about." I keep my voice hushed, afraid of alerting any nearby creatures to my presence. "Where the first residents of Halloween Town lived before building our current town."

A creak of wood to my left makes me jump. Zero growls, his long ears pinned back. The creak comes again, followed by a strange, steady rhythm.

I whip around to face a tumbledown cottage, where two elderly figures sit in wooden rockers on a ramshackle front porch. The chairs' steady rocking is the source of the creak.

They're skeletons, like Jack.

Only, these two are weathered with age, their bones a faded yellow brown, like the brittle husks of autumn leaves. Their skulls aren't shiny cue balls anymore but rather dull and porous, stripped of any former gleam. Moss grows on their kneecaps, and old cobwebs span their cracked rib cages.

"H-hello?" I call.

Their two heads, dry and brittle, creak toward my voice at the same time.

"Well, Abner, you see?" the one on the left says. "I

told you. I had a feeling in my bones we'd get a visitor today!"

"Lewin, I guess you were right."

I throw glances at the forest around us. I'm a rag doll—a child's toy. People in Halloween Town have come to know and respect me, but the monsters out here might think I'm something to play games with.

"I'm Sally." I clear my throat. "Queen Sally, co-ruler of Halloween Town, which includes Recluse Woods. I'm sorry that I haven't come to visit yet—I haven't been the queen for long, and much of our realm is new to me."

"A queen!" The skeleton called Lewin leans forward, his old bones creaking. "Is that so? Step closer, Majesty. Even closer. We don't see so well these days."

"Nor any other days, come to think of it." The other, Abner, chuckles. "No eyes!"

They wheeze laughter, grinning good-naturedly as they rock back and forth in opposite rhythms.

The tight stitch in my chest eases. "May I ask why you live all the way out here?"

"Oh, this has been the Grave brothers' home forever! Never saw any reason to leave," Lewin says. "Years ago, the other creepy-crawlies around here picked up and built that fancy brick town you hail from, Majesty. But we Grave brothers? We were plenty comfy right here."

Abner pats his yellowed rib cage. "It isn't as though we need to come to town much—skeletons don't need to eat!"

They laugh again, their bones softly rattling.

I can't help smiling, though I still throw nervous glances toward the woods. "Maybe you can help me. I'm searching for a woman who might live in Recluse Woods—someone not from here. A princess. Her name is Dahlia Dark."

Their rocking chairs continue to creak, filling a long silence, before Lewin clears the cobwebs from his throat. "Don't know anyone by that name, Majesty. Certainly no princesses. Then again, folks come out here to be alone. To live on their own terms. Not everyone wants to be found—and some will do just about anything to keep it that way."

I hug my cloak tighter around my shoulders.

"Oh, don't scare her, Lewin." Abner slaps his rocking chair's wooden arm. "We aren't all fearsome things. Say, what about that sweet hedge witch who comes to dust off our bones? She's never told us her name, just smiles when we ask."

"A hedge witch?" I ask.

"Hedge witches are healers," Abner explains. "They practice wild magic beyond the borders of towns. Beyond the *hedges*, get it? Some say they live between worlds."

A whisper of excitement licks up my spine, because someone living between worlds sounds exactly like who I'm seeking.

"She's a kind little thing," Abner continues. "She comes when the seasons change to dust off our cobwebs and oil our chairs. But don't let that fool you—I once watched her turn a biting fly to ash to teach the others in the swarm a lesson."

I tug on the loose string around my wrist, attention sliding to the woods. I can't help being curious about Dahlia Dark, the mysterious ruler who tried to save her town from her brother's tyranny. Does she have Shadow Magic, like her brother? Does she fear him? And of all places, why did she choose to flee to Halloween Town?

"Do you know where she lives?" I ask.

"Out beyond the bone yard—look for a rusted mailbox."

I thank the old skeleton brothers and continue along the path, my steps more purposeful now. The farther Zero and I venture into Recluse Woods, the darker it grows. Towering pines curtain off sunlight.

The ground is damp and spongy. I feel like, at any point, my foot might sink into a mud pit and I'll never get out.

Zero flies ahead of me, his pumpkin nose lighting up the darkest shadows. I draw my cloak tighter against the chill that wraps itself around my ankles and seems to want to hold me here.

Soon, we come to a large patch of bare ground where dusty bones poke out of the soil. *The bone yard.* I'm relieved to find a well-kept bridge on the other side. Orange sunlight winks ahead on something metal, and we push through until we come to a small cottage with a tin roof.

Along the path, there's a rusted mailbox on a locust wood post.

I pause to take it in.

The cottage is old but in good repair; the windows are freshly washed, and a hammer and nails rest on the front porch where someone's been replacing a rotten board. There's a picket fence around a garden that's bursting with plump tomatoes, round pumpkins, and sky-high stalks of golden corn. Several fishing poles lean against the front porch, and just down the hill, a trout jumps in a lily pond.

"Hello?" I call, daring to raise my voice.

There's a rustle in the woods behind me, and I

twirl around, my hand plunging into my pocket for my needle-sword, but it's only a chipmunk hopping along the tree roots.

My shoulders ease. I swing open the fence gate and cautiously step onto the porch.

"Hello?" I knock on the door. There's no answer.

I peer into the windows, pressing my face against the glass, and see a kettle over a low fire—someone has been here recently. Bundles of fresh herbs rest on a wooden worktable. A basket holds shed deer antlers.

"I'm looking for Princess Dahlia Dark," I call. "It's urgent I speak with her."

Again, there's no answer, and I pull myself away from the door, pacing as I tug at the too-loose thread on my wrist. Considering the kettle is still on, the resident must have left only a moment ago.

I hear a soft humming in the distance and hurry to the end of the porch, where I see a woman coming out of the woods. She's wearing a wide-brimmed hat and carrying a basket filled with walnuts. Hair the color of bluebells cascades over her shoulders and complements her light brown skin tone, and it gives me pause—I expected that, as Dorian's twin, she would have his same white-streaked black hair and purple skin. But perhaps not.

I press on, calling in a friendly tone that I hope

won't scare her away. "Hello there! I'm looking for someone—do you happen to know Prince Dorian Dark of Shadow Town?"

The woman's wide-eyed attention snaps to me, and the basket falls from her grasp, walnuts rolling across the front path.

For a second, she only stares. A flicker of recognition crosses her face—strangely, I almost think she knows *me*, until I realize that Dorian's name must have triggered the look.

She takes an unsteady step backward, her eyes never leaving mine. Her gaze darts briefly to the forest—as if she's weighing her chances of fleeing.

But then she seems to change her mind and straightens. She studies me.

"What do you want with Dorian?" Her voice is cool, wary. As though she expects lies to pour out of me.

The suspicion in her words takes me aback, and I study her more closely—her light brown face dotted with freckles, a thick scar visible on her breastbone just above her collar. I search my memory, trying to place her.

But she's as much a stranger as old Abner and Lewin.

"It's you, isn't it?" I dare a step forward, slowly, so

I don't spook her like a wild animal. "You're Princess Dahlia. Dorian's sister."

She scoffs, looking away as a strange ripple of hurt crosses her eyes. "Haven't you done enough damage? Are you going to report me again—only this time to Dorian?"

The air seems to still around me, as though even the dancing june bugs are trapped in time. Something tickles at the deepest folds in my brain, but I can't quite drag it up to the surface.

"Report you . . . again?" I breathe. "Do—do I *know* you?"

She barks a mirthless laugh, full of pain she's trying to mask, but when her eyes turn back to me, they waver with uncertainty. "Do you really not remember?"

"Remember *what*?" I throw my hands wide, shaking my head. "Tell me—have we met before? Maybe in Dream Town when I was young, or . . . at an All Realms Gathering?"

This time, her eyes narrow more with curiosity than ire. Her rosewood lips part, on the verge of spilling some long-withheld secret, but then she snaps her mouth firm.

"More tricks—well, what did I expect, given who raised you? I have nothing to say to you, Sally. You'll leave Dorian alone if you know what's good for you. As for me, I don't wish to be found."

She draws a long, thin willow wand out of her pocket.

Before I can move, she jabs the wand in the air like a dagger, and ivy sprouts from the ground at my feet. It crawls up my shoes. Tangles in the laces.

I cry out and jump back, freeing myself, but my feet still tingle in an odd way that I can't seem to shake.

"So don't bother trying to find me again," she continues. "Because those rag doll feet of yours won't be able to set foot in Recluse Woods. I'm banishing you, Pumpkin Queen."

She cuts a sharp line through the air with the wand, and my body goes strangely numb; it's swift and all-consuming, like I've been plunged into ice water. My vision blurs. I feel my limbs swaying with minds of their own, and I spin in a drunken circle, balance tipping sharply to the right—

Then, I blink and everything is bright.

Zero is beside me.

Sunlight warms my forest-cooled skin. Zero and I are outside of Recluse Woods now, back on the path near Oogie Boogie's old lair, staring at the edge of the forest where we first entered.

Zero's ears prick upward, a curious whine cork-screwing from his snout.

"I—I'm not sure what happened, either," I admit, resting a steadying hand against my still-reeling head. I blink a few more times, then run my hands down my dress to make sure I'm unharmed. Once I assure myself I'm okay, my hands fold into determined fists. "But I'm going to find out."

I march straight back toward Recluse Woods, yet as soon as I've reached the first tree, my foot simply *stops*. Rooted to the ground like before, as though phantom ivy is coiled around me, holding me back. I reach forward, but it's like pressing against invisible glass.

I step back, breathing deeply, and try again.

Only to run into the same invisible wall.

Zero lets out a worried bark and darts forward, easily slipping between the trees that wouldn't let me cross. He vanishes into the branches, and for a second, I'm alone at the edge of the dark wood, shivers quaking the curled leaves in my chest.

"Zero!" I call out, voice breaking—and am immediately relieved when a flash of ghostly white floats back out, circling around me with a wagging tail. I nearly fall over my own feet to run my hands over his ghostly head. "Well, it seems you aren't banished, but I am."

I bite my lip, sliding a look into the darkest part of the forest, wondering what secrets Dahlia has buried coffin-deep among the shadows—and how I'll uncover them to save Jack and the others.

But a whisper stirs inside me that the real secrets might not be in the woods at all. I can't stop thinking about what she said. About Dorian's strange words, too.

The real secrets might be buried in me.

8

My house is too quiet. Too empty.

I'm in our kitchen, normally a place filled with clattering pans, the warm maple smell of fresh pancakes, and Jack's laughter as Zero's wagging tail stirs a draft.

But now?

It's just me. My parents and Luna are with the witches in their apothecary, scrying with Santa Claus to check in on Dream Town. Jack is gone.

Zero curls in my lap, snoring softly, but his little ghost body doesn't give off any warmth. Soft rain batters the kitchen windows—regular rain, thankfully, at least for now—and I turn to look at the black-cat clock on the wall.

It's barely late afternoon, but the dark clouds outside make the world look as dark as midnight.

With each jump of the tail-shaped hand, new questions take root in my mind. I realize that my search for answers isn't just about Dahlia. Or even Prince Dorian.

As fiercely as I want Jack back, it's not just the fear of losing him that keeps me moving. It's fear of losing myself. The fear of my nightmare—trapped in a pit of darkness, no way out.

Someone knocks on the door, and my head jerks up. Tugging at my loose wrist thread, I make my way into the hall, frowning at the rain battering the windows.

Cautiously, I unlock the door. "Hello?"

"It's us!" Luna and Scorch huddle together at the top of my rickety front steps, Scorch's left wing extended as an umbrella over Luna's yarn hair. My parents stand behind them, holding up newspapers to keep their yarn hair dry.

I quickly let them inside. The wind blows in rain at a sharp angle until I can close and lock the door behind them. Gathering my hair, I wring out the dampness. "What did Santa Claus say?"

"Not much to report," my father rattles off. "Which is a *good* thing these days. Town is quiet. The gates remain firmly shut. So far, all residents accounted for."

"But we do have something to tell you." My mother's eyes gleam, bright and sparkling. *"Luna found something."*

I cock my head, curious.

"It's about the Grimoriel." Luna's voice is hushed, as if she's trying to hold in a burst of excitement. Now I can see that she has the magical book clutched tightly beneath her robe. She tromps farther into the foyer, wet boots squelching, and shrugs out of her rain-soaked robe, hanging it on a scorpion-tail hook.

I grab a towel to dry Scorch's scales, then usher them into the living room, where I turn on lamps and stoke the dwindling fire back to a roar. Scorch plods over to Zero's dog bed by the hearth, turning in a circle before attempting to squeeze his backside onto the tiny cushion.

"I'll get us warm drinks," I say. "Wait here."

I head to the kitchen and soon return with three large mugs of rosemary bone broth, but when I set the tray on the coffee table, Luna is so excited she hardly glances at it. Clutching the Grimoriel, she paces excitedly in front of the fireplace.

"After scrying with Dream Town," she buzzes, "I

got to thinking about other types of portals. I remembered how Thorna emerged from the Grimoriel. Then I remembered one of the other stories in the book."

She thumbs open the book to where it's marked with a chewed-up pencil and slides it across the coffee table for me to read.

I lean forward, the mug of bone broth warming my hands against the frigid wind slipping through the wall cracks.

Softly, I read aloud, "'Night Magic's Impossible Riddle.'" And then, the first sentence. "'Only one being is made of the night—she is called the Night Mare.'"

My gaze shoots up to meet Luna's.

Her eyes gleam like pearl buttons as she leans forward, gripping her knees to contain her excitement. "Remember when Scorch led us through Fable Town? There was a statue in Villain Village of a—"

"A horse," I finish as the memory returns to me. "I remember. A horse painted as black as midnight. The tall witch mentioned it just the other day. Said it had powerful Night Magic. The Wolfman said it was only a legend."

Luna shrugs, undaunted. "Well, let's put it to the test. If Thorna can be summoned out of this book, maybe the Night Mare can, too."

My skin prickles with the whisper of magic as I

pull the heavy Grimoriel into my lap. Outside, the storm pounds harder, branches clawing against the windows.

Luna and my parents press in to read over my shoulder.

"'In the never nowhere,'" I read, "'there lived a horse called the Night Mare. Her black coat was sleek as oil, her hooves forged from obsidian. No one knew from what realm she came—or if she came from a realm at all. It was rumored she belonged only to the night, which spans all realms, linking them all yet belonging to none. In this in-between existence, the Night Mare alone had the ability to harness Night Magic, the strongest magic of all.'"

Out of the corner of my eye, the room's light takes on a rich golden hue, growing so intense that I have to squeeze my eyes shut against the brilliance.

Luna gasps softly. My father murmurs something under his breath, full of awe. The golden light warms my fabric skin, and I dare to open my eyes.

When I do, I feel the world shift.

A creature stands in my house, straight out of the Grimoriel's ruffled pages. A black horse—no, not just black. Her coat is the deep velvet of a moonless night sky, yet golden strands wink and glow softly. Her mane flows as if caught in an invisible breeze.

Her dark eyes are large, deep, ancient. And somehow gentle.

All of us in the room can only stare in awe.

"You're here," I whisper.

"Why have you summoned me?" The Night Mare's voice echoes in the air, though her lips don't move a fraction. It's as though her voice comes from everywhere and nowhere at once.

I'm so rattled that I drop the Grimoriel on the braided rug—it falls closed, but the mystical horse doesn't vanish. Not like Thorna did.

My brows pinch together as I look between the horse and the closed book. "You're . . . you're still here."

The answer comes from all corners of the room. *"My powers extend far beyond the Grimoriel."*

My skin prickles, ticklish and alive. "Is it true that you can wield the most powerful magic of all?"

"Yes."

I tug on the loose thread on my wrist, pulling it tighter, needing the grounding feeling of control. "Powerful enough to defeat Shadow Magic?"

The Night Mare takes her time studying me with her dark eyes as my heart rattles hard in my chest. *"Yes."*

I pluck at my dress collar, feeling suddenly warm, as though I'm an inch from the fire instead of six feet away. Excited, I wet my dry lips, scooting to the edge of the velvet couch.

"Our friends have been abducted to Shadow Town. Will you help us bring them back?"

In her ghostly projection, her ethereal mane moves around her neck, swaying and magical, like she's underwater. She peers at me as if she can see straight through my linen exterior to the shy, lonely girl in a tower who gazed out at a town she desperately wanted to be a part of. The girl who finally got everything she wished for—and will do anything to get it back again.

The Night Mare tips her head toward the Grimoriel. *You did not finish reading my story. If you had, you would have learned that I am bound by the Night Rules.*

My hands tighten over my knees. "What are those?"

"My magic works in a delicate balance with the three elements of night: the moon, the stars, and the witching hour. If you wish for my help, you must, in turn, maintain the balance. You must perform three impossible tasks."

I stand up, setting the Grimoriel aside, pacing circles around the spiral-pattern floor until I notice the overturned mug on the rug. Offhand, I set it back on the table, staring at the small puddle of spilled bone broth, wishing saving Jack were as simple as mopping up liquid.

Impossible tasks?

Well, haven't I faced impossible odds before? Rescue Santa Claus? Put the Sandman to sleep? Turn time from past to future and back again?

Taking a deep breath, I ask, "What are these tasks?"

The Night Mare lifts her head, her ink-black mane swirling. *"You must fly without wings. You must solve an unsolvable maze. You must catch a star."*

My mom swallows a sharp gasp.

The tasks tumble through my head with all the dizzying chaos of fire ants. Moving too fast to catch. It feels as though an invisible hand curls around my throat, threatening to squeeze.

"But those are . . . well . . . they're . . . *impossible!*" I sputter.

The Night Mare flicks her tail in gentle amusement. *"Yes."*

I feel the prickle of coming tears needling behind my eyelids, and it's all I can do to hold back my sob. Fly without wings? Catch a star? How could anyone even begin to solve such riddles? I twist my bone wedding ring on my finger, pacing to the window, gaze pinned on the dark clouds.

"What about your spells, Sally?" Luna suggests.

I shake my head, biting back the flood of tears. "My spells couldn't even point me in the right direction."

"We'll call on the other town rulers for help," my father says. "They'll come to our aid."

I shake my head. "They're needed in their towns to defend against Prince Dorian."

My mother sputters, "Our Sally can't do those tasks—no one can!"

The Night Mare turns to her, the scent of iron shifting toward our direction. *The Night Rules are nothing if not fair. If she wants magic, she must give magic.*

My mother's face twists as she holds back tears, her eyes glistening with doubt, but I quickly squeeze her hands.

"I can do it, Mom. I don't know how, but I can." I meet the Night Mare's stare. "Tell me how to accomplish the tasks." I force my voice to be steady and firm, for Luna's and my parents' sakes if nothing else. "I'll undergo any quest to save my town."

"They are your riddles to solve, not mine." The horse

blinks slowly as though she has all the time in the world—and perhaps, as a creature of night, she *does*.

But I don't have the same luxury. Jack and the others are trapped in Shadow Town. Prince Dorian is coming for the rest of us. One by one, he's going to pick us off until there's no one left.

The invisible hand tightens more around my throat. "How long do I have?"

"Sally," my father whispers urgently, chewing so anxiously on the inside of his cheek that I'm afraid he'll gnaw a hole straight through. "You can't be seriously considering this. No one could do those tasks. As a ruler, you need to be reasonable."

"I have to try." I brush the glistening tears off my lashes, then draw myself up to full height to address the Night Mare again. "I'll do it—I'll find a way."

"You must complete all three tasks before the next full moon."

Scorch plods over to Jack's wall calendar, where Jack penciled in the phases of the moon in each box's corner. Luna joins him there, running her finger over the boxes, counting. "According to this, it's twelve days until the next one."

Twelve days?

The strength goes out of my knees, and I sink onto

the couch, swaying like a scarecrow in the wind, hollow and straw-light. But I can't let Luna and Scorch see my doubt. This isn't just about me; it's about protecting those I love, about not letting Prince Dorian steal what I've fought so hard for.

I plant my feet on the rug as I lift the Grimoriel back into my arms. "I'll do the three tasks. I'll find a way."

I feel the weight of the impossible tasks settling on my shoulders, pressing me down, but I refuse to break. Rag dolls weren't made to shatter, after all. We aren't bone china, easily broken—I was made to be tossed, thrown, cuddled, played with. I was made to be *loved.* And love doesn't come without tatters and tears.

The Night Mare slowly lowers her head in acknowledgment. *"Before the full moon, then, Pumpkin Queen."*

"Before the full moon." I mirror her nod.

The Night Mare fades until there's nothing but a faint, lingering shimmer of gold dust in the air—I could almost convince myself I imagined it all.

Except everyone else in the room saw it, too.

Luna tugs on her pajama sleeves as she turns back to the wall calendar. She chews on a porcelain fingernail. In a quiet voice, she asks, "How, Sally?"

I give my dress a sharp, sensible tug. "The same way anyone accomplishes anything: by starting at the beginning, of course."

I grab an eraser and scrub Jack's diagrams of pumpkin-catapulting machines off the chalkboard. Taking up a piece of fresh chalk, I write the Night Mare's three tasks in big bold letters, then stand back to take them in.

Fly Without Wings
Solve an Unsolvable Maze
Catch a Star

As I stare at the chalkboard, my lettering blurs with Jack's half-erased brainstorming schematics. He's always been so certain. So unwaveringly optimistic. How many nights have I seen him scribbling away until dawn on one plan or another, not sleeping a wink?

My fingers tremble, leaving white chalk smudges on my dress. The immensity of the tasks before me hits me all at once: these aren't just tasks; they're *tests*. Each one designed to push me to the breaking point.

My stitches groan, straining under the weight of what I've taken on, but seeing Jack's half-erased plans inspires me. How many times did Jack's plans fail only for him to pick himself back up and try again?

I step forward purposefully, dust the chalk powder off my hands, and underline the first task with bold strokes.

Fly Without Wings

O ver the next few days, my parents, Luna, Scorch, and I put our heads together to think of every possible way to fly without wings.

"Sew a hang glider," Luna suggests. "Out of owl feathers, the lightest there are. Then jump off Spiral Hill and try to fly."

"Goodness, no." My mother presses her hands to her cheek patches. "Sally will crash into a headstone and burst a seam!"

"Scorch will fly Sally as high as she wants to go," the dragon offers.

I give him a soft smile. "Thanks, Scorch, but you have wings, remember? I can't use those."

This rules out several other ideas. If wings are off the table, I can't barter with the cave bats to lift me into the air. Likewise, I can't use my spell for creating winged boots out of crow feathers and ribbon.

"Borrow one of the witches' brooms," my mother suggests.

Sadly, I shake my head. "Each broom only works for the witch who manages to charm it."

"What about Dr. Finkelstein's flying reindeer skeletons?" Luna asks.

Another headshake. "I already checked Hemlock Hall—nothing left."

My father heaves a heavy sigh, rubbing the bridge of his nose. "You simply can't do this on your own. We should reach out to the other rulers. Santa Claus would gladly lend you his sleigh."

Yet when we send a message by crow to Santa Claus, he regretfully responds that his reindeer fly only in December. Likewise, letters flood back from Tooth Town, Time Town, and Easter Town—everyone wants to help, but no one knows how to fly without wings.

With every day that passes, Luna marks a black X on the calendar. Every one of those marks chills my stuffing, curls my dried leaves, makes me feel as claustrophobic as my nightmare of being trapped in the dark.

What happens when the entire calendar fills with X's?

As I'm staring at the calendar, a wolf spider plods her way across the slick paper, her many eyes reflecting back my tight-set face.

"Ew, a spider," Luna says, shuffling out of her shoe. She picks the shoe up and pulls her hand back, ready to smoosh the spider.

"No, don't!" I catch her wrist an inch above the calendar. "Spiders are misunderstood," I explain as I take the shoe out of her hand and bend down to tie it back on her foot. "I came to know them well when I lived in Dr. Finkelstein's house. They were my only companions. I left the window open each day so they could catch bugs for their supper. I'd never hurt them. In fact, they once spun a silken string for me when I ran out of thread...."

My voice trails off as an idea weaves itself into my skull.

Slowly, I grin.

Then we set to work.

My latest plan? A parachute. But not just any parachute. This one will be made from pound after pound of silver-gray spider silk, painstakingly woven into a windproof net by the ninety-nine orb weaver spiders that live in our attic.

The spiders agree to help, and fan out across the couch, coffee table, and fireplace mantel, spinning silk until their little legs sag from exhaustion.

When they're done, we admire their handiwork together.

"Thank you." I clasp my hands in front of my chest. "It's a work of art, truly. A masterpiece. I really can't express how much your help means to me."

The orb weavers bob up and down as though saying goodbye before marching off in single file up the door trim to a crack in the ceiling, back to their waiting egg sacs.

"I still can't believe you convinced spiders to help." A shiver runs from my mother's head to the hem of her plaid pajamas as she watches the last spider disappear. "In Dream Town, we sweep away their cobwebs. Nothing disturbs a good night's sleep like a spider crawling on your nose!"

"I'm the queen of Halloween Town, remember?" I gently remind her. "Here, spiders are our neighbors. Our friends."

My mother gazes up at the gargoyles carved into

our crown molding. "Sometimes I forget you aren't a part of our town anymore." She gives me a reassuring pat. "At least, not officially. You'll always be our daughter, of course."

My father pulls me into a hug. "Don't forget, your people are relying on you—don't take any unnecessary risks. We'll watch from the garden. Ready to catch you, should we need to."

As Luna and I climb the ladder to my roof, the parachute tucked under my arm, my hands feel clammy, slipping against the rungs. The leaves in my chest crackle and rustle, poking me with their sharp edges to remind me of all the things that could go wrong.

"Goodness!" As we climb onto the roof tiles, the wind blusters against my delicate cheeks, chapping my exposed skin. A few slate tiles slide off and fall into the garden. I peer down at the ground far below, and a chill spreads through my fabric.

What if I'm not high enough? Or worse, too high?

Scorch flies to the rooftop and lands beside the chimney pipe. His tail fire sputters, struggling to provide us with warmth and light while the wind keeps blowing it out.

"It's too windy!" A sudden gust nearly steals

Luna's voice, so she cups her hands and yells in my ear, "We should wait until tomorrow!"

I shake my head fiercely—I can't bear to see another black X on the calendar. Another failure. Another day further from Jack. Cupping my own hands, I call back, "Wait here, Luna! Hold on to the ladder so you don't blow away!"

I pull myself the rest of the way onto the roof, steadying myself by leaning into the wind. Its frigid chill stings my eyes, making them water, but I squint and push on.

"Hold on to Scorch!" Scorch extends his paw, and I grip his talon as he pulls me safely to the chimney. He peers nervously down at the three-story fall. "Queen Sally is sure about this?"

Well, am I?

I've fallen before. From windows. From doors. From rooftops. I want to tell him that falling isn't what I'm afraid of—broken seams can be sewn back together. What I fear most is what *can't* be mended: losing a person you love, forever.

"As sure as I'll ever be."

"Climb on Scorch's back." The dragon lowers himself so I can throw one leg over his rough scales, clutching the parachute tightly with one hand and wrapping the other around his neck.

I've barely adjusted my position when his haunches bunch, and suddenly, he's charging toward the edge. I'm so lightweight, nothing but fabric and stuffing, that if I don't hold on, I'll be bounced off. My teeth rattle in my skull with every step. My heartbeat gallops along with the *thunk-thunk* of his paws on the roof tiles—until he jumps, wings fanning out on either side of us.

My stomach shoots to my throat as Scorch soars upward over the garden, circling higher and higher.

"For Jack," I whisper to myself.

Squeezing my eyes shut, I grip the edge of the parachute—

—and slide off Scorch's back.

Down, down, down.

Above me, the parachute opens, and for a second, I feel a tug as it lifts me. Hope fills my lungs. But there's something wrong. Soon, I start falling again—fast. The chute is too small. Or I'm too heavy. Even as a lightweight rag doll, I weigh much more than a spider. There must have been something wrong with our calculations. It isn't enough to hold me.

As I plunge downward, a scream tearing from my throat, the parachute catches on a branch and shreds. A ripping sound tears through the night.

The ground rises up sharply as my rag doll body

cartwheels down to the front yard, limbs tangled in tattered spider silk. I frantically kick my feet, trying to right myself, but all I see are the sharp spikes of our wrought iron fence coming at me fast.

With a cry, I land squarely on one of the spikes.

It punches through my flimsy fabric skin, through leaves and stuffing, through my patchwork dress. Pain blooms around the wound as I dangle backward over the fence, flailing, but I can't get myself free.

"Sally, hold on!"

My parents are there, ready. They hurry to lift my floppy body off the iron spike, taking care not to snag my delicate skin on the thorns that tangle around the fence, and then lower me to the ground.

Scorch lands in the garden at the same time that Luna climbs down from the roof.

"Sally is okay?" Scorch frets, flicking his tail back and forth, sparks sputtering.

I wince as I carefully sit up, a headache bursting through my skull, and touch the hole in my chest.

My mother kneels in the winter-dead grass next to me. "Easy. Don't move too fast. That hole is too big to stitch back together." She shrugs out of her plaid robe. "But I can patch it. You'll be good as new in a moment, I promise. Just hold on."

Tears begin to sprout from the corners of my eyes. I only have this one body—and it's already been so bruised and broken. How many times can I be patched over and repaired?

I wipe a tear off my bottom eyelashes. "The parachute didn't work—oh, what are we going to do?"

Undaunted, my mother focuses on healing my wound. With skilled fingers and a salvaged pair of scissors from Scorch's pouch, she cuts a circle of fabric from her robe, then stitches it over my torn torso.

One patch in the front. One in the back.

"You're patchwork now, like your dress," Luna says encouragingly, with a bittersweet note.

Patchwork? The word pokes and prods around my stuffing as I trace the chunky black stitching holding my homespun dress together.

On impulse, I snatch up my mother's cast-off robe, holding it toward the sky, peering through the hole she cut to mend my punctured chest.

"That's it, Luna! Oh, you're a genius!" I take both her hands in mine, already pushing to my feet and tugging her toward the house. "I know how to fly now!"

From dusk to dawn, working off only a few hours of sleep, I'm glued to my sewing machine. Guzzling tar-black coffee like water. My eyes are bleary, but I only rub them with fraying knuckles and keep at it.

While I sew, Luna and Scorch strip every curtain in the house. My parents pull off the bedsheets. The tablecloths. Towels. Soon, I have a small mountain of fabric beside my sewing table—even down to Jack's beloved old Santa Jack costume.

If this works, Jack, I promise, *I'll make you a new suit even cozier than this one.*

When the first hazy rays of morning knock at the window, I finally take a step back from my sewing machine, stretching my arms high overhead as my seams creak and pop. I pat my chest and back, adjusting my stuffing back into place after hunching over my sewing machine all night.

Everyone else is asleep on the floor or sofa, snoring softly. Otherwise, the house is as quiet as a graveyard.

Silencing a yawn, I start to gather blankets to drape over them—only to remember that we scrapped all the blankets.

I push open the living room window. Clouds crouch along the western horizon, but in the east, a tangerine sun breaks across the early morning sky, still dotted with twilight stars.

"Sally?" My mother yawns awake, stretches, and comes to join me. She frowns up at the clouds. "You really want to try this again, after what happened with the parachute?"

A shadow briefly eclipses my hope as I think of my failure. *Falling, falling, falling. Down, down, down.* Without intending to, I find myself rubbing the patch on my chest beneath my mended dress.

"This isn't like the parachute." I try to sound confident for her sake—and mine. "With that attempt, I didn't have anything to provide propulsion. I was relying on wind alone. Really, if you think about it, using a parachute isn't flying at all. It's simply falling in a controlled way. I'm not sure it even would have counted." A stitch pulls tight in my stomach, and I flinch as I remember free-falling toward metal spikes.

Greta presses her lips together and looks worriedly at the wrought iron fence.

"This, however, is *real* flying," I assure her. "I'll be completely in control at all times—not just in terms of raising and lowering myself, but moving horizontally, too. Come on. Let's wake the others. The sun is up—it's time."

All together, we gather the plentiful folds of patchwork fabric in our arms and make our way to the garden. For the basket, we're using a scrapped basket the Easter Bunny lent us last Halloween for storing pumpkins. It's perfect—the size of a large barrel, made of hollow river reeds, so it's lightweight yet sturdy.

I test out the makeshift controls, a rudimentary system of ropes and levers: a rusted scythe as the rudder, a length of black ribbon as the tether, and an hourglass from Time Town to measure altitude. The main lever—a salvaged jawbone—groans smoothly as I turn it.

I nod in satisfaction. "Help me lay out the balloon."

We unroll the giant swath of fabric stitched together from bedsheets and curtains. There's a piece of our bathroom mat. The Santa Jack coat. A portion of my black chiffon queen's gown. The quilt I sewed for our wedding anniversary. In fact, this project is a little bit of my whole life all sewn together. Every frayed edge, every faded patch—it's all here, a map of me.

"That's all of it." We stand back, dusting off our hands, and I take in the colorful hot-air balloon rolled out in our garden. "I *know* it will fly."

This time, I've thought everything through. All my trial and error has led me to this. The balloon's colors don't match—blacks, golds, and oranges taken from market awnings and bedsheets—but it will fly because it has to. The thought of staying immobile weighs heavier than any fear of falling.

"Let me come with you," Greta pleads, a mother above all else.

I tug on the ropes one final time. "Thank you, but I'm afraid I have to do this on my own. The hot-air balloon basket is only large enough for one person."

"Then we'll follow you," my mother vows with a definitive nod. "From the ground—the Mayor will let us borrow his hearse. We aren't letting our daughter take such a risky voyage without someone watching out for her."

Even though I'm far from their little girl now, I find tears pressing behind my eyelids again, and I tumble forward to fold myself into their open arms. Their skin is freshly laundered, and they smell like the lavender fields back home.

I clasp my hands together in front of my chest, nearly bursting with love for them. After so many years of thinking my only parent was a coldhearted scientist, it means the world to me to have my true parents' love.

Even if—sometimes—they doubt me.

My mom's smile wobbles as she gazes at the large unfilled hot-air balloon rolled out over the garden.

My father pulls in a breath. "You're certain it's airworthy?"

I shade my eyes against the rising sun, looking at the clouds encroaching from the west, stalking the horizon like foxes. "Only one way to find out."

I try to ignore my heart's pounding as we fasten the hot-air balloon to the reed basket, weigh it down with dream-sand bags, then test the knots twice to be sure. Scorch ignites his tail fire and carefully holds it under the large brass ring at the base of the balloon. Gradually, the hot air from his flame inflates the fabric. It fills slowly, expanding until it's round as a full moon.

The basket wobbles, held to the ground by a single stake.

"Zero," I call. "Here, boy!"

The ghost dog zooms out of his gravestone doghouse, tail wagging. The basket might only hold one person, but at least Zero can float along beside me.

I cast one last look up at the sky as I slide my satchel, filled with supplies for my flight, over one shoulder. *This is for you, Jack. You said you always wanted to be by my side. Gazing at the stars together, now and forever. Well, today, I'm going to the stars for us both.*

In the west, the storm paws closer, sneaking in

fast and hungry. My eyes flick to the weather vane on the roof, where the skull and crossbones swings wildly between north and west, its movement jagged and wrong, and something inside me hollows out.

If I'm going to do this, it needs to be now.

Hiking up my skirt, I grip the ropes and swing one leg into the basket, then the other. Zero hovers by my side, his long ears rippling in the wind.

Clutching the ropes with all the strength in my doll arms, I nod to Scorch.

"Cut the tie!"

Scorch holds his tail flame to the tie, which eats through the twine rope until it snaps. The basket gives a strong lurch, and I stumble forward, holding myself steady by the ropes.

Zero yips, tongue lolling.

With a stomach-flipping rush, we're airborne!

We rise, higher and higher, the world slipping away beneath us. The nightshade garden falls away at our feet. The wind plays with my hair, tossing it like live wires, and I gaze down at my parents, their figures growing smaller with every second. Luna bounces on her toes, waving, her voice carrying a thread of encouragement in the wind.

A rush of air fills my lungs, cool and clean, and I feel weightless. We rise over the rooftop's sharp angles, the soot-streaked chimney pipe, and the weather vane spinning out of control in the shifting currents.

From this vantage point, I can see my home in a way I never have before, the way a bird sees it. Jack's telescope pokes out of his window like a curious eye, its brass components gleaming. My overgrown herb garden sprawls below, looking like the scraggly fur of some winter beast.

My fingers grip the ropes tightly, trembling—not with fear, but with something wild and bright.

"We're doing it, Zero." My voice wavers, thick with wonder. "We're really flying!"

<h1 style="text-align:center">10</h1>

As I fly, all of Halloween Town unspools beneath me, the crooked streets and winter-barren fields forming a patchwork quilt over rippling hills. From this high, I feel like a cloud. Like an angel. Like the stars and moon themselves, gazing down on a toy-box world.

The houses' crooked rooftops look small enough to pluck from the ground and put in my pocket. Even Lock, Shock, and Barrel's tree house, whose massive branches seem to claw at the sky, looks more like a child's tiny hand reaching out for something lost.

I grip the main lever, angling it sharply for the balloon to catch a stronger breeze.

Wind fills my chest, pushing out the heaviness that's lingered there for days. For the first time in what feels like forever, my head is clear—no tangled thoughts or scratchy fears. Just this. The steady lift of the balloon, the world unrolling below me, and the hum of possibility.

I realize, in this moment, that I've spent so much of my life grounded—by fears, by doubts, by the weight of everyone's expectations. But up here, above it all, I'm *free*.

Zero's sudden bark pulls me from my thoughts. He flies in a circle around me, his pumpkin nose burning bright, and then zips toward the east to warn me of a towering pine tree closing in.

"Hold on!" Moving fast, I untie one of the dream-sand bags, letting it plunge to the cornfield below. The hot-air balloon sweeps skyward. I grab the jaw-bone lever, pulling with all my strength to turn us sharply to the right.

The pine tree surges closer, its jagged branches ready to snag my balloon. My teeth grind together so hard that it's a wonder they don't shatter. My free hand clamps onto the edge of the basket, knuckles white as I brace for a bone-rattling impact.

The bottom of the basket brushes so close to the tree that I hear leaves whisper against the woven reeds, but then–*then*–we're rising. Floating higher. The branches fall away beneath us, and the balloon's flight steadies.

A ragged cry of relief tears from my throat as my limbs give out. My knees buckle, and I collapse to the bottom of the basket, where I close my eyes as I let the fear slowly drain out like water from a cracked cauldron.

I'm okay.

And then, I start laughing and crying because I'm doing the impossible–a task that everyone told me couldn't be done. Here I am, flying over Halloween Town without wings.

I'm doing it, Jack!

A deep longing in my heart opens up, and I hug my legs close, resting my cheek on my knee. I wish Jack could see me now. I think about him trapped deep underground, in a kingdom of rocks and caverns. In this moment, flying sky-high, I've never felt farther apart from him, worlds away from each other, without even the ground connecting us. It feels impossible that we'll ever find our way back together.

I fish out the broken shard of the Mirror of Reverie, smoothing my thumb over the surface. *Jack, I want to talk to you again. To see you.* But I don't dare speak the words to open a communications portal. The risk is too great that Dorian has taken possession of the other piece.

I put away the shard, then take a deep breath and dry my tears on my skirt.

"I can do the impossible," I whisper to myself.

From outside the basket, Zero growls, low and warningly.

My head snaps up. Something has shifted in my brief moment of calm. As soon as I grip the sides of the basket to pull myself upright, a blast of wind knocks me back. The gust catches my dress like a kite, threatening to blow me out of the basket. I clutch a rope, bracing myself, trying to tuck myself into the basket's protective corner.

Zero barks again, his vicious snarls snapping in the air.

The wind blurs my vision. I wipe my eyes. Squint into the sky. It's grown dark in the span of only minutes. The storm clouds from the west are right on top of us, pressing down like grave dirt. Below us, now, is the vast expanse of Recluse Woods—the storm has blown us far off course. Freezing rain bites at my skin, plastering my hair to my face, as I struggle to pull the jawbone lever to steer us back to Halloween Town.

"This storm came out of nowhere!" I yell to Zero over the wind.

A dark shiver travels through my body.

My stomach lurches, fear twisting like a tight fist in my gut. I seize the jawbone lever with both hands.

"It's him!" I cry to Zero. "It's Prince Dorian—he's coming for us!"

I yank the lever hard, hoping to turn the balloon away from the shadows that are closing in by the second. The whole contraption groans in protest, the basket lurching sideways as ropes snap taut.

Wind rushes past, stinging my cheeks.

The scythe rudder swings confusedly, caught in uneven gusts. I reach for the black ribbon tether, fumbling to tighten it, but the slick material slides out of my fingers. The balloon jolts, its frame creaking ominously as I haul the controls toward the east, where the hills below us drop into a jagged ravine.

The horizon tilts sharply. My breath catches as the whole basket tips precariously to one side. I grip the jawbone lever tighter, muscles burning, desperate to right us. Below, the rooftops of Halloween Town spin into a mismatched blur.

The wind tosses me around like two children fighting over a toy ball, and I'm thrown violently against the basket's edge. The air is thrust out of my lungs. As I cling to the railing, my vision centers on a small clearing below.

A lily pond.

A vegetable garden.

A rusted mailbox on a crooked locust-wood post.

A figure is down there, hurrying through the swaying trees with an herb-collecting satchel slung over one shoulder. She wears a woolen cloak, but the wind blows it back to reveal long bluebell curls.

Somehow, my threadbare lungs pull in a small gasp of air. Dahlia might have banished me from setting foot into Recluse Woods, but not from flying over it!

And this moment—this wild moment of sheer frenzy—might be my only chance to get the answers I desperately need.

"Dahlia!" I shout, leaning as far as I dare over the basket edge. "Please, I need to talk to you!"

The hedge witch pauses, throwing a guarded look up toward me, her long curls whipping behind her like a battle banner. Her hand thrusts into her pocket for her wand—but stays there, at the ready.

Waiting to hear what I have to say.

"You seem to think I harmed you," I shout down, cupping my hands against the wind. "You must be mistaken. You've confused me for someone else. Or—or else I simply don't remember."

The strings in my stomach pull taut, spreading a deep, familiar ache that stretches to my core. I have to force the next words out. "My memory is filled with holes from my childhood. My tormenter . . . he made me forget everything."

Dahlia stares up at me, her hood fallen back and forgotten, rain pelting her face. Her eyes narrow at first, still suspicious, but then her whole posture shifts.

"What?" Her wariness flickers. "Your tormenter? I . . . I thought you–" The wind steals the rest of her words off her pursed lips.

In that moment, a gale throws the basket violently to the right, and Zero and I are tossed like a leaf in a whirlpool. Frantic, I dart from one end of the basket to the other, studying the encroaching clouds coming in fast from the west.

"I'll try to land!" I cry.

"No–those are Dorian's storm clouds!" she shouts back up. "Fly away–as fast as you can, or he'll capture the both of us!"

Before I can call to her again, she bolts, disappearing among the quaking leaves. The basket lurches violently to one side, the ropes groaning under the strain. I grip the edge to steady myself, my knuckles bone white, and shout over the chaos, "Hold on, Zero! I'm going to try to take us down!"

I fight to angle the balloon into a descent. The jawbone lever stutters and jerks, the ropes tangling in the frenzy, but I refuse to stop. Sweat stings my eyes, and my heart pounds in sync with the balloon's tortured groans.

We pitch sharply downward, and the basket swings like a pendulum. I cling to a rope as the wind nearly lifts me right off my feet. My hair whips in my eyes, blurring my vision.

The roar of the storm is so loud I can't hear my own breathing. Can't hear Zero–

Oh, no.

"Zero!" I rake the hair off my face, screaming into the wind for him. The hot-air balloon is falling fast. The ground is rising up to meet me with dizzying speed.

"Zero!"

In the distance, I spot a little white body spiraling off, caught in a wind gyre, as hard raindrops pelt against my skin.

A dark laughter booms across the purple-tinged clouds.

I glance down at the basket, where iron raindrops are collecting inch-deep in the bottom. "No!"

The basket suddenly collides with a tree, jerking me violently to one side. There's an awful ripping sound as the hot-air balloon tears. A rope snaps.

As iron rain bites against my skin, I crash to the ground.

And everything goes black.

"*Sally, dear. Wake up.*"

My mother's voice calls to me across an ocean of shadows, and I slowly rise up from the murky depths to answer it. But the surface is farther than it seems. I feel trapped, hemmed in by the weight of shadows pressing from all sides, the air heavy with the scent of wet dirt and decay.

I feel like I'm being buried alive.

I wake with a jolt, jerking upright, a hand tightly clasping my throat. But—I can breathe. I'm not trapped in my nightmare. In the bleak, unforgiving darkness.

Blinking fast, I take in my surroundings.

I'm in my own bed, covered in a borrowed Dream Town quilt that is soft and star-studded. Morning light streams through the windows, which are now free of dust—someone must have cleaned them. Probably my parents, who stand on either side of the bed, their faces pinched in concern. The sun's rays touch on objects that feel like they must have come from another life.

Jack's chalkboard with my three tasks spelled out.

The Grimoriel, closed on the floor.

My sewing implements strewn about the room.

And . . . Zero's empty dog bed.

A sob tears out of my throat as I press my hand to my lips, trying to hold in the heartache. The last thing I remember is Zero's ghost-white body pinwheeling away on a draft while iron raindrops stung my skin.

I was reaching out for him—but fell instead.

"Zero." I hiccup the name, throwing off the covers dizzily, trying to get to my feet. "Zero's been taken. The storm captured him, and now he's in Shadow Town with Jack and—"

"Sally, dear, breathe. Just breathe." My mother rests a firm hand on my shoulder, easing me back against the pillow.

"How long have I been asleep?"

She hesitates. "Three days."

"Three days!" I try to jolt upright, but she eases me back again.

"You were exhausted. You needed the sleep."

My mind whirls. If I lost three days, then I only have five days left to solve the riddles. My eyes dart around the bedroom. "Where's Luna? Scorch?"

"They're fine," my mother reassures me. "In the kitchen, boiling some water for tea."

It's a relief, but I latch on to her hand, squeezing fiercely. "Mom, you don't understand. Prince Dorian took Zero."

Her eyes crease at the corners, the sadness in them deep and unflinching, as if this was news she had expected all along. She lifts her gaze to my father, and the two of them share a heavy look.

He nods slowly, the gesture solemn like the closing of a grave.

"We saw it happen," he says quietly. "We were on the ground, following your hot-air balloon in the Mayor's hearse. We saw poor Zero get swept away before your balloon came down. Once we had you settled here, we went back to search for him. We looked everywhere. But there was nothing—only these."

My father opens his hand to reveal a palmful of iron raindrops.

A wail creeps out of my throat as I twist on the bed, tossing back and forth, wanting to tangle myself in the quilt until the pain goes away. But I can't surrender. I can't wail or moan. I can't hide out in bed.

Now more than ever, this town needs me.

I pull a deep breath into my lungs, filling the stuffing with fresh air, then fasten my attention on the window. "When you were looking for Zero, did you see a blue-haired woman? A hedge witch?"

My parents both frown, shaking their heads.

"What about a cottage with a lily pond?" I press.

My mother's eyes brighten. "Yes, but it was empty. It looked as though someone had packed and left in a hurry."

I sigh, sinking into the bed pillows. Did Dahlia flee again? I can't shake the sharp wonder about what she said in the woods, how her whole demeanor changed when I mentioned a tormenter who made me forget things.

The thought twists uneasily in my stomach, but signs of her packing mean at least one thing—she escaped the storm. Wherever she's run to this time, it isn't Shadow Town. I recall the expression on her face when I called down to her from the hot-air balloon. That startled-rabbit look in her big eyes. But beneath the fear, there had been something else. A glimmer of hesitation, like she was on the verge of answering me.

Of trusting me.

But then her brother's storm clouds rolled in, black and ominous, and whatever courage she'd found slipped away again.

"You were lucky." My father eases himself onto the edge of the bed, patting my hand. "The basket broke your fall. Other than a bruise to your head that knocked you out, you're just a little out of sorts. Nothing a bit of fluffing can't fix."

I run my hands over the quilt, feeling my lumpy body beneath it. I don't like this feeling—like I'm not myself. Like my body isn't my own. I climb out of bed, working my way from one wrist up my arm, then down to the other, rearranging my stuffing. Finally, after a good bit of poking, I get myself back into proper shape.

That's better.

I roll out my neck, closing my eyes, and when I open them, something catches my eye on the chalkboard.

"Mom? Dad?" I ask. "Did you write on the board?"

Their salt-and-pepper eyebrows rise in unison as they shake their heads. "Haven't touched it," my mother adds.

I step closer to the chalkboard, tilting my head.

The three impossible tasks are still there in my careful, blocky handwriting, just as I left them. Only, now, there's a gold-dust chalk line through the first task:

~~*Fly Without Wings*~~

Curious, I run my finger through the chalk dust and come away with some of the shimmering golden powder mixed with it. Holding it close to my nose, I pick up the faint, clean scent of nighttime.

Hope takes root in my belly. I spin around, squeezing Jack's bone ring on my finger as my mind races.

"The Night Mare was here." My voice is breathy, trembling, as I pace over the rug. "She marked off the task, see? Mom, Dad, I did the impossible!"

My mother offers a warm smile. "You did, Sally." But there's a hitch in her eyes. She clears her throat, then glances at my father, but I'm too keyed up to think about what her hesitation means.

Pacing in quick steps, bare feet padding softly on the floor, I rattle out plans.

"The second task is to solve an unsolvable maze. But nothing is actually impossible, right? Not with some cleverness and help from friends. I can get Jack back, I know it. Zero, too. All of them, and prevent Prince Dorian from stealing anyone again."

"Sally, dear . . ." my mom says, so softly that I barely hear her.

I stop at the wall calendar, tapping my finger on the full moon at the end of the month.

Five more days to complete the second and third impossible tasks.

But I refuse to be daunted, and with a bounce in my step, I reach for my shoes, plopping down onto the sofa to quickly lace them up. "I'll write letters to the other rulers to ask about the maze. Surely one of them has heard of it. There's a hedge maze in Fable Town, so I'll start there—"

"Sally, dear, stop!"

My mother captures my face between her cotton palms, tilting my gaze to meet hers. My body goes still. I don't like what I see in her eyes. The same sadness and regret that haunted her when the Sandman threatened Dream Town and they had to burn all the doorways to protect their people.

"Mom? Dad? What's wrong?"

My father sits on the sofa next to me, carefully resting his palms on his knees. "Your mother and I don't think you should continue with this quest. No one knows if this magical horse can even be trusted. Even if she can, it's too dangerous to risk yourself again. You could have been torn apart in that storm.

Scattered to the four corners so that we could never put you back together."

I let go of my half-knotted laces. My cheeks warm with a flush of irritation. "I didn't ask for your advice."

"We're your parents. We just want what's best for you. We can't lose you!"

"But you will! Don't you see?" I explode to my feet. "If I don't do this, Prince Dorian will continue to take everyone. He almost got me once—he'll return to finish the job. Or maybe he won't, but he'll come for you two instead. Take you to Shadow Town, where you'll never see the moon again."

My mother wipes her tear-stained cheek, looking away.

"I'm the Pumpkin Queen. Don't you believe in me?" I ask haltingly.

"Oh, Sally, we know you can do incredible things," my father reassures me, his voice wavering with pride. "But the Hinterland Maze is beyond even your ability."

"The Hinterland Maze?" My feet drift to a stop. "Wait—you *know* about the riddle's maze?"

My mother plucks anxiously at her uppermost pajama button, worrying the thread so hard that I'm afraid it'll snap.

"We didn't think you'd make it past the first task,

so we weren't going to mention it," she explains quietly. "But yes. We discovered the maze when we were destroying all the doorways into Dream Town to keep the Sandman from returning. A traveling pixie from Tooth Town warned us about it. It's a maze of living brambles with thorns as long as your fingers. That's deadly for a rag doll made of cloth—but that isn't the worst part. The maze changes. Every hour, the brambles shift. There's no way to know where you're going. Or where you've come from. If you enter the Hinterland Maze, you might be trapped there forever."

My skin prickles with the phantom pain of scratchy briars. I rub my bare arm, trying to wipe away the feeling. I believe my parents; it's clear to see that their worry is genuine. But how can I stop now when I've come so far?

"Mom, Dad, I understand, but I can't give up." I let my hands fall at my sides. "There's danger in any dream worth chasing. I can beat this Hinterland Maze."

"How?" My father's concern is practical. He holds out his hand palm up.

It's a fair question. One I need to consider carefully before undergoing the second riddle. But the wall calendar is already filled with too many black

X's. There's no other way to rescue Jack and stop the prince.

My breath feels shallow, like I'm back in the murky dream—trapped in a tight space, swallowed by darkness, fighting to get out.

As I pace, my foot knocks into a bag of dream sand from the hot-air balloon supplies, sending dust spilling out in a shimmering cascade. The dream sand catches the morning light filtering through the window, each grain scattering tiny rainbows that dance across the floorboards.

It triggers a memory from somewhere deep.

"When I was saving Dream Town from the Sandman," I start slowly, a tentative hope blossoming in my chest, "I got a four-leaf clover from St. Patrick's Day Town. The leprechaun who gave it to me said it was for luck. Maybe I can use that again—a little luck to help me through the Hinterland Maze."

My parents exchange doubtful looks with each other, but then my father squeezes my mother's hand and gives me a nod. "Good luck, then, Sally. We won't try to stop you. Just know that we love you."

Feeling more confident, I finish lacing my shoes and then pull my cloak around my collar, fastening the black-widow clasp.

"Go home to Dream Town," I tell my parents. "Take Luna and Scorch with you. I trust that you'll keep them safe. Before I go, I'll make sure the Mayor and the rest of the council watch over everyone here in Halloween Town."

The three of us fold into a hug, all yarn and patchwork and rustling stuffing, a safety net around one another—but how long can it hold?

Luna begs, pleads, and wails to go with me, and Scorch drips molten tears onto the floor. But I say my goodbyes to them and my parents. Then, I pack my satchel and sit at my desk. There's one final thing I have to do before leaving for the Hinterlands.

I take out paper and a quill, then start writing.

To Princess Dahlia Dark,

Since I cannot enter Recluse Woods, this is the only way I could think of to reach you. I wanted to write because there's so much I don't understand—and I think you might hold some of the answers. You acted as though we had crossed paths before, but the truth is, my memories of childhood are foggy at best. My abductor gave me a potion many years ago to make me forget. He said it was for my own good. I believed him.

But when you looked at me like you knew me, I felt that something was missing—something important. I want to remember. If there's anything that went poorly between us, I will work night and day to make things right. Even if I don't remember what went wrong.

With hope,

Sally

On the way to the Hinterlands, I post the letter by crow, addressed to the rusted mailbox outside her cottage, just in case.

I take a deep breath as I stand before the door with a four-leaf clover carving, the slanting light of the Hinterland grove warming my back. I've passed through this door dozens of times, but I've never felt more determination than I do now.

I'm coming, Jack.

I step through the doorway into the leafy green forest that surrounds St. Patrick's Day Town, bathed in the glow of morning light–and freeze.

Every town has its own time zone, and here, it's already morning.

Another day gone.

I take a steadying breath to ease my nerves, and stride forward. By now, I know the pathways through the fields by heart. I take the one that leads straight into town, past the waist-high thatched houses and miniature park benches. A countdown clock above the pub that doubles as town hall declares that it's mere weeks until St. Patrick's Day. This close to its holiday, the town should be a flurry of activity. I'd expect the fiddlers to be rehearsing their Irish reels. The claddagh-knot pretzels to be baking away. The river to be dyed green.

Yet it's oddly quiet. Smoke rises from the brick chimneys, but few people are out on the cobblestone streets. I pass a small elderly leprechaun with gray hairs threaded through his red beard, who barely glances at me as he lugs a heavy sack of harvested clover. Two schoolgirls whose heads barely come up to my knees quietly walk by, keeping their eyes low. Extra locks gleam on all the doors. All the storefront windows are boarded up.

There's an air of fear tunneling through this town.

"Excuse me." I step directly in front of the clover farmer to get his attention.

He jumps nearly a mile before relaxing, though his fingers pluck anxiously on his sack as his eyes dart from side to side. "A visitor? Haven't gotten many of those recently. You know there's a travel restriction, yes?"

"I'm aware, but it's urgent, and as a ruler, I have a pass. Where might I find Cathal Shamrock?"

The clover farmer points out a thatched-roof house on the street corner, with a cozy line of smoke winding out of the red brick chimney. I thank him and stoop down to knock on the wooden door.

The murmur of worried voices comes from inside before a hesitant voice calls, "Who is it?"

"Cathal, it's Queen Sally from Halloween Town."

There's a rumble as the locks unfasten, and then the St. Patrick's Day Town ambassador throws open the door. His broomstick beard and cherry-round nose are familiar, but there are new lines etched into his face that weren't there at the last All Realms Gathering.

"Queen Sally, indeed!" His eyes light up with real joy. "Come in, come in. What an honor. Niamh, put a kettle on!"

He waves me inside, but I hesitate, crouched over with my hands braced on my knees. I stoop lower to peek inside at a living room that is more suited for Zero's size than my own.

"Erm . . . perhaps it would be better to speak outside?"

As the realization hits him that I'm too large

to comfortably fit inside, he slaps his cheek with a chuckle. "Right you are!"

He ducks out of his doorway, and I follow him to one of the clover fields on the outskirts of town. Pretty delicate white butterflies flit from blossom to blossom. A few farmers harvest clover in the distance, but I still can't shake the eerie feeling that something bad is about to happen at any moment.

Knitting my hands together, I gaze at the pub's countdown clock. "St. Patrick's Day will be here before we know it."

Cathal sighs, rubbing his round red nose. "Aye. The Council of Leprechauns fears we might have to cancel the holiday this year."

I swallow a gasp. "Cancel St. Patrick's Day?"

He holds out his hands, motioning to the nearly empty fields as butterflies dance around us. "People are too afraid to leave their homes. We've already lost four leprechauns to Prince Dorian's storm clouds. No one wants to risk being taken next. It might be a sad, dreary, colorless March around the world."

I pace tensely, the clover brushing my ankles, each step kicking up the fresh scent of earth and grass. But the sweetness doesn't calm me. I tug on the loose string at my wrist, and my chest tightens as his words settle like cold stones in my stomach.

Cancel St. Patrick's Day.

I stop, digging my heels into the ground. "I'm trying to stop Prince Dorian and bring home everyone he's taken. But to do so, I need something special. I need . . . *luck*."

Cathal strokes his beard thoughtfully. "Luck, you say? Well, luck is no simple thing. There are four-leaf clovers. Rabbits' feet. Horseshoes. Ladybugs. Each has a different angle on luck. What kind of luck are you looking for specifically, Majesty?"

I explain to him about the Night Mare's three impossible tasks.

His eyes travel into the middling distance as he nods slowly. "Ah. I'm afraid the kind of luck that you need to solve the Hinterland Maze, you won't get from a four-leaf clover. They can be lucky, it's true—for finding lost buttons or remembering your shopping list. But for your purposes, you need two things: skill and *Prime* Luck. The strong stuff."

I comb my hair behind my ear, trying to look more confident than I feel. "How do I get Prime Luck?"

"I'm afraid you won't find it in St. Patrick's Day Town." He turns up his green velvet coat collar against the chill blowing in from the west, then plucks a four-leaf clover from the ground and spins it between his fingers thoughtfully. "The kind of luck you're seeking is only found in Chance Town."

I cock my head as curiosity tugs at the loose threads in my mind. Jack and I have spent the last year cataloging most of the doorways in the Hinterlands. We've mapped out the holiday towns. The ancient realms. Even a few phenomenon towns, like Weather Town.

But I've never heard of this one.

"Chance Town?" I repeat, blinking blankly.

"It's a place unlike any other," Cathal informs me, hands thrust in his pockets. "Where the streets are paved with dice. Markets trade in probabilities instead of wares, fortunes rise and fall on a coin toss, and at its heart lies the Luck Factory, a warehouse that distills pure chance into jewel-toned luck drops—quite delicious, I hear. But let me give you this warning: In a town where everything is decided by chance, the odds are rarely in anyone's favor."

A line of worry creeps up my spine. "How do I get there?"

He barks a chuckle. "You need luck even to find it." He extends me the four-leaf clover. "This should be powerful enough. Go to the Hinterland grove, spin three times in a circle, and see where your feet take you."

I take the clover gingerly and tuck it into my dress

pocket, patting the fabric to make sure it's secure. But my hand lingers over my pocket, my fingers smoothing the folds of fabric again and again.

Finally, I blurt out, "Will you come with me?"

Cathal sighs. "I'd like to, Queen Sally. Yours is a noble mission. But St. Patrick's Day Town needs all the protection it can get. I don't dare leave now. I have a family, you know. I have to keep them inside. Away from the storms."

He motions to his cottage at the field's edge, where his brood of tiny leprechaun children huddle at the door, watched over by their attentive mother, who keeps a close eye on the clouds.

"I understand." I touch my chest in gratitude, though the idea of going at this alone fills me with anxious knots. "Thank you, Cathal."

He bows deeply, tucking his hand to his midsection, before returning to his family.

I look longingly at his quaint family life, wondering if I'll ever have the same. Will Jack ever again be waiting for me in our doorway, his smile broad, his kiss warm and welcoming? Or is that kind of happiness something meant for others? Always out of my reach?

My mind is mired in such thoughts as I tromp back along the path that leads through the spring-green forest. Sunlight filters through the canopy, dappling the ground in shifting patterns, but even that gentle beauty can't loosen the tangles in my stuffing.

Stop it, I think, forcing myself to take a deep breath, filling my lungs with the scent of blooming wildflowers. I think back on the bandleader's words: *Nothing's ever lost. There are echoes from every note ever played. You just have to close your eyes and listen.*

My chest sinks, my worries eased. One of the butterflies from the clover field flits around my face. Distracted, I gently wave it away. But it returns with such insistence that it nearly bumps into me.

"I'll thank you not to swat me away, Your Majesty!" a tiny voice chirps in my face. "I'm no insect!"

"Oh!"

I rear back, startled, as I recognize that the tiny winged creature isn't a butterfly at all.

"Pearl?" I say in surprise.

It's a pixie from Tooth Town—and one I know all too well. Her wings are the greenish-white color of a cabbage butterfly, and her white locks hang loose around the two feathery antennae that rise from her head.

Keeping herself in place with gentle flutters, she gives me a bow. "Finally—I've been following you since the Hinterlands, trying to get your attention!"

My hand instinctively plunges into my dress pocket, checking on my belongings.

If I've learned one lesson from my time in Tooth Town, it's that tooth pixies are expert thieves. The first time I met Pearl, she stole my needle and thread right from my pocket. Fortunately, everything seems to be there.

"Why are you following me, Pearl?" I ask suspiciously.

"To help you, silly!" She flits in lazy loops from one of my ears to the other like a nectar-drunk bumblebee. "The Tooth Fairy sent me to assist you in whatever way I can. We've had three pixies go missing from Tooth Town in the last week. The rest of us are too scared to leave home and collect children's teeth. Incisors are stacking up left and right!"

"*You* want to *help*?" A touch of skepticism laces my voice.

Though the Tooth Fairy ultimately proved trustworthy when I was trying to reset our holiday clock, I'm not sure I can say the same for her pixies.

Pearl zips so close between my eyes that her face blurs. "Queen Sally, I lost my brother, Cusp. He's in Shadow Town now. You aren't the only one who wants their missing people back."

Her words smooth the hard, untrusting edges

of my heart—but don't erase them. Is she telling the truth? It's hard to say. Pixies are known for their tricks. Still, there's something about her big round eyes that makes me want to believe her—while keeping an eye on her.

I nod. "Okay, Pearl. You can come with me. But we'll have to be careful—we can't assume the ruler of any town will be our ally, just as Prince Dorian isn't our friend."

Her wings flutter excitedly as she swoops circles around my head, then grabs the shell of my right ear and tugs me down the pathway back toward the Hinterland grove. "Follow me! We pixies know how to be careful. You wouldn't believe how many children set traps for us before they go to bed!"

She zips ahead, and I break into a jog after her, hoping beyond hope that I'm making the right choice—that on the other side of this pixie's promise is a way to save my people.

I stand in the center of the Hinterland grove with Cathal's clover pinched tightly between my fingers, trying not to pin all my hopes on four little leaves.

"What are you waiting for?" Pearl whispers, fluttering her iridescent wings, flitting around like a spot of dancing light. "What's wrong?"

I'm unsure how to explain the doubts hanging over me like a funeral shroud. Luck is such a slippery thing—just when you think you've caught it, it's already gone. Not long ago, I was lucky enough to have everything I ever wanted. Jack. Friends. A purpose.

And I lost it all.

"N-nothing. Nothing's wrong." I banish my worries, pushing my shoulders back, squaring my stance, and hoping I sound believable.

Holding out my arms for balance, I spin three times as Cathal told me to do. The Hinterland trees swirl at the edges of my vision. When I stop, the world still seems to go on spinning without me for a minute, like a toy top that never slows.

I catch myself on a low branch to stop spinning, and once the world stops whirling, I hold out the four-leaf clover.

"Take me to Chance Town's door, please," I ask, my hopes as fragile and precious as a whisper.

The air grows still around us. Pearl lands on my shoulder, her wings unmoving now, as though she can also sense the change in the grove.

"Ow!"

An acorn suddenly thumps against the top of my head, leaving my ears ringing.

A squirrel chitters overhead like it's laughing at me, and I scowl up at it while I rub my scalp's sore spot.

"That wasn't very nice," I scold the squirrel. "I have friends who eat fuzzy little things like you for breakfast, you know—"

"Queen Sally—look!"

Pearl tugs on my left ear, pulling my head down and forward. I blink, not sure what I'm supposed to be looking at. The forest floor is the same twisted map of roots and divots as always. But then, I spot the acorn rolling down a dry creek bed, where it bumps along over moss-covered rocks.

"Follow that acorn!" I cry.

Pearl takes wing, and we follow the acorn's bumpy path as it picks up speed, plinking against rocks as the dry streambed zigzags. When the acorn reaches a fork, it rolls to the right. I hop from one stream bank to the other, trying to keep the acorn in sight. The ground slopes downward even more sharply, and the acorn rolls faster.

We run beneath trees that arch overhead like cathedral spires, their branches forming a natural rooftop, dappling the ground with shifting patterns of light and shadow until, suddenly, I'm blocked by brambles.

I stop short, craning my neck. "Do you still see the acorn?"

"I'm on it!" Pearl zips skyward confidently, but a moment later, I hear a tiny cry. Straining on my tiptoes, I see that she's caught in a gossamer spiderweb. I pick my way through the brambles, then break off a stick to sweep through the web to free her. She tumbles downward, wings tangled in spider silk, and I dart forward, hands outstretched, to catch her before she hits the ground.

"Whew! Close one. Thanks, Your Majesty," she murmurs, plucking long strands of spider silk off her wings. Her mouth purses. "But we lost the acorn!"

"Maybe. Maybe not." I plunge my hand into my pocket, twirling the four-leaf clover's stem between my fingers, squeezing as hard as I dare.

The wind shifts, and as if by magic, the acorn rolls out of the brambles, curving in a graceful semicircle to land at the base of an elm tree, where there's a doorway that's partially hidden by greenery.

"That must be the door!"

I grin, already heading toward it—but then pause. As I move around the brambles, I see that the tree's massive trunk is split in two. Its two trunks tower overhead, each one thick enough to block out the sun, plunging me into sudden shadows.

And there's not just one door.

Two doorknobs.

Four hinges.

"Wait. There are *two* doors?" I exclaim. "On one tree?"

Pearl and I step back, my feet softly rustling fallen

leaves and twigs, as we try to get a better view of the situation. The forest air smells faintly of damp bark and something metallic, like coins left in the rain.

There are two symbols carved into the doors: On the left side, a coin symbol is etched with a queen's head. On the right side, a coin symbol shows a pair of high-heeled shoes.

"Heads and tails," I murmur. "These must be the doors to Chance Town. Or, rather, *one* of the doors leads to Chance Town. I suppose which one you pick is, well, up to chance." I tap my finger on my chin stitch. "So, which one do we go through?"

Pearl shrugs her glitter-dusted shoulders.

I fold my arms across my patchwork dress, tilting my head. Other than the carved coin symbols, the doors are identical. Both are chin height to me, their brass knobs polished to a bright sheen. The hinges look freshly oiled.

Something Dr. Finkelstein used to say about probability wriggles into my mind: *A coin toss does not determine the outcome; rather, it reveals hopes that were already present in the decision-maker.*

I straighten, arms falling at my sides.

"A coin flip," I murmur. "That's how we'll decide which doorway to enter."

I turn out my pockets—needle and thread, a spare

button, but no coins. I pace over the twisting roots, turning my wedding ring on my finger. If I don't pick the right door, where will I end up? What if I'm taken to a realm even farther from him?

Exasperated, I drop my hands. My wedding ring knocks against the wooden button inside my pocket. It gives me an idea, and I fish out the button.

It's made of rough oak. Four uneven holes. Jack carved this button for me when I was in a pinch last Halloween after my witch costume tore on a branch.

The front side is plain and polished, and on the back, he carved our initials.

J+S

"We can use this!" I sink to my knees in the fallen leaves, balancing the wooden button on my thumb knuckle. I look briefly up at the hazy sky, thinking of Jack, and then hold my breath and flip the button.

Pearl flies close, her wings fluttering in anticipation. The slanting light hits the smooth, timeworn wood as it spins in the air.

I catch the button with my other hand, heart skipping a beat, for a moment afraid to look.

Afraid of what I'll see.

But I must.

Slowly, I open my palm.

J+S

"Heads!" My gaze jerks to the trunk on the left. I swallow down my last trickle of doubt, pushing back to my feet, and stow Jack's button in my pocket.

With a deep breath, I open the door on the left . . . hoping luck is in my favor.

In the next breath, I'm tumbling down, down, down.

The rush of falling into a new world always makes my heart pull tighter than a button. There's no way to know what I'll find. Rushing rivers or serene pastures. Monsters or new friends. Usually, Jack is free-falling beside me, all dry-bone elbows and knee-caps, his skull grinning from the stomach-churning thrill of it. His enthusiasm for new worlds is infectious. When I'm exploring with Jack, it's easy to grin along with him.

But when I crash-land on a stone courtyard that leaves my molars rattling around in my jaw and my body flopped over like a pile of old laundry, the last thing I feel is adventurous.

I'm not here to explore, I remind myself.

I'm here to save *Jack*—and everyone else.

Pearl lands beside me with substantially more grace, her wings folding tidily along her back as she straightens her dress's windblown ruffles.

She wrinkles her nose as she peers up at a gumball-blue sky. "Well? Did we pick the right door?"

I stand up, straightening my dress, checking myself for any broken seams. A shrill whistle suddenly blasts behind me, and I spin around with a start.

We've landed in front of a cheerful-looking train station with a long list of stops on its rotating platform display. I glance over the first ones:

SPINWHEEL MANSION

FATE'S CROSSROADS

LUCKY BREAK STATION

My heart flutters, rustling the leaves in my chest. "We made it to Chance Town! Oh—but look at the sun." My voice climbs into a wail.

Pearl squints at the flush of sunrise pink on the horizon. "What about it?"

"It's sunrise again. We lost another day traveling between realms!"

Pearl flaps her wings, shooting into the air. "Well, then, we'd better get going!"

I run after her toward the station.

The train station's courtyard is made of large smooth white squares, each with between one and six shiny round black dots—just like the sides of a die. Similar dice-paved pathways run over rolling hills in the distance. One path leads into a rawboned, shadowy forest. Another disappears into a valley. Where a third path forks, a woman in a checkerboard dress sets down her suitcase to give a directional street sign a spin. When it comes to a stop, it points toward the fork that leads to tall city gates.

She primly picks up her suitcase and sets off toward the town.

"There!" I say to Pearl, pointing in the woman's direction. "That's where we need to go, into downtown. That has to be where we'll find the Luck Factory."

We make our way along the dice path, Pearl flitting over my head while I stride from square to square. At the fork, I veer the same direction the woman in the checkerboard dress did, yet to my surprise, the path twists and turns, and I'm right back at the same spinning street sign.

"Why didn't the path lead us to the town gates?" I ask.

"Because you didn't spin the sign first, of course!" a friendly voice calls out behind me.

When I turn, a dashing young man in a checkerboard suit makes a spinning motion in the air with one finger. "You must be new here. I'm Gamble. Gamble Oddfellow. Just arrived from the village of Lucky Penny, yonder over those hills, and I'm headed to the big city myself."

He proudly pats a shiny suitcase covered in blue question marks. His sandy brown hair is carefully combed, his chin so freshly shaven that there's a nick in his dimpled chin. His bow tie is a checkerboard print to match his suit, but his shoes are mismatched, one brown and one black. Given the careful attention that went into the rest of his attire, I can't help feeling the choice was left up to chance.

Pearl flies over to his suitcase, poking around at a loose shirtsleeve bulging out of the side. I know how she loves to pickpocket, so I give her a warning look.

She sheepishly flies back over to my shoulder.

"It's a pleasure to meet you, Gamble." I give a curtsy. "I'm Sally from Halloween Town, and this is

Pearl, a tooth pixie." I look up at the clear blue sky. Not a trace of storm clouds. "This might sound strange, but is everything okay in your town? Has anyone gone missing?"

His eyebrows climb high. "Missing? Why, no, not that I'm aware of."

I feel my chest ease, the tight threads loosening. Prince Dorian, it seems, hasn't made it this far. *Yet.*

"Can you tell us what path to take to the Luck Factory?" I ask.

The young man chuckles. "Well, that's up to chance, isn't it? Give the sign a spin. Maybe you'll get lucky." He shrugs good-naturedly. "If not, you can come back and try again until you get to where you want to go!"

Anxious, I glance at the sun overhead. "Isn't that toilsome? It could take all day, and we're in a hurry."

He scratches his head. "I've never thought about it quite like that. Chance is chance. Even if a path takes you somewhere else, you might find that was the right course all along. Go ahead. See where fate takes you."

Still frowning up at the burning sun, I approach the street sign and give it a spin. It whirls around and around and around, and I wiggle my toes as I wait, hoping it points to the town center. The sign slows, finally stopping to point right back where we started: CHANCE CENTRAL STATION.

"The train station?" My voice rises like a squeaky wheel. "That's back the way we came!"

Gamble gives me a reassuring wink. "See where the train takes you—you might be pleasantly surprised."

He digs around in his pocket, then tosses me a coin before stepping up to the directional sign himself to give it a spin.

I catch the coin and fold it into my palm.

I turn to Pearl, who shrugs her tiny shoulders. Since we don't seem to have a choice, we follow Gamble's advice and return to the train station. There's only one platform, lined with wooden benches, half of which are filled with waiting riders. I spot a yawning attendant at a ticket booth and look down at Gamble's coin in my open hand.

"Hello. Two tickets to—"

Before I can finish, the ticket collector plucks the coin from my palm and pushes two flimsy tickets in my direction, printed with the train company's question mark logo.

She rubs her tired eyes as she calls, "Next!"

I'm nudged out of the way by a portly grandmother with dangling ladybug earrings. "Step aside, deary, step aside! The train arrives in one minute!"

A shrill whistle punctuates her words, and in the distance, I see a line of smoke chugging our direction. Everyone shuffles to their feet as an ink-black train with a question mark logo on its side pulls into the station and squeals to a halt.

I hand the conductor our tickets and we take a place in the first passenger car, which has smooth wooden bench seats and wide open-air windows.

The conductor rings his bell, and the train lurches forward with enough force that I have to grab the windowsill to keep from sliding right off the polished seat. Pearl perches on my shoulder, clutching a handful of my hair to keep from being blown away. Outside, the hills surrounding Chance Town rush by in a blur.

"All right, folks, first stop is . . ." The conductor pulls a lever that creaks like a rusted old slot machine. Destinations whirl past on the flickering display—JACKPOT CROSSING, FATE'S CROSSROADS, SPINWHEEL MANSION—before the display slows with a clunk, landing on . . .

"Coinflip Square!" he announces.

The train suddenly lurches to the left as it shifts onto a second set of tracks, which pitch down a steep hill. Wind rushes by, sending my hair trailing behind me. My ears pop, and my breath catches as the train plunges into the valley.

Fields streak past in slanted patches of green and gold. My vision bounces with every jolt of the track, but I catch glimpses outside of oddities—a windmill spinning backward, a laundry line strung with sheets that look like giant playing cards.

The train lurches again, throwing me to the side. I grip the edge of the seat with blanched fabric knuckles, wondering how everyone isn't panicked. The other passengers merely sway and shift along with the rocking car, having spent a lifetime getting used to the wild ride.

A rosy-cheeked couple in the seats across the aisle calmly rest their hands on their hats to keep them from blowing away as they read a newspaper. Though my vision is bouncing, I squint to make out the headline: MAYORAL DRAWING TO TAKE PLACE TODAY IN COINFLIP SQUARE.

"Look, Sally!" Pearl tugs on my ear, pointing outside. "There's the factory!"

A large collection of warehouse buildings loom behind a tall iron fence with a gate that reads LUCK FACTORY. I grip the windowsill, leaning forward eagerly.

Gamble Oddfellow was right—chance took us in the right direction, after all!

The Luck Factory's buildings are draped in twinkle-light strings, and each entrance sits beneath a golden horseshoe arch. The windows are mirrored, so I can't see inside, but the tantalizing smell of caramelized sugar on the air makes me lick my lips.

Guards in stiff chessman uniforms—complete with chessboard breastplates and cloaks that billow like a chess piece's broad, round base—stride back and forth along a high fence. A sign over the main gate declares in bold letters: NO ADMITTANCE, BY ORDER OF MAYOR LUCKWELL.

"Stop!" I shout, looking for a signal rope to pull. "Stop here, please! We'd like to get out!"

The conductor doesn't seem to hear me, though, whistling away to himself as he shovels fresh coal into the firebox.

We plow straight through Luck Factory Station without stopping. I hold in a breath as I watch the station fly by, my knuckles going bone white as I grip the window. I stare at the Luck Factory disappearing in the distance.

Ahead, the train track stretches endlessly, curving sharply from one side to the other. This whole town is so bewildering that I'm not sure if I should laugh or scream.

Suddenly, the train comes to a screeching halt. I'm thrown forward, barely catching myself before I thud against the next seat.

Outside, the station sign reads COINFLIP SQUARE.

I gasp. "We have to get off here, Pearl—it's only one station away from the factory. Hurry, before the train takes us to the end of the world next!"

13

The conductor nods the brim of his checker-board cap to us as we make our way down the stairs, still reeling from the ride.

From the platform, we pass through a bustling open-air train station to join a growing crowd headed toward Chance Town's gates. The gates are forged from shiny brass, smooth and stately, with curlicue question marks topping every other bar.

As I pause to marvel at the gates, the young woman from the train glances at the wall clock and turns to her companion. "We'll have to hurry if we want to watch the results of the mayoral race. What are the chances Fortuna Luckwell wins again?"

Her young man blows out an exasperated puff of air. "Infinitesimal—it would be the tenth time in a row!"

The couple takes a branching dice path toward what looks like the town center, and I signal to Pearl and whisper, "Come on—let's follow them."

Once we're through the gates, the town unfolds like a board game, with pathways weaving between neighborhoods that seem to crop up as haphazardly as if a child scattered a handful of toy blocks. At every intersection, spinning street signs whirl in a way that leaves my head turning like a top but seems to make sense to everyone else.

The curving path takes us toward the town center, where a Victorian house with a wide wraparound porch presides from the highest point on a hill, its turret capped with a spinning roulette wheel. That must be Spinwheel Mansion.

We pass by boxy buildings made from giant domino bricks, which have been carefully arranged to have matching black dots.

The path steers us past Haphazard Books & More, where teetering stacks of antique books spill from crooked windows. Next door is the Domino Diner, where a chalkboard sign announces, "Come in—every order a random surprise!" On the corner, a white-haired fortune-teller in a lucky red cape flips cards for passersby.

A trumpet blares from a few streets over, making me jump and press a hand to my chest to steady the rustling leaves within.

"Hurry!" The young woman takes hold of her friend's hand. "The mayoral race is starting!"

We follow the young couple into a tree-lined town square, where a fountain flips an enormous coin into the air in sporadic bursts, water cascading around its edge as it lands with a splash on heads or tails.

A bandstand draped with black-and-red streamers holds an official-looking line of men and women, fashionably dressed in sequin checkerboard prints and peacock-plume hats. They wave to the crowd with wide smiles, hope sparkling in their eyes, like children wishing to be picked for a prize.

A squat woman at the head of the line catches my eye as she whispers with an announcer whose mustache is curled into twin question marks. Her blond hair is pinned into an impossibly tall beehive twirl. She has red playing card diamonds painted on her cheeks, and her pantsuit matches.

The trumpet blares again, and the announcer steps up to the podium. "Ladies and gentlemen, I'd like to present our current mayoral candidates. Come, come! Don't be shy! Step on up! Maybe *you* will be our next mayor—just write your name on a paper, and chance will determine the results!"

He motions to a table draped with a lucky red velvet cloth, holding a round glass fishbowl filled with dozens of slips of paper.

My own eyebrows twist into question marks as I murmur sidelong to Pearl, "They determine their ruler by chance?"

She points her feathery antennae toward the coin fountain. "How else?"

She's right, but something about this method sits uneasily with me. As the crowd pushes in around us, voices rising and falling in excitement, I'm rooted to the spot, plucking anxiously at the loose string around my wrist.

It wasn't that long ago that *I* was named as Halloween Town's co-ruler with Jack. I remember so clearly when the eldest vampire placed the crowfeather crown on my head. The crowd's cheers still echo between my linen ears. Since that day, I've tried to be the best ruler I can, not only defending my town but paying close attention to the little needs: offering advice when townspeople bicker over a costume, helping with the pumpkin harvest, keeping the Haunted Bed and Breakfast stocked with fresh rosemary soap.

Still, a wicked thought pushes up from my mind, telling me that I didn't *earn* the crown. That I'm only queen because I married Jack, not from my own merit. That my position is as much happenstance as a name drawn from a fishbowl.

I tug harder at the string, my insides flip-flopping like a tossed coin that can't seem to settle on one side or the other.

No, I tell that naughty voice. *That might be how it started, but I've proven myself now.*

The announcer taps the loudspeaker mouthpiece twice before proclaiming, "Now, the moment you've all been waiting for!" He plunges his hand into the glass fishbowl. "Chance Town's new mayor will be …"

With a showman's flourish, he lets a pause linger, wiggling his corkscrew mustache as he swishes the slips of paper. Finally, he snags one at random and holds it high.

Everyone around me holds their breath, leaning in toward the gazebo.

"Well, well. For the tenth year in a row." The announcer chuckles heartily but dabs at the sweat on his brow with a dice-dot handkerchief. "Fortuna Luckwell!"

The air grows thick around me, a heaviness pressing against my fabric skin that makes me rake my hair back off my sticky forehead. Amid scattered applause, waves of discontented murmurs spread through the crowd.

The couple in front of us swap angry looks. "I can tell you precisely what the chances are," the young man murmurs. "One in five hundred billion."

The young woman folds her arms tightly. "I'd say those odds are decidedly *odd*."

The losing candidates stomp down from the gazebo, shaking their heads and throwing glares at the woman in the playing card pantsuit.

However, Fortuna Luckwell is nothing but wide-stretching smiles as she grabs the podium loudspeaker. "Another year in my beloved role as Chance Town mayor—what good fortune!"

Someone in the front row shouts, "Was it fortune— or *cheating*?"

Fortuna Luckwell's red-diamond cheeks slacken. A bead of sweat runs down from her towering blond beehive as her eyes dart anxiously among the crowd.

She grips the loudspeaker tighter. "Who said that? Who said I cheated? It's a vicious lie spread by my competitors. I would never interfere with the political process!"

Her eyes pop wide as her plump lips snap shut—as though she's said too much. Her dangling diamond earrings quake as she shifts from one teetering high heel to the other.

"Someone check those paper slips!" another angry voice calls. "I bet every name is her own!"

Fortuna Luckwell and the announcer exchange furtive looks as the loudspeaker goes limp in her hand. She gives a curt nod, and he swipes the glass fishbowl off the table, cradling it under his arm like someone would have to wrestle it away from him.

He calls out with forced cheer, "Yes, yes, wonderful drawing, everyone. Now, Mayor Luckwell and I are needed in Spinwheel Mansion for the celebratory dinner—"

As soon as they head for the steps, someone hurls a pair of dice at the stage. One of them plinks against Fortuna Luckwell's sequined suit lapel. She gasps and staggers backward.

"Quick, Prosper, head to the mansion!" she shrieks. The two of them rush offstage while the crowd is still buzzing with suspicions.

I turn to the pixie. "Pearl, don't let them out of your sight—we need to speak with her!"

Fortuna and Prosper are hustling so hard that they're already halfway across Coinflip Square, headed for the zigzag stairs that climb to the Victorian mansion overlooking town.

Standing on tiptoe to keep them in sight, I try to push my way through the agitated crowd but keep bumping into men and women arguing over the mayoral race results.

Pearl zips overhead for a clearer view. She points toward the rear of the gazebo. "This way, Queen Sally—there's a path!"

I slip between the Chance Town residents to skirt around the back side of the gazebo, where a path winds through the park's lucky bamboo grove. I break into a jog as Pearl keeps pace alongside me, her cabbage-butterfly wings flapping swift and sure.

With my long legs and Pearl's strong wings, we're able to cut off Fortuna Luckwell and the town announcer just as they reach the bottom of the staircase. I pop out from behind a cluster of glossy green bamboo leaves, blocking the path to Spinwheel Mansion.

"Excuse me, Miss Luckwell!"

She screeches to a stop on her stocky legs, eyes wide like a trapped rabbit's, as she takes the fishbowl from Prosper and hugs it protectively to her chest.

"Who are you? I won, fair and square, and I won't have anyone claiming otherwise!"

I hold up my hands to defuse the tension. "Whether you won fairly or not is none of my business. My name is Sally, Queen of Halloween Town. As one ruler to another, I've come because I need your help."

Her beady eyes dart over my shoulder toward the safety of Spinwheel Mansion on the hill. She shifts the fishbowl from one arm to the other while the announcer leans down to whisper something urgent in her ear.

She gives a curt nod.

"I'm quite sorry, Your Majesty," she says breezily, "but it isn't a good time. I've just been reelected mayor, and there's far too much work to be done to get this town shipshape. You may set up an appointment with me for next week with Prosper."

The announcer produces a notebook and checkerboard pen from his pocket, blinking at me expectantly, ready to take down my information. I hesitate, tugging on the loose thread on my wrist. Fortuna Luckwell tries to nudge around me on the path, but I take a sharp step to my left to cut her off.

"I'm afraid this can't wait." I keep my voice firm. "My town is in trouble."

"Condolences! If only I *could* help, but you see, I'm

quite unfamiliar with Halloween protocol. May I suggest you speak to someone more knowledgeable? Your town's ruler, for example?"

"I *am* the ruler—I already told you that!" Frustration rustles my stuffing as I widen my stance, holding my hands to either side to block any escape.

She looks me up and down like she's inspecting a suspicious package. "Who sent you? Was it Lucky Goldwin? That trumped-up board game salesman is sore every year that I win over him!"

I've tried to play nice, but beneath my pretty rag doll face, I'm the queen of frights—and it might be time to prove it.

I drop my voice an octave, hollowing out my cheeks and letting my hair slither snakelike around my shoulders. "You don't understand. I *need* a luck drop."

One look at my frightening face, and the fishbowl slips from Fortuna's hands. She barely catches it before it crashes to the path.

Her throat bobs in a thick swallow. "A–a luck drop? I'm sorry. That's quite impossible. Luck drops are reserved for very exclusive uses. We take our job regulating chance across the realms very seriously, doling out luck drops only when and where they are necessary—not to any town ruler who shows up out of the blue, hoping to win a hand of cards."

I cry, "I don't want to win a card game—I want to save my *town*!"

She straightens her back, eyeing me closely. "Do you think you're the first town ruler who's come here after our luck drops? Why do you think our Luck Factory security is unmatched? Raw luck is the most dangerous substance in the world. It spoils the soul faster than gold ever could—makes men and women believe they're invincible, untouchable. The mayor before me developed an addiction. Drop after drop until he was a gibbering mess, mumbling all day about his big lucky break that was always just around the corner."

Pearl flits close to my ear to whisper, "And she thinks she's a better ruler? Let's see about that."

Without warning, Pearl dives down into the glass fishbowl, sending paper slips flying. Her wings flutter like a tornado in a teacup, and from one blink to the next, she shoots out with two slips clenched in her tiny fists.

Fortuna Luckwell staggers backward, mouth gaping. "That's—that's no butterfly!"

The town announcer shrieks, "A tooth pixie!"

before tightly sealing his lips to protect his teeth from Pearl's sticky fingers.

Pearl ignores their dramatics as she passes me the first paper slip, which I smooth out and read in a loud voice. "Fortuna Luckwell."

She hands me the second slip, and I read, "And . . . Fortuna Luckwell."

I fold the entry slips in my fist, blinking hard at the mayor. "Well, isn't that curious? How many more paper slips have your name written on them—*all* of them?"

Fortuna steps back, her body quaking precariously on her too-high heels. "What are you suggesting?"

"I'd bet that your townspeople would enjoy seeing proof of your cheating."

"You—you wouldn't!" In a snap, her wide-eyed panic breaks into a toothy smile as she suddenly turns friendly. "We rulers have to support one another, you know."

I fold my arms squarely over my chest as Pearl lands on my shoulder. For once, I'm grateful for Pearl's sneaky ways.

I tip my chin upward. "A luck drop, please. Or I show these paper slips to that suspicious crowd back in Coinflip Square."

Fortuna adjusts her charm necklace, dangling

with tiny red diamonds, as she glances back toward the gazebo. For what I imagine is the first time in her life, she looks uncertain of what to do.

The announcer, Prosper, whispers something in her ear. Her eyebrows lift and her eyes light up with renewed hope and perhaps a spark of mischief.

"Prosper here is quite observant," she says. "He remarked that neither of you has a passenger stamp on your hands. Riding the Chance Town train without a stamp is a serious offense."

I draw in a sharp breath as I look at the backs of my hands, bare as freshly woven cotton. "I didn't know we needed a stamp to ride—we had tickets!"

"Unvalidated tickets, it seems." Her lips press into a smug line as she reaches into her suit pocket. "It seems we both hold something over the other, doesn't it? *Tsk tsk.* Quite the quandary." She pulls out a deck of glossy gold playing cards. "What do you say we leave the solution to our predicament up to chance?"

I rub the back of my neck. "Chance?"

"You draw a card. If it's red, I'll give you the luck drop you need. Black, and you give me those paper slips. Either way, we both walk away with our information to ourselves." Her lips quirk in a smug half grin. "A fifty-fifty chance isn't bad odds, you know."

I tilt my head, fumbling with a worn patch of

fabric on my nape as I give a questioning look to Pearl.

The tooth pixie whispers in my ear, "Don't worry, I'll keep an eye on her. Make sure they don't cheat again."

I sigh before extending my hand to the mayor. "Deal."

Fortuna grins wider as she gives my hand a shake so strong that my molars rattle in my skull.

She hands the deck to the announcer, who shuffles the cards with a magician's skill. He passes them back to Fortuna, who holds out the deck with a flourish.

"Any card you like," she says.

I fight the urge to pluck at the loose thread on my wrist as I debate. Ultimately, I settle for the second card from the top, and give Pearl one final glance, relieved when she nods that no hanky-panky is going on.

Slowly, my heart thumping a rat-a-tat rhythm in my chest, I turn over the card.

Seven of spades.

"Black." Fortuna tuts in sympathy, plucking the card out of my left hand. She tries to snatch the duplicate entry slips, too, but I hold firm to those, and her face darkens. "Too bad for you. But fate has decided. I'm afraid you're on your own, Majesty." Distracted, she whips back around to her assistant. "Quick,

Prosper, before they change the locks on Spinwheel Mansion!"

This time, I let her barrel past me. Fortuna's and Prosper's footsteps echo up the winding stairs until they fade from hearing.

I collapse on the bottom stair, burying my face in my hands, rubbing my cheeks so much that I'm afraid they'll fray. What was I thinking? That I could outwit fate? That I was lucky enough? My chest tightens until it feels like I'm shrinking, every inch of me drawing inward like linen in the dryer.

The paper slips crumple in my hand. I fold them, then slip them through a gap in the seam running along my arm for safekeeping.

"What are we going to do now, Pearl?" I whisper.

Pearl lands on my knee and gently pries my hands away from my button eyes, a trace of mischief on her silvery lips as she wiggles her deft fingers.

"Now, Queen Sally, it's time to set aside your royal airs and let a tooth pixie show you how *real* work gets done."

In my travels with Jack, I've toured many factories. Santa's workshop at the North Pole, with its gingerbread awnings and warm cinnamon scent pumped throughout the toy-making floor. The Chocolatery at Valentine's Town, where Amore Buttercup concocts the most mouthwatering confections. Even in Halloween Town, our broomstick mill is always buzzing with the sound of freshly whittled wood.

Still, I've never seen *any* place like Chance Town's Luck Factory.

As I press my linen cheeks against the brass gates, the first thing that comes to mind is a toy box filled with castaway blocks. The buildings are connected by a dizzying network of glass tubes and brass pipes, which carry bubbly liquid from one building to the next. At the last building, a series of chutes delivers cellophane-wrapped luck drops into the open back of a truck parked in a fenced-in courtyard.

The spinning sound of a wheel of fortune whirs from inside the mysterious mirrored windows. A second later, we hear the melodic clatter of luck drops plinking down the system of chutes.

I stare through the bars at a rotating golden coin the size of a door, which silently and smoothly spins between heads and tails, allowing workers into the Luck Factory's foyer.

"Do you think you can fly through that rotating door and carry out a drop?" I ask her.

"Worth a try!" She zips toward the factory, disappearing through the coin-flip door. I wait, fingers wrapping tight around the bars.

Other than the glass pipework, the factory is shrouded in secrecy. The mirrored windows hide any view of the operation within. The tall spired brass fence keeps out looky-loos, like us. Guards in stiff chessman uniforms flank the horseshoe-arch gate. Most telling of all, a prominent sign beside the gate reads NO ADMITTANCE. NO TOURS. NO SAMPLES.

Pearl soon flies back, landing on my shoulder with drooping antennae. "I can only make it into the entry hall. All the other doors beyond there are too heavy for me to open on my own. You'll have to be the thief this time, Majesty. Those luck drops sure must be something to need all this security."

"Think about it," I murmur. "With enough luck, a person could win fame and fortune. They could luck their way into unbelievable power—and power like that can't fall into the wrong hands. Fortuna Luckwell was telling the truth about that, at least."

It's a lesson I know all too well. It wasn't that long ago that I was tied in knots in Oogie Boogie's lair. His obsession with rigging games ruined him, too.

The lure of fortune can ruin anyone.

Pearl cracks her tiny knuckles. "Guess we'll have to make sure it falls into *our* hands, then."

I take a close look at her, from her tooth-collecting satchel to her feathered curlicue antennae. I'm not ready to trust her entirely.

With one last glance at the cloud moving across the sun, I tighten my hold on the polished brass bars. "So, how do we get in?"

"We could climb in through a roof vent," Pearl suggests.

I shade my eyes to peer up at the mirrored roof

tiles. "Too steep—I'd slide right off. My fabric skin has no grip."

"What if we say Fortuna Luckwell sent us?"

"With no note from her? No proof? No escort?" I point to the bold black letters on the NO ADMITTANCE sign. "No chance they'd believe us."

Undeterred, Pearl suggests brightly, "Oh! We could bribe one of the guards."

Uncertain, I run my hands up and down the bars as I consider the chessman guards. Their uniforms are gray with red piping in the outline of a knight piece, and they wear helmets topped by a rook piece's crenelations.

A bell chimes from within the factory, and like clockwork, the guards pivot toward the building as their replacements march to meet them.

"It was worth a try with Fortuna," I admit, rubbing one hand up my other arm. "But these guards don't look like they'd take cheating lightly."

A horn blares at the end of the fence, capturing my attention. A train with four boxcars rumbles to a stop while a chessman guard approaches from the guard booth to check for the proper delivery paperwork.

I can't see inside the first three closed boxcars, but the fourth is a flatbed car where wooden crates stacked three high are stamped with blocky text: FRESH FROM LUCKY LEMON GROVE.

An idea takes root in my mind.

"Pearl!" I whisper urgently. "Follow me—this way!"

We weave among the pedestrians to the end of the factory fence, where the train driver and the guard are arguing over the odds of the Lucky Ducks beating the Chance Town Players at the evening's basketball game. I duck behind the last train car, hidden from sight by the lemon crates.

"We can stow away in one of these crates," I whisper.

Pearl's feathery antennae curl inward in a show of joy. "Now you're thinking like a proper sneak! But I hate to point this out—Queen Sally, how will you fit?"

The lemon crates are indeed on the small side. Add up their width plus height plus depth, and it wouldn't even reach the tip of my chin. Still, I smile as I fish out my needle from my pocket, holding it like a wizard's wand.

"You'd be amazed at how a rag doll can be squished and folded—no bones! Now, keep watch for those guards, okay?"

Pearl flutters her wings before skyrocketing overhead to keep the lookout. I sink to my knees, my heart making bat-wing flaps inside my chest. I run one finger down the gleaming needle.

Outside of sword fighting practice, the last time I used the enlargement spell on my needle was to intimidate Scorch. His out-of-control tail fire had threatened to ignite my dry-tinder stuffing into a bonfire.

Poor Scorch. He hadn't meant any harm, but I didn't know that at the time. After all, even the gentlest dragon might be unpredictable when cornered.

Am I so different? A bribe, a break-in, a theft—these are the choices I've made to save Jack and our town.

The needle trembles in my hand as I imagine Jack's face when he learns of my crimes, his lopsided smile melting away to something darker.

I tuck these fears into a deep pocket in my mind—there is a time for such worries, and it isn't now.

"Expandere," I whisper.

The needle begins to swell in my clasped fingers until its rounded base fits comfortably into my palm. The tip grows until it's the length of my forearm, sharp and sturdy as a sword. A flash of sunlight gleams off its steel plating.

I insert the needle-sword's point below the lid of the closest crate, which is nailed down tight. With a quick intake of breath, I heave my weight down on the needle-sword's rounded end.

My makeshift crowbar pries open the lid, nails popping off left and right as the boards groan.

"Quick!" Pearl advises as she dive-bombs to land on my shoulder, grasping tiny fistfuls of my hair to steady herself. "The conductor just climbed back in the engine."

The train engine rumbles as the mechanics groan, winding back up. I throw handful after handful of lemons into the gutter. Pearl strains, using all her strength, but she can't manage to lift a single lemon.

Soon, I've emptied half of the crate. I toss my needle-sword in among the remaining lemons, then throw one leg over the crate's edge and climb in. Pearl was right—it's a tight fit. But I've folded myself into all kinds of tight spaces before.

Moving fast, I twist myself into a pretzel, tucking my knees close to my chin, tilting my feet at odd angles. My cloth body bends awkwardly to fit the tight corners, but I know I can always fluff myself back into shape again.

Pearl wrings her tiny hands. "I'll find you inside once it's safe—I can fit through the barred gate into the warehouse."

The train rumbles forward, and I barely drag the lid back over my head in time.

Darkness sweeps over me, broken only by a circle of light from a knothole in one of the boards. My lungs feel as closed as a coffin, crammed uncomfortably between my ribs and spine so that I can only sip small breaths. I wriggle my corkscrew body until I can press my eye to the knothole.

Between steady blinks, I watch the train pull through the Luck Factory gates. We rumble across a courtyard and into a warehouse that smells of fresh ink, as if game tickets or fortunes are printed here. From my pinprick view, I can make out giant brass machinery churning away, twirling finished luck drops into printed cellophane wrappers.

The train whistles, and I jump, hitting my head on the crate's lid.

A barred gate rumbles open ahead of us, and the train pulls into a second warehouse. Even from inside the crate, my ears pick up on the burble of boiling liquid, popping like soap bubbles. The most delicious smell of warm caramel and crisp citrus wafts out from the giant metal vats. I can taste the tang of citrus zest on my tongue, and for a moment, I'm overcome by the memory of sipping lemon-peel tea on the porch with Jack.

I'm still thinking of Jack, hugging my knotted knees as close as I can, when a worker gives a crisp whistle. With a hiss, the train pulls to a stop. I hear the clatter of footsteps as more workers come closer and then a rumble as the crate beside mine is lifted away.

They're emptying the flatbed car!

I pinch my mouth closed, holding in any sound that might give me away. After some wriggles, I manage to get my eye back to the peephole, where I see workers in white overalls unloading the train, one crate at a time.

Before I can think of a plan, my own crate suddenly jostles. I clamp my hand over my mouth as I'm lifted, then carried across the warehouse, the remaining lemons rolling awkwardly under my legs. Still, my chest sinks with relief. No one seems to notice the slightly ajar lid, or shouts that my crate feels significantly lighter than the others.

My crate is roughly stacked somewhere in the warehouse. I don't know how long I wait, cramped and uncomfortable, peering out the knothole for any signs of Pearl.

After what must be hours, a whistle blows and the workers begin clearing out for the day. They stow away their brooms, finish polishing the liquid luck vats, and lock up the gates, all while cheerfully making predictions on the Lucky Ducks or the Chance Town Players.

As the last worker leaves, she turns out the light. I'm suddenly plunged into a shadowy blackness that the crate's tight walls only make reaper dark. My seams groan, not used to being twisted up for so long, and a tickle tiptoes up my spine.

This darkness.

This is what Jack is experiencing in his underground prison. All I can think about is the glimpse through the mirror of my dear husband swallowed by morose darkness. It's so terribly similar to my own nightmare. *Darkness, darkness, everywhere.*

Before I know it, my hand plunges into my pocket with a mind of its own and takes out the broken mirror piece. It's a gamble to use—but in a place drenched in the sweet scent of luck, I'm feeling hopeful.

I have to twist and contort to get it to my face, but eventually, I can angle it in front of one eye. My breath hitches, because I know it's a risk to open a portal. There's a good chance Dorian took Jack's piece of the mirror. I can't let him know where I am or what I'm attempting to do.

Then again, trapped in the crate as I am, all he would see is my close-up eye.

"Eye o' shilver, wizdom's gleam, show me the trooth un-sheen. I'd like to shee Jack Shkellington." My words come out smooshed but effective, because the mirror's surface begins to ripple.

I smother my breath as the surface clears, showing darkness once more. But as my eye adjusts, I see what looks like a tangle of ropes. Strange music pumps through the air, whimsical but rusty, churned out by a pipe organ.

"Jack?" I keep my voice whisper soft.

There's a rattle and clatter, and then, Jack's face appears in the mirror. The glowworms in his eyes deepen his sockets even more, making him look positively hollow. Dirt streaks his cue ball skull. One of his teeth is dented. "S-Sally?"

"Jack, watshappened? Where—where are you?"

"Sally, listen." He rattles out a dry cough. "I don't have long. Dorian will be back at any moment. Whatever you do, don't come here. I can't bear the thought of you locked away without the stars overhead. Promise me that you'll forget about me. Take Dr. Finkelstein's swamp-water potion. It will be like I never existed."

I tighten my fingers around the broken mirror so hard it slices into my fabric skin. "I would never forget you, Jack! Not in a hunred and one yearsh! You're my ozer half. You're hard where I'm shoft, 'member?"

His eyes soften, loaded with a trace of bittersweet sadness. "My beautiful patchwork princess. Then I fear we will both be doomed."

My heart pounds so hard it nearly bursts out of my chest, clawing its way closer to Jack in the mirror. I rub my sternum, holding in the pain. "Jack–"

But I hear footsteps on the other side of the mirror. Jack's face goes a shade whiter. There's only enough time for him to catch and hold my eyes once more—electric, bright, powerful—before he cuts off the portal.

The mirror ripples until I'm staring back at nothing but my own smooshed face.

"I'll save you, Jack," I murmur.

"Queen Sally? Majesty? Are you there?" Pearl's small voice comes from just outside the knothole.

I can't begin to guess how long I've crouched here in the lemon crate, more tangled than a ball of yarn in the bottom of my sewing kit.

"Ahm hee-uh, Pch-uhl," I call, though it comes out garbled from my smooshed throat.

"What a relief! I was afraid you'd been juiced— they took half the crates to the processing room!" She fits her tiny head through the knothole, so close that her feathery antennae tickle my eyelashes. "The factory is closed up for the night. Most of the workers have left. We just need to watch out for a few night guards patrolling the fence outside. Can you get out of there?"

"Yesh," I answer. "Jush a mih-nuh."

I didn't think it was possible to contort my poor stretched limbs any more, but I shimmy and twist until my left arm is circling my right ankle, my long neck twisted around like an owl's, so I can use my back to lift the heavy lid.

The lid creaks open an inch, letting in the metallic, sharp smell of the metal vats. I push the lid the rest of the way off and pop out like one of the pumpkin-headed jack-in-the-boxes we made as Christmas gifts, slumping over the crate's edge, letting my poor crushed stuffing slowly puff back up.

"There, there." Pearl frets around me, straightening out my bent fingers and tugging my features back into place. "Good as new!"

Once I feel more like myself, I stretch my arms toward the mirrored ceiling, arching my back, savoring the ability to move freely. Now that I know how it feels for Halloween Town's graveyard dead to be trapped in their coffins, I'm going to declare a biannual coffin-raising day so they can get some fresh air.

Once I'm fluffed back into shape–minus a few stubborn wrinkles–I take in the dark factory. The machines loom like the fossils of giant metal creatures, quiet and immobile now. The glass tubes winding around every corner of the warehouse are empty. A single cellophane wrapper blows across the tile floor.

I pull a length of packing twine off a supply shelf, fasten a makeshift belt around my waist, and tuck my needle-sword into it so it hangs at my side, at the ready. If we encounter any of those frightening chessman guards, I want more than a two-inch embroidery needle to defend myself.

"Right." I crack my knuckles, the soft fabric rustling as it adjusts. "Let's find where they store those luck drops."

I tiptoe across the factory floor while Pearl silently glides at my side. We weave our way around the massive brass vats fitted with temperature gauges and measuring lines. I spare a moment to peek in the back of a delivery truck, but it's empty–no boxes of finished luck drops ready to cart off to other realms.

We leave the delivery warehouse and enter a hallway with buzzing neon question marks on the wall that cast magenta and tangerine lights on our faces. The hall leads us into a space marked TESTING ROOM, filled with game of chance stations that, I assume, are meant to verify the luck drops' potency.

Heavy footsteps echo from down the hall, and I duck behind a roulette wheel while Pearl hides behind a stack of playing cards.

Carefully peeking above the wheel, I watch as a chessman guard sweeps through the room, his cloak billowing silently around his feet.

I hold my breath, counting my thudding heartbeats until he leaves.

"This way," I whisper to Pearl once the coast is clear.

We pass through another door, its sign announcing we're entering the Distillation Room. Its sterile glass beakers and steel utensils are too reminiscent of Dr. Finkelstein's workshop for comfort, and I'm all too happy to hurry through the space.

After the chill of the Distillation Room, it's a relief to enter a warm oak-paneled hallway with red velvet ropes lining the walls. We follow the zigzag path of the velvet ropes, back and forth, until we abruptly turn a corner and find ourselves in front of a giant round door, closed now, polished to a fine gleam like an enormous golden coin. Locking bolts circle the door's edge, with a brass wheel in the center.

A sign written in curving red letters reads THE VAULT.

"Pearl, I think we found where they store the luck drops!" It's hard to keep my voice hushed when all I want to do is yell from the rooftops that I'm one step closer to saving Halloween Town.

Pearl turns a cartwheel loop in the air to show her excitement.

My giddy smile fades, however, when I look closer at the intricate system of bolts that keeps the door locked. A pinprick of doubt in the back of my head grows until fear radiates through my leaf-and-cotton stuffing.

"It's locked," I croak. "Do you know how to break in?"

Pearl flies in a slow circle around the door's perimeter, examining each of the bolts. Her wings droop. "This is much more complicated than taking a tooth from a pillow."

Worries rattle around my hollow chest, and I tug on the loose thread on my wrist, as though if I pull hard enough, I'll wrestle out the answer. We can't have ventured so far only to be stopped now by nuts and bolts. If I don't get that door open, then I'll never solve the Night Mare's second riddle. *I'll never see Jack again!*

My vision starts to blur, the strength bleeding out of my cotton-stuffed legs, and I slump forward over the vault door's wheel, listing toward the floor—

And the wheel spins with me.

Giving a shriek of surprise, I fall to my hands and knees, tangling the needle-sword on my belt in one of the velvet ropes. When I finally free myself from the velvet knots, I check my sword, comb the mess of my hair off my face, and gape at the door.

"It's . . . it's unlocked!"

My words hardly even seem like my own.

Pearl lands on my shoulder, gripping a fistful of my hair, her tiny jaw hinged open. For a few seconds, all either of us does is stare in disbelief.

"Well, what are you waiting for? Open it." Pearl's voice is breathy, bubbling with hope.

Swallowing down a cotton lump, I gently pull on the wheel, not daring to trust it could possibly be this easy. There must be a second door inside. Another lock. Yet the vault door swings open on silent hinges, and a warm, honey-colored light from within cascades over our faces.

Inside, large glass jars packed to the brim with luck drops line the shelves. I feel like I've just uncovered a tomb's stash of gold. I do a quick calculation—there must be tens of thousands of drops in all. Each tidily wrapped in cellophane. Packed and ready to go to other realms.

Despite our good luck, a shiver snakes through my threads, shouting at me that something is wrong.

This is too easy.

"Why would they leave the vault unlocked?" My voice rises to an uncertain pitch as I tug even harder at my wrist thread.

Pearl's eyes, wide and hungry, reflect the soft amber glow of the luck drops, as though she's been charmed by a golden-eyed serpent. Her wings beat in smooth rhythmic pulses, everything else forgotten except the floor-to-ceiling shelves full of luck drops.

"Who cares?" Her tiny shoulders lift in a shrug. "So a guard forgot to lock up—that's our good fortune!"

She flits toward the vault on fluttering wings, but I lurch forward to pinch the hem of her tiny dress between my thumb and index finger, stopping her. She flaps her wings harder, trying to free herself from my grasp.

"Queen Sally, let me go—the drops are right there!"

Holding back a shiver, I look over my shoulder at the dark wood-paneled hallway. "Something doesn't feel right."

"Bah! Let me tell you the thief's motto: *When luck knocks, don't ask why*. Sometimes, a little boy or girl forgets to put their tooth under their pillow. They leave it on the nightstand instead. Or it rolls out from under their pillow while they're tossing and turning. Do you know what we tooth pixies do in that case?"

I shake my head, my stomach still all twisted up in knots.

"We don't need to steal what is freely given—and this is practically dropped in our lap!"

She bats her wings hard enough to tug her hem free from between my fingers and zips into the vault.

Alone at the doorway, I pin my bottom lip between my teeth, throwing uncertain looks between the vault and the dark hallway. I run my hand up my other arm, over the goose bumps that have cropped up there to pucker my skin.

What would you do, Jack? I whisper in the quiet corners of my mind, but only the silence of a black hole answers. My head fills with a vision of him in Shadow Town, in the dark underground realm I saw through the mirror. Shadows coil around him like living chains, his skull's beautiful smooth dome untouched by moonlight ever again.

My hand tightens on the wheel, and I straighten

my needle-sword on its makeshift belt. Then I step decisively inside.

The vault's backlight bathes the amber drops, their golden glow washing over us like an autumn sunset. I turn slowly, eyes drifting over the wall of luck drops stretching twelve feet high, jar after jar brimming with electric power.

What would I do with this much luck at my fingertips? How strong of a queen could I be? I could keep the pumpkin harvest from ever rotting–keep every stem green, every rind unblemished. There would be no more broken skeletons after a bad fall; they'd rise, dust themselves off, and walk away grinning. And any villains that dared to prowl too close to my beloved town? They'd miss their mark every time.

With so much luck, I could make everything right–forever.

Pearl lands on a jar, wrapping her arms around the lid, bracing herself with her feet against the shelf as she strains to open it.

A bolt of fear rushes back into my cotton-stuffed veins.

No. No one needs that much power–least of all a queen. Look what happened to Fortuna Luckwell.

"Move aside, Pearl," I whisper in an urgent hush. "Let me. Remember, we only need one."

The pixie flies up near my shoulder while I tuck the jar under my arm for grip and twist the lid. A tantalizing lemon scent pours out, the smell so full of promise that something about the air already feels lucky.

Pearl squeals with delight and dives into the jar, disappearing amid the drops with the rustle of cellophane, like a miser bathing in his pool of golden coins. Her head pops back up, white-blond hair falling in messy tangles, wearing a goofy grin as she playfully tries to wrap her arms around as many luck drops as she can.

"Pearl," I scold, darting a look over my shoulder at the hallway. "Stop that. We're getting one drop and leaving."

Pearl groans. "But, Your Majesty—"

"No." My voice is firm, holding the line against the temptation I feel tickling my own fingers.

I don't trust myself against the unchecked luck-power—that Fortuna warned about. I don't want to end up ruined by its promise like Oogie Boogie. What's more, I still don't know if I can trust Pearl with one drop, let alone more.

"One drop," I repeat. "That's all we need. Any more will only cause trouble."

I dip my hand in the jar and come out with a single drop, its wrapper printed with a white question mark.

More wrappers rustle as Pearl wriggles her way out of the jar, still pouting with her cabbage-green bottom lip jutted out, like a child who left out their first lost tooth and found nothing beneath their pillow.

My heart softens because I know that resisting theft is a tall order for my sticky-fingered friend. Maybe I've been wrong to be suspicious of her and she really is doing this to save her brother.

"I'm proud of you, Pearl," I say with a gentle smile. "Wait—you know what? I'm proud of *both* of us. The last thing I want to do is steal, and it's all you think about. I guess, in a way, we had to meet in the middle. Find a way to get the job done that stretched both our boundaries."

My good mood is suddenly shattered by heavy footsteps in the wooden hallway. Immediately, the threads of my stomach pull tight as I whip around to find searching light beams projected on the hall's wood paneling.

Someone is coming!

Sure enough, a second later, two men turn the corner, chatting between themselves so that they haven't yet noticed us. The one holding a flashlight is a chessman guard, and the other is a portly business-man in checkered suspenders, holding a clipboard in one hand.

Scraps of their midstream conversation reach my ears, tidbits about quantities and quotas drawled out with businesslike formality.

I realize why the vault door was left unlocked: *They were in the midst of taking inventory!*

I shove the luck drop into my pocket while my other hand flies to the hilt of my needle-sword.

"Pearl," I choke out. "We need to get out of here—"

I've taken a single step toward the hallway when a blinding beam catches me right in the face, and I freeze like a needle mid-stitch.

A gruff, surprised voice shouts, "You there—don't move!"

The leaves in my chest curl up tightly, sharp and shredding against my thin fabric skin, until I feel like I'm about to be torn apart from the inside out.

The worst possible thing has happened.

We're caught!

"Stay right there!" the chessman guard orders. "By my authority as the Chief of Factory Security, I am placing you under arrest for thievery!"

His flashlight blinds me, turning my whole world into a blazing white haze as my chest rises and falls in waves of panic.

I slowly lift my hands like they're on puppet strings, palms open toward the guard to show I'm all stuffing and stitches—not a threat. As my dress shifts, the luck drop in my pocket rustles.

We have it, I remind myself. *We have the drop—we just have to escape.*

All that stands between me and victory now? *The Chief of Factory Security.*

"Pearl," I whisper, low and urgent. "What do we do?"

Her featherlight weight lands on my shoulder, where she grabs the shell of my ear with both her tiny hands and leans in to yell in my ear's cavern: *"Run, Queen Sally!"*

I don't hesitate. I don't second-guess. I'm too close to saving my town—I can't stop now. When I drop my hands and bolt toward the opposite end of the hallway, the guard cries out in surprise. There's a curse and fumbling before his gruff voice shouts into a radio.

"I need backup. At the Vault. A rag doll is stealing luck drops!"

As I race down night-dark hallways, Pearl flaps her wings in powerful pulses, matching my speed.

"Did you hear that, Pearl?" I say between heaving breaths. "He only mentioned me. I don't think he saw you. That means you can escape—save yourself, go back to Tooth Town."

She darts ahead, turning a frenetic cartwheel in the air, her feather antennae twitching. "Are you kidding? I'm not leaving now; it's just getting *fun!*"

Her pinprick eyes glimmer with notes of excitement that I wish I could match—but this chase is no thrill for me. Nothing about this is a game. Desperation pushes my feet forward blindly. My knees feel loose, ready to buckle, but I don't let them.

The hallway doesn't go on forever, so I pick a door at random and plunge through it, finding myself in a break room with a box of ladybug cookies on the checkerboard table. I can picture factory workers resting here, celebrating birthdays and swapping odds for upcoming basketball games. Pearl and I dive through the next door, which takes us into a large open room full of office desks.

Brightly colored posters on the wall read:

Chance Never Knocks Twice—Safety First!
Leadership Is Fate's Calling.
Don't Wish for a Lucky Star—Be One!

At the end of the office, a flight of switchback stairs takes me down to a lobby where an enormous brass horseshoe arches over an information desk. At the far end of the lobby, an elderly janitor wearing a wishbone-print apron pushes her mop over the domino floor tiles, humming softly to herself.

"Excuse me, ma'am! Coming through!" As Pearl and I hustle past her, she looks up with round eyes, her mouth forming a perfect O of surprise—I imagine that a fugitive rag doll and a tooth pixie aren't something she often sees after closing hours.

The guards' boots echo behind us as we turn down a hallway that leads us into a large sorting room, filled with giant machinery that towers over us like sleeping monsters in the moonlight. Brass tubes run throughout the room, some of them covered with a light coating of frost, others blasting hot steam from their rivets. Conveyor belts, off for the evening, form a haphazard tangle overhead to connect the various machines with sorting bins.

I pause, heart pounding, as I search the shadows for an exit.

Footsteps thunder down the hallway behind me, and a flashlight beam pins me in its blazing spotlight. "She's here!"

I rush forward, weaving through the maze of machinery, ducking under conveyor belts, and climbing over brass pipes. My shoulder grazes one of the steaming pipes, and I gasp, flinching away from the intense heat—the pipe must transport boiling hot water.

A burst of steam from the pipe rises up, up, up, to the highest of the conveyor belts far overhead, near where a single rooftop window is cracked open to let out the steam.

There!

If I can get to that open window, I can make it out onto the roof and glide down the angled glass tiles like a playground slide. My stuffing tingles, filling me with a pins-and-needles urgency that has me looking around for something to climb up. My gaze falls on a nearby frosty pipe rising vertically over the sorting bins. I tap it with the back of my hand to double-check that it's cold, then grip it with the soft fabric of my palms and climb hand-over-hand.

"There she is—Miss, stop at once! It's too dangerous to climb around this machinery!"

The guards' flashlight beams sweep back and forth as I swing from the first pipe to a second one, avoiding any of the hot-water pipes leaking scalding steam. Pearl darts ahead of me, still avoiding the guards' notice, easily looping around the tangled knot of pipes.

"The conveyor belt below you—drop down!" she advises as she seizes a small lever and pulls with all her strength.

The gears suddenly crank with a metallic groan, and the zigzag system of conveyor belts rumbles to life.

I let go of the pipe and drop onto the conveyor belt. The rumbling belt carries me speedily over the sorting vats, high above the guards' heads. My arms ache from climbing the pipes, feeling yanked and stretched like a doll who's been played with too roughly. I take a moment to catch my breath and look down at my palms. The fabric is soaked through from frost, my fingers numb and stiff, curled into claws I can't quite straighten.

Jack's smooth fingerbones flash into my mind. In the evenings, I used to trace the delicate lines of his bones, whispering to myself their names: *carpus, radius, phalanx*. Like magical words from one of my spell books. As though if I could memorize him inside and out, I would never lose him.

"Queen Sally—the belt!" Pearl cries.

Her tiny voice hits me just before the conveyor belt comes to an abrupt end at a steep drop-off into a low sorting bin—where I'll be trapped, an easy catch for the guards. I suck in a breath and, looking overhead, jump for the first pipe I see.

"Wait!" Pearl yells. "That's the wrong pipe!"

My fingers curl around a pipe that's practically blazing red, giving off fat curls of steam. The burn sears through the delicate fabric of my palm faster than I can react.

My entire right hand slips off. Two fingers on the left.

I'm dangling by only three fingers.

Another finger slips, then another, and suddenly, I feel myself plummeting downward. Pearl gives a shrill shriek as I tumble toward the domino floor, pinwheeling my arms, desperate for something to grab hold of.

Pearl rockets downward, latching on to my thumb with both arms. Her wings buzz with frantic effort, feet braced against my knuckle, pulling as if she can slow my fall. Well-intentioned but pointless.

Gravity wins, and I hit the floor with a near-silent thump, body flopping like spilled laundry.

The chessman guards rush in to check on me, their flashlights sweeping over my rag doll limbs. "Miss—don't try to move. That was a hard fall!"

"I'm . . . okay," I breathe, wincing as I sit up. My stitches groan in protest, but when I pat myself from chin to ankles, there are no torn seams, only a wisp of stuffing that pushed out from one of my ears, which I poke back into place.

The guards gape like I've risen from the dead—they must not see many rag dolls in Chance Town.

Seeing that I'm okay, the Chief of Factory Security pulls himself together and shines the flashlight in my eyes. "Arrest her!"

The others surround me, taking my needle-sword, seizing my wrists, and hauling me to my feet.

"She was in the Vault," the Chief of Factory Security states. "Search her pockets!"

As they paw through my pockets, I frantically think through what to do next.

I can't let them find the luck drop. Without it, I'll never complete the Hinterland Maze. I won't solve the Night Mare's riddles. I'll never make it to Shadow Town to rescue everyone I love from Prince Dorian.

But it's too late—they're already pulling out a spool of blue thread and a spare button, and I wince against the bitterness slicing through my stuffing.

This is it. The end. Everything I've worked for, and it all ends here with a single luck drop.

"Nothing," one of the guards reports after examining my pockets' contents. "She's got nothing."

I blink hard, fishhook lashes clinking together as I scramble to hide the bald surprise on my face.

Nothing?

The Chief of Factory Security shifts his weight, head cocked like he's working out a riddle. After a beat, he clears his throat. "Regardless, trespassing is still a serious crime. Mayor Luckwell will want to speak to her. Take her to the Chance Town Jail."

As I'm dragged away, confused and panicked, I spot two feathery antennae twitching like tuning forks from behind a temperature gauge.

Pearl's head pops out, a naughty half grin on her face. She hefts her tooth-collecting satchel up just enough for me to spot the luck drop peeking out.

My breath hitches. Was this her plan all along? Lure me in with those big round eyes, then walk off with the thing I need most?

I should have known better. *Pixies.*

"I didn't steal anything, Mayor Luckwell!" I insist. "The guards found nothing on me—ask them again!"

We're in the Chance Town Jail, a small window-less brick building with seven cells—a lucky number, they tell me, though I'd imagine lucky for the *guards*, not for the prisoners.

Currently, I'm the only occupant, not counting a few ladybugs flitting between the bars. On the wall opposite the cells, just out of reach, hundreds of hooks hold an odd assortment of keys. There's everything from rusted skeleton keys to shiny new mechanical-cut keys.

Fortuna Luckwell stands on the other side of the bars, shaking her head regretfully. "Even if you didn't steal anything, you broke into the Luck Factory. You could have damaged valuable equipment. You wasted the time of our chessman guards when they could have been patrolling for *real* threats."

Her eye twitches, and she looks away at the wall, where a guard outside is hammering a board over the window. *Real threats?* I wonder. What could be a greater threat to the Luck Factory than someone trying to steal drops?

"You know what Prince Dorian Dark is doing to our towns, don't you?" I say. "That's why you're boarding up the windows. You're worried that Chance Town is next. That he'll start stealing away your residents, too."

She stiffens, tugging to straighten her diamond-shaped lapels, but her eye keeps twitching. Curtly, she admits, "There have been reports of strange storm clouds in neighboring towns, it's true."

I wrap my hands around the bars, squeezing tightly. "From one ruler to another—send me back to Halloween Town. I'm sure there are extradition rules somewhere in your law books. If I stop Prince Dorian, then I'm helping Chance Town, too."

Her lips knit together as she watches the ladybugs crawl up the brick wall. "I'm afraid that's impossible. The people of Chance Town trust me to uphold the law. How would it look if I let a criminal go?"

My face goes flat. "You mean that you don't want

to be viewed as a cheater even more than you already *are.*"

Anger flashes in her eyes, quick and bright, before she composes herself by patting an escaped strand of her beehive hairstyle back into place.

"Ten days," she says in a clipped voice. "That's your sentence. Truly, I'm being lenient—I could have made it three times that. Besides, you'll find that we take excellent care of our prisoners. The guard outside will provide you with a deck of cards to pass the time. You'll find the lucky clover crepes that Sheriff Wishworth makes are so tasty that you'll probably beg us to stay longer!"

I press my forehead against the cool bars, swallowing back the lump of panic rising in my throat. "You don't understand. I can't stay here ten days. That will put us far after the full moon, and I have urgent tasks to complete before then—if I don't, Prince Dorian might keep my townspeople forever!"

Fortuna breezily adjusts her red diamond necklace, not meeting my eyes. "I suppose you should have thought of that before attempting to steal from Chance Town."

Her tottering heels clomp down the hallway as she leaves me alone in the jail.

The front door slams behind her.

I sink to the floor, back pressed against the bars, and hug my knees close, as though I could fold myself small enough to disappear. Hot tears prickle against my eyes, but I blink them back, hard and fast, because once they start, I'm afraid they'll never stop.

All I can think about are the people I love dearly. Jack. Zero. Everyone Prince Dorian has taken from across the realms. They're trapped in Dorian's lightless kingdom like misfit buttons in a screwed jar. Taken to a land of forgetting. Reduced to *missing things*.

I nuzzle my face against my knees, breathing in the familiar scent of worn fabric, and I swear I can hear them calling from that cold, hollow land beneath my feet.

But what can I do from here? Ten days will be too late. The full moon will come, and my deal with the Night Mare will be void.

My shoulders shake as my tears spill onto the domino floor, adding a fresh sprinkle of dots, making a mess of this town's careful sense of order. But I can't hold them back anymore. I'm exhausted. Worn through as an old rag. So tired I could fold in half and never wake again . . .

A tiny tug on my hair jolts me upright.

I sputter, blinking hard, my limbs stiff—I must have fallen asleep.

"Oh, look, you've stained your cheeks with your tears!" a small voice chastises. "Why so sad, Majesty? You didn't think I was going to leave you on your own, did you?"

A gentle breeze ruffles the hair off my face, and I look up with a hiccup to see a pixie's greenish-white wings. For a moment, all I can do is stare. She lands on my knee, her tooth-collecting satchel heavy over one tiny shoulder. Her wings give a quick, proud flutter, and the soft crinkle of cellophane in the satchel makes my heart squeeze tight.

"Pearl! You came back! You didn't steal the drop!"

Pearl grips my thumb with both hands like she's anchoring herself to me. Her face is serious in a way I'm not used to, her sharp little features set like stone.

"Nobody trusts a tooth pixie," she says, eyes locked on mine, her voice steady but edged with something raw. "For good reason, sure. But remember, I lost someone to Shadow Town, too." Her grip tightens just a little, her wings twitching behind her. "Rescuing my brother Cusp is more important to me than anything else. So yeah, this adventure's fun and all—but don't think for a second I'm not taking it seriously."

Tenderly, I wrap my thumb around her in a gentle hug. "I shouldn't have doubted you."

A smile breaks across her face as her antennae rub together mischievously. "All is forgiven. Now, let's get you out of here."

She purses her lips, tapping her chin as she looks around the jail cell with an escape artist's keen eye.

I dry the last of my tears and slide into a cross-legged position, tucking a strand of hair behind my ear. "How? These bars are too narrow for me to fit through, even if I squeeze. I could detach my limbs, but my head would never fit."

"True, true." Pearl wraps her arms around the bars, testing their strength as though her tiny power could bend them. *Oh, my kingdom for a pixie's self-confidence.*

"There's a guard outside," I add, thinking back to when the factory security team brought me in. "And the cell's key is one of hundreds on that wall. It would take you days to try them all to find the right one." Laughing dryly, I add as an afterthought, "Unless you got really lucky—"

My words fade. Pearl and I swap wide-eyed looks.

She grins impishly, patting her heavy satchel. "You've nailed it, Queen Sally. Luck! That's exactly what we need to get you out of here!"

I push up to my knees, gripping the cell bars, squinting at the wall of keys just out of reach. "It might work, but I can't use the luck drop to get out—I need it to solve the Hinterland Maze, and we only have one. There's no way we'll be able to steal a second one."

Pearl's antennae droop as she nods, considering this, and paces back and forth across my knee. I'm about to sink back into a pit of hopelessness when her antennae shoot upright again.

"Maybe *you* can't," she says with one finger thrust in the air. "But maybe *I* can. I'm one one-hundredth of your size! Surely, just a lick of the drop will be enough for me to find the key."

I twist my wedding ring around my finger, looking uncertainly between the luck drop in Pearl's satchel and the wall of keys. Finally, I let out a long-held breath. "I guess we don't have a choice."

Pearl claps her hands excitedly before shrugging off her satchel's strap. I balance her on my palm as she tugs the luck drop, which is more than half her size, out of the bag.

Slowly, I unwrap the cellophane wrapper with the printed white question mark. I feel like I'm hanging by a single thread—one I hope doesn't snap.

"Okay," I whisper, holding the drop in my palm. "Give it a go."

Pearl grips the sides of the drop with both hands and licks it with her cabbage-green tongue. Her antennae twist into feathered ringlets. "Scrumptious! Like a lemon meringue pie fresh from Sweet Tooth Bakery."

"Quick now." I hastily rewrap the drop and tuck it into my pocket. "Try to find the key."

Pearl dusts off her hands and flies over to the wall of keys. She glides in studious loops as she inspects them, running her hands along the thin brass ones, the shiny double-sided ones, the antique barrel ones with their smooth cylindrical shafts.

When she reaches a long copper key with a handle in the shape of a four-leaf clover, her wings start fluttering as if they've gained a life of their own.

"This one!" she exclaims. "This is it!"

I grip the bars, swallowing hard. "How can you be sure?"

"I–I just *know*. It's like a tug on the outer part of my ear—the same sense I get when a child's lost tooth is near!"

It takes all her strength to unhook the key—it's nearly taller than she is—and bat her wings to carry it over to me. I thrust my hand through the bars, catching it in my palm just as her strength gives out.

Driving up to my feet, my heart pitter-patters as I push the key into the lock, holding my breath, wishing on every lucky star I've ever seen that this will work.

"For Jack," I whisper as I turn the key.

16

With a click and a clatter, the key turns in the lock. The jail cell door swings open.

For a moment, I'm rooted to the domino floor, unable to believe my good fortune. It feels too easy. Spreading down my spine is the same uncanny itch that I felt in the Luck Factory Vault right before chessman guards caught us. Only this time, I'm not afraid.

I know the reason why.

I pat the outside of my pocket to feel the luck drop's cellophane crinkle.

Pearl claps her hands, zooming in loop-de-loops

outside the cell bars. "Best. Jailbreak. *Ever!* Wait until the other pixies hear about this! Come on, Queen Sally—let's see how long my luck lasts."

She barrels toward the exit, but I step out of my cell more cautiously, my heart thumping a warning in my chest. No matter how gently I step, my shoes clatter on the floor, and it feels impossible that the guard outside doesn't hear and come running.

Still, no one comes.

Maybe this *is* our lucky day?

I stride more confidently down the hall, past the meandering ladybugs, and my gaze falls to a cardboard box on the intake desk marked EVIDENCE. Inside, I find my needle-sword, along with the spare thread and mirror shard confiscated from my pockets. Thank goodness I tucked the paper slips away in my arm seam. Fortuna Luckwell would have never given those back.

I retrieve my objects, running my thumb thoughtfully over the broken mirror. Then I stash the needle-sword in my makeshift belt and follow Pearl.

She lands on the doorknob, pulling hard, but it doesn't budge under her teeny effort. I peer out the window first.

Beyond, I can see the guard seated on an entryway

bench, keeping careful watch. I'm about to tell Pearl to wait, that our luck has already run out, when the guard's head droops to one side.

A sawing snore tears out of his nose, loud enough to rattle the window.

He's . . . asleep?

"What are the chances?" I murmur wryly. I twist the knob, and Pearl and I step out into morning sunlight. I keep one hand on my needle-sword, just in case. But when no one shouts or even glances at us, I slowly let it fall.

We're in downtown Chance Town, yet none of the passersby in checkerboard suits, headed to work for the day, stop to notice our jailbreak. Everywhere I look, there's a tweeting bird or a honking car to distract anyone who almost looks our way. A loud whistle blares a few blocks away, where a train is pulling into Chance Central Station.

"I guess it's true what they say," I whisper to Pearl. "Luck is what happens when preparation meets opportunity."

"Or meets honey-lemon luck drops," she adds, licking her lips.

I look at the rising sun, judging the time. I was in jail overnight, and given the days we've lost traveling between realms, I only have two days left to solve the Night Mare's final two riddles. I plunge my hand into my pocket to curl around the remnants of the luck drop.

So much hope rests on something so tiny.

"This way," I tell Pearl, nodding toward the train station. "When we arrived, the train station was the first thing we ran into, so the Hinterlands should be just over that hill."

My pulse hammers steadily beneath my linen skin with every step, but impossibly, our escape couldn't be more successful—we walk right past the sleeping guard.

I'm almost giddy with excitement when, just as I'm about to cross the road, a cough sounds behind us.

"Hey. Hey, stop, there!" a disoriented voice commands. "Prisoner escaping! Repeat, prisoner escaping—with a pixie accomplice!"

I toss a startled look over my shoulder, where the guard is hastily pushing to his feet, still yawning, his radio in one hand as he shoves his brass helmet down over his tow-colored locks with the other.

Even worse? Strange dark storm clouds are just cresting on the horizon and moving in quick.

"Uh-oh." Pearl's nose wrinkles like she's smelled rotting pumpkins. "I think my luck just ran out."

"*And* now they know you're with me. Which

means we need to get out of here. Fast!" I pivot sharply toward the distant line of trees, and we rush through town, upsetting townspeople who are now all too aware of our presence. Shocked shoppers nearly drop their lucky red parcels as I speed by, stumbling over my own feet as I throw watchful looks back at the guard.

"The guard is closing in!" I cry.

His cloak billows behind him, his heavy leather boots clomping on the pavement. This time, there are no copper pipes for me to climb. No conveyor belts to whisk me away. Coinflip Square, just ahead, is filled with more guards approaching from the other direction.

Breathless, I duck into Fortune Cookie Bakery's alcove doorway to think about what to do.

"They're all around us," I breathe.

Pearl flits back and forth, her wings trembling. "I'll lead them off. You run to the Hinterlands."

I'm about to tell her that her plan is too dangerous, and that besides, she's just a tiny pixie. But I catch myself. Pearl has already done so much, regardless of her size.

"I'm worried they'll catch you," I croak.

Unbothered, she blows a puff of air, waving one hand as though it's child's play. "We train our whole lives not to be seen when we don't want to be. Trust me, Queen Sally, I can do this."

As I peek around the corner at the guards closing in, I'm not sure I have much choice. If I wait here another minute, I'll be surrounded.

I give a nod, feeling worried tears in my eyes. "Whatever happens, Pearl, I've been lucky to have you for a friend. I never should have been suspicious of you."

"Oh, pish! Luck has nothing to do with it. A friend doubles your luck and halves your troubles."

She swoops in to hug the soft fabric apple of my cheek and then, without another word, zips into the street.

That's when I notice them—hundreds, no, *thousands* of ladybugs clustered along the sun-warmed bricks of the bakery's side wall, their tiny spotted shells gleaming like red gemstones.

Pearl lets out a sharp, trilling whistle.

Instantly, the swarm erupts into motion, rising as one cloud of glittering wings. The air fills with the hum of tiny bodies as they stream down Main Street.

Townspeople cry out and bat them away, ducking behind carts and into doorways. Cars slam on their brakes as the ladybugs coat their windshields.

This is it—my chance.

I grab an empty flour sack from the bakery's alleyway and wrap it around my patchwork dress to disguise myself.

I dart down the opposite street, keeping my head low, hoping no one peers too closely beneath my makeshift cloak. Fortunately, everyone's attention is on the ladybug brigade currently clogging Main Street.

I dare another look at the horizon. At the storm clouds coming in *faster*. So fast, in fact, that the sun is eclipsed, casting the town in heavy shade. Strong curls of wind bluster through town, stealing people's newspapers. A warning thrums through my veins.

I'm about to turn back, to call for Pearl to call off her plan, when a powerful gust of wind smacks into me with the force of a stampeding horse, knocking me backward. I catch myself against a bench, my hair blustering around me. Blinding me.

When I finally manage to tame my locks, I immediately search the skies.

Roiling dark clouds.

A streak of lightning.

And no Pearl.

"No," I murmur, as my heart thrashes in the cage of my ribs. "Please, no. Not Pearl."

But I can't stick around to see her fate.

Pulse pounding, I hurry to the train station, where I fall in with the stream of travelers pouring through the gate and hurry past the platforms to the dice paths that lead out of town. Holding my breath, I spin the street sign and wish hard for it to land on the Hinterlands.

To my horror, though, the wheel begins to slow, about to stop on the path right back to Coinflip Square.

No, no, no . . . I have to leave or the storm will get me!

A last-ditch idea seizes me, and I pull out the luck drop, popping it into my mouth. A burst of citrus and honey hits my tongue, tickling all the way down my throat. As soon as the drop settles in my belly, the street sign gives one final, extra squeaky turn as it comes to rest just past COINFLIP SQUARE.

HINTERLANDS, the sign now reads.

"Yes!" I start to jog down the path but am distracted by familiar faces. The sweet young couple from the train walk arm in arm, a basket of fresh produce from the farmer's market slung over the woman's shoulder.

All at once, I do something bold.

I pull Fortuna Luckwell's duplicate entry slips out of my arm seam and, running after them, press them into the woman's hand.

"You'll know what to do with these," I say breath-lessly, then jerk my chin toward the approaching storm. "And tell everyone they need to stay inside when that storm hits."

They give me surprised faces as I double back toward the woods and disappear.

As the path leads me between thick pines that gradually bleed into strange barren trees, the light shifts. It's silent as a graveyard, not a single bird call-ing or rustle of leaves. I can't see the heavyset dark clouds anymore on the horizon.

There's something about the wink of mottled light through the trees that tells me I've left Chance Town behind.

The temperature drops as I plunge deeper into the Hinterlands.

The winding paths could lead even the best map-maker astray, but with the sparkle of luck on my tongue, my feet somehow know exactly where to go. At each fork in the path, I feel the same swift *tug* that Pearl described, like someone giving my ear an extra pull to tell me which direction to take.

Before long I slow as that mysterious tug of fate tweaks both my ears this time.

I stop at the crest of a hill, pausing to catch my breath, legs burning and worn through. Below, a tangle of boxwoods and thorns unrolls as far as the eye can see, forming passageways that feel shrouded in secrecy, the fallen leaves rustling in a windless valley as if they're still alive, beckoning, calling to me.

The second impossible task: the Hinterland Maze.

The maze's bramble walls tower twice my height, the snarled branches packed so tightly that not even a whisper of daylight cuts through. Thorns as large as my needle-sword poke out at all angles as if to warn off anyone who would be so foolish as to enter.

As I stand outside the entrance, the air hums with the bitter snap of frost and the rotting sweetness of old leaves, but beneath it all is the faint scent of something older, made of iron and dirt. Something that I have the uncanny feeling has lingered in these Hinterland woods for a long, long time.

When I first saw the maze from the hilltop, its paths seemed straightforward enough. Like solving a wooden toy labyrinth with a metal ball, I merely needed to avoid the dead ends to find my way through to a pair of crossed spruce trunks forming an X at the exit.

Now, however, standing at the entrance, it's clear

that the paths ahead are never the same for long. The groan of shifting wood echoes like an old door swung open, and every so often, a vine uncoils and bursts into bloom, setting a new wall into place. Thorns slide against one another with the slow scrape of knives being sharpened, and roots underfoot coil like they're hungry to trap my ankles.

I know I must enter the maze. But my parents' voices whisper in the back of my head that I might never exit again—that every turn will be a mistake, that I'll spend my final days here, forever separated from everyone I love.

I squeeze my wedding ring, finding strength in its sturdiness.

"Luck and skill." I repeat Cathal Shamrock's words to me, then add under my breath, "I have both."

With nimble fingers, I weave my hair into a braid as I stride into the maze, stepping over the twisting roots and ducking under vines. With every step, my heart squeezes tighter. Brambles snag at my patch-work dress, thorns catching the fabric like greedy little claws, and every yank free means a fresh tear to mend—*when* I get out.

At the end of the first row, I turn sideways through a narrow gap, my back scraping against branches just as vines weave across the opening, sealing it closed right behind me.

I take a deep breath, smoothing my hands down the length of my braid.

I guess there's no turning back now.

As I move down the next row, the air is thick with the spring-green smell of growing hedges. Maybe if Pearl were here, she could fly overhead and tell me where to turn. Yet every time I look up, the sky is thin and gray, never changing. A pain stabs straight into my stuffing at the memory of her being swept away.

Now, there's no help coming. I must face it on my own.

Without the sun as a guide, it's impossible to tell which direction I'm headed in, or if I'm walking in circles.

Or rather, that *would* be the case, if I didn't have the luck drop's sweet zest on my tongue. I can feel its energy—its Prime Luck—fizzing through my stuffing like fresh, light bubbles. At every turn in the maze, I wait for the gentle but certain tug on one of my ears to show me the way.

Turn by turn, row by row, I advance through the unsolvable maze. I slip through every fork, every gap, and every jagged snare of thorns like threading a needle on the first try. When a root rises to block my way, it suddenly stops short of my knees as if it's changed its mind. A path that looks ready to close ahead of me stays open just long enough for me to duck through.

My heart feels lighter than it has in days, and the rush of it makes me bold.

Time blurs as I speed my steps, more confident now, trusting in the *fizz* and the *tug*.

As I turn the next corner, easily dodging a branch reaching out to snag me, I nearly laugh with the ease of it. For days, life has felt so heavy. Dreary, like the sky. I could almost be stuck underground with Jack for as weighed down as my heart has been.

It's dangerous, this feeling.

It would be so easy to crave more of it. How effortless luck makes life seem—no tough decisions to mull over, no long nights pacing in indecision. If I had an endless supply of luck drops, being Pumpkin Queen would be a snap.

I understand now why Fortuna Luckwell was so protective over the Luck Factory. Why they dole luck out so carefully to other realms, in doses small enough to feel like happenstance—not a promise of forever.

I slip through another gap in the hedge wall, and as soon as I'm clear, the groan of shifting wood creaks behind me. Ahead, the brambles look thinner. Sparser. I crane my head to peek between the branches, and my breath hitches.

The two crossing spruce trees rise just on the other side of this hedge wall—the same ones I saw from the hill overlooking the maze. The ones that mark the end. They're so close that I can almost reach my arm through the brambles and touch freedom on the other side.

I'm not sure which skips faster, my heart or my feet, as I search the wall for the final gap that will let me out. I've almost solved the Night Mare's second riddle. Once I set foot on those rustled leaves beyond the maze, I'll be that much closer to rescuing the people I love.

When I blink, in the brief darkness behind my eyes, I can already see the chalkboard in my living room with the second task crossed out in gold-dust chalk.

The *tug* leads me around a corner, and my feet drift to a stop.

Ahead, as I thought, an opening in the wall leads out of the maze. Beyond it, there are no slithering vines or thorny brambles. There are only those two towering spruces crossing each other to mark a finish line.

"I'm coming, Jack!"

My face breaks into a grin as I sprint for the exit, mind already turning to the third task—catch a star— which I *know* will be possible now that I've flown without wings and solved an unsolvable maze.

Ten paces from the exit, however, a vine as thick as my waist slithers across the opening, slow and smug, like it knows I'm coming.

In a flash, the opening closes.

The smile drops off my face, my confidence sinking all the way to my toes. I blink hard, trying to hold back a coming rush of panic.

"No, no, no." I grab the thickest vine, trying to pull it free, but it snaps back and hits me square in the chest, knocking me backward.

I press my hand to my chest, rubbing away the sting, fighting to catch my breath. Panic drips thickly down the length of my throat. This is the first time the maze hasn't opened up to me as though by magic.

I clasp my left ear, tugging on the soft fold of fabric, trying to bring back the uncanny tug of the luck drop.

But I only feel my own worn fingers plucking on my ear.

"I guess my luck ran dry," I whisper hollowly.

The shock of it has me sinking to my knees on the knotty roots, shoulders slumped and folded inward. This can't be happening. Another ten feet and I would be free right now, already halfway to the Halloween Town tree to tell everyone the good news!

Tears bubble from deep within me, and I soak them up with my dress sleeve, letting myself linger in this moment of pity.

Then, I pull in a ragged breath. *That's enough.*

I can't wallow here, not when Jack and the others are counting on me. Luck carried me this far, but now it looks like I'm going to have to finish the maze on my own.

Luck and *skill*, I repeat to myself.

I dry my tears, straighten the wrinkles of my dress, and push to my feet. I pace the hedge wall's length as my mind turns circles to try to plan my exit.

I carefully test the brambles, tugging on vines and pushing aside thorny branches, but they only push right back. So I draw my needle-sword and hack at them with all my strength, again and again until a small hill of pruned branches piles up around my feet.

But for every branch I cut, two more grow back faster than I can cut them again.

I brace my hands on my fabric knees, taking a moment. If I don't figure this out, I could be in this maze until long after the full moon. Time passes strangely in the Hinterlands. I won't know how much has gone by until I'm back in Halloween Town.

And it could be too late by then. . . .

I push those fears away like cobwebs, then peer up at the top of the wall. Maybe if I can't go through it, I can go over it? Yet every time I try to climb, thorns poke and shred my fabric hands until stuffing spills out like blood.

After a few efforts, I sit cross-legged on the ground to mend the tears in my palms with my spare needle and thread. I focus so intently on the stitches that I hardly notice when a gust of wind blows the spool of thread away. I tie off the final stitch, snapping the thread with my teeth, and then stand up to search for the lost spool.

I follow the thin unraveled line of blue thread over the roots like a treasure map to where the wooden spool has rolled under a leafy vine.

"There you are."

I collect the spool, hefting its familiar weight in my hand, almost like a part of myself. Because it *is* a part of me—half my body is held together with this tough blue thread.

I look back at the unraveled line of thread on the path, and an idea unspools in my mind.

Could I mark the path as I go, like some lost princess in a fairy tale?

But the second I turn back to the writhing wall of thorns, twisting like tangled threads themselves, I know the idea won't work. What good is marking a path that is forever changing?

So it's pointless to mark the path.

But what about marking . . . me?

The maze keeps changing around me—the only thing that stays the same, I realize, is me. If there's no compass here, no way to tell directions, then what if I become my *own* compass?

I know where the exit is, after all. Right under the two crossing spruce trees. I just have to wait for the opening to reveal itself again.

Moving quickly, I loop the end of the thread around my wrist and knot it tight—tighter than I need to, but I'm not taking any chances. Then I drop to hands and knees and roll the spool under the hedge wall. Peeking through the brambles, I can just make out where it comes to rest against one of the spruce trees' trunks.

My spool is free, even if I'm not.

I give the spool a gentle tug, and it rolls an inch back toward me, lodging itself on the far side of a root.

I tug a little harder, and it holds fast.

Then I step back, letting the spool unroll.

As branches creak, the wall to my left opens wide as though inviting me in for a stroll, but now I know not to heed the maze's tricks. I hold the thread like a lifeline, my tether to Jack and everyone I love. After a few minutes, the opening closes back up. I hear a distant rustle as a new one opens farther in the maze's interior.

Roots suddenly rise at my feet, knocking me off balance, and I stumble backward. Fresh bramble saplings burst free from the ground right where I was standing, whipping out their thorns toward me, slicing my skin until I have no choice but to retreat.

"I know what you're trying to do," I scold the brambles.

The maze wants to steer me away from the exit—it's pushing me back, growing barriers between me and the end. But I hold the thread firm, the steady tether reassuring me that I'm still connected to the exit.

My center point.

My way back.

The maze changes again, brambles stretching out from the wall on my right to close behind me, but it doesn't matter. I stand tall, squaring my feet against the shifting ground. Let the maze change all it wants.

I have my thread. I have my center. I have *me.*

A long groaning creak comes from behind me, like an old house settling after a storm. I'm used to the shuddering walls now, though, and I clutch the thread taut while the branches slither around me.

Minutes pass. Maybe hours. Without the sun as a guide, time feels like an eternity in the maze, like Father Time has trapped me in an hourglass that spins in endless circles. At some point, my eyes shutter with exhaustion. Jack floats into my head, the way he tiptoes up to my side of the bed on frosty mornings with a bright candle and fresh-baked spice cake. I miss him so much it aches to my toes. His love. His light–

With a cock of my head, I realize that light isn't just in my memories.

My eyelids snap open.

There is real light ahead–the golden hue of the Hinterlands filtering through the leaves. It isn't much at first, just a slim crack, but it widens as the brambles creak and groan.

I push to my knees, holding tight to the thread around my wrist.

I give a tug, and it stays taut and strong.

The brambles ahead give one final shiver before fanning open. I have no idea where I am in the maze now—how far off course the walls have pushed me from the exit. But I still have my tether.

I break into a run, winding the thread around my wrist as I follow its path back to the exit. It leads me around a corner where thorns try to snag my fabric skin, but I tear free and keep running. The light grows brighter ahead, washing over my face and arms. Warmth pours into my skin like liquid sunlight. My knees go slack, threatening to give out, but I force myself to keep moving.

And ahead, the final wall slowly begins to part, vines pulling back to reveal the exit.

The two crossed spruces are *right there*; I can almost feel the scrape of their bark on my fingertips. I count the time the exit has been open.

Three seconds.

Four.

Five.

I close in on the exit, hope propelling me forward, so close now that I can see my wooden spool resting in the spruce root's nook. I want to cry out, to laugh, to scream.

A step before the exit, one final root snags the tip of my shoe, and I stumble forward, arms clawing at the air like I can catch myself on the wind, but I fall. And I feel like it's over, that I've lost, that I'll never get out—

But this time, I don't land on twisting boxwood roots.

I fall on soft autumn leaves instead. *Hinterland* leaves. As my hand closes over my spool of blue thread, I roll over to see the Hinterland Maze exit weave closed behind me, the vines pulling corset tight.

I made it. I solved the unsolvable maze.

17

I race back to Halloween Town so fast that I feel like I have wings. The air feels alive, as if the trees themselves are cheering me on. It doesn't take me long to find the grove of holiday trees, and then I'm plunging downward through the familiar jack-o'-lantern door to land in the cornfields outside of Halloween Town.

I whip around to find the moon, holding my breath as I peer up at it. It's bright and round, but not *quite* full.

I still have one day left.

As soon as I'm on my feet, I speed past the scarecrow and don't stop until I'm at the gates.

"It's me! Let me in!" I shout between heaving breaths. But today, there's no creak and clatter of chains. No one comes to open the gate.

Frowning, I shade my eyes to peer through the bars—the town looks deserted. A worried stitch pulls in my stomach, but I reassure myself that everyone is just safely inside their homes.

So I climb the gate myself, as Jack has done a hundred times.

The sky is dark as I make my way into town. A few raindrops plunk onto my face, soaking through to dampen the stuffing beneath.

Despite the heavy weather, I pump my arms as I run, the exhilaration of solving the maze making my steps featherlight as I stride into the town square.

It's quiet. Even Cyclops's café is closed up tight, all the lights turned off. A few lamps shine in some of the homes overlooking the town square, but the whole place has an eerie stillness.

I climb my steps and open the door, headed for the chalkboard. But as soon as I enter the living room, I wheel to a halt.

My parents sit on the sofa, speaking in hushed whispers, while Luna and Scorch pore over my maps and notebook on the floor.

"Mom, Dad." I rush in to join them, attention

jumping from one person to the next. "What are you doing here? I told you to go back to Dream Town!"

"Sally!" Luna jumps up from the rug. "You're back!"

"Thank goodness!" Albert pulls me in for a fierce hug, so firm that my leaves crunch in my chest, and I can barely manage to extricate myself from his arms.

"You're all supposed to be in Dream Town," I sputter. "It isn't safe to travel now!"

"We went there, but we had to come back." My mother wrings her hands. "We were so afraid for you."

"Dream Town is under control," my father explains. "We advised all the Dream Town residents to go to bed. If there's one thing our people excel at, it's sleep and dreaming! The entire town is snoring away under quilts, safe and secure in their homes, where Dorian's storms can't reach them."

My mother presses her palm to my cheek. "*We* couldn't sleep. None of us. We kept waking up, worrying that you'd get lost in the Hinterland Maze. So we asked Santa Claus to watch over town again and came here to search your maps and notes. We were about to form a search party to look for you."

Luna bounces on her toes. "But here you are! Does that mean—"

The thrill finds its way back into my seams, traveling through me until I can't help smiling. "Yes. I did it. I solved the unsolvable maze!"

Luna gasps in delight. My parents blink, their eyes so big their pupils are pinpricks, as their lips droop open in disbelief.

"Look," Scorch says. "The chalkboard!"

All of us pivot toward the chalkboard where I've written the Night Mare's three impossible tasks.

~~Fly Without Wings~~
~~Solve an Unsolvable Maze~~
Catch a Star

"See?" I say. "The Night Mare crossed it off! I flew without wings, I solved the maze, and there's still time left before the full moon to solve the third riddle! To catch a star!"

But my mother's tight face says she's holding something back as she glances at my father with a look that says everything and nothing all at once.

Luna and Scorch fall oddly silent.

"What?" I blurt out. "What aren't you telling me?"

My father releases a long exhale, pinching the bridge of his nose beneath his glasses. "Sally, there's something you should know." He returns to the window, pushing the curtain open the rest of the way. "Those storm clouds rolled in shortly after you left. They haven't moved since. While you were gone, Prince Dorian has waged war on Halloween Town's residents—he's been taking someone every day, including most of the council. The Mayor. One of the witches. The town musicians and the entire Mummy family. And many more. Now, the few who remain stay locked up tightly in their homes, afraid to step outside for even a moment."

I feel my eyes stretch wide as saucers as I stumble to the window, pressing my palm against the cool glass as a bolt of lightning strikes outside, briefly lighting up my beloved town.

Now it makes sense why everything was so quiet when I returned. Most of the town is *gone*. Taken to Shadow Town. Stolen away.

My only comfort is that my beloved townspeople are most likely imprisoned somewhere near Jack, who I know will look after them as best he can.

A sharp *plink* comes from the window, followed by another. Small objects land on the outside sill, and I recognize them as iron raindrops.

I hiss and pull my hand back as if the glass is burning hot.

"I'm afraid Prince Dorian hasn't only focused his efforts on Halloween Town," my mother says, a hitch in her voice. "These letters were delivered by crow."

She signals to Scorch, who shuffles over with a stack of opened letters gently clamped in his jaw.

"Letters?" I repeat.

My eyes glaze over as I grasp the letters reflexively, too stunned to take in the swirling writing. I blink hard to focus on the words that seem to swim on the parchment page.

My dear friend,

It is with grave sorrow that I share that twelve more Valentine's Town residents have been abducted, including our lead chocolatier, Amore Buttercup. We've decided to seal the town gates. Cherub archers stand at every entrance, ready to defend our town. I wish we could send you reinforcements—but we are barely holding on to our own town.

Yours,

Queen Ruby Valentino

A dull pain throbs deep in my chest, as if an animal has burrowed into my stuffing and is scratching at an unreachable itch.

My knees are weak, wobbly things as I sink onto the wingback chair and let the letters slip out of my fingers and scatter onto the floor. My eyes fall on Zero's little dog bed by the fireplace, empty still, and a sob bubbles from my lips.

"There, there, dear." My father rubs my back. "All is not lost—a few of us remain."

"I'm the Pumpkin Queen," I say. "I'm meant to look after everyone, and I've failed!"

My mom takes my cheeks in her hands, tipping my chin up to make me look at her. "You're also just one person. Darling, you can't hold up the world with just your own two shoulders. Part of being a ruler is knowing when to retreat. Listen to your father and me on this—we've been at the game a lot longer than you have. Is this what Jack would want for you? To risk tearing your town down to its bones, or to preserve what little is left and rebuild over time?" She sighs deeply. "Sometimes, you have to leave people behind. Cut them loose—as awful as that sounds."

She makes the gesture of scissors cutting through an imaginary thread.

My stomach curls inward, leaves hardening inside. For a moment, I can't even find words. Since the moment I donned my crown, they've been pouring out advice as freely as weak tea. Advice I never *asked* for.

"You always do this." My voice grates, hoarse. "You try to wrap me up in protective blankets and bury me in pillows and tell me safety and prudence are most important. You want me to be like Luna." I motion to the rag doll girl—stitched like me, stuffed like me—but the resemblance ends at our fabric skin. "Luna, you have the potential to be a great ruler, but our hearts are different. I have my own way."

Luna nods softly, acknowledging and accepting this.

My parents, on the other hand, exchange startled looks. Mom says, "Sally, we're only trying to help."

I toss my hands up and groan. "I know you mean well, but I'm not your little rag doll anymore. You're mentoring Luna, not me. And I'm not hiding behind Jack or waiting for someone else to decide what's best. I love you, but I'm *not* you. This is my kingdom, my fight, and my choice. I need you to trust in me that I can solve the final riddle and save my town." I take a breath, my hands clenched tightly in the fabric of my dress. "So please, either help me stand, or stand aside."

Silence falls thick as cotton.

Slowly, my father's brows lift, eyes wide. He opens his mouth but closes it again. My mother's gaze, sharp with worry, softens.

Luna's moss-green eyes gleam brighter, a proud smile tugging the corners of her mouth.

My mother's silence breaks. "Oh, Sally. I hear you. I—I just didn't see it the same way. That all this time, you saw it as us holding you back, when we were really just afraid of losing you again."

"If it's what you need of us, we'll follow your lead." My father pats my shoulder, his voice suddenly thick.

They both reach for me at once, their arms folding me into a warm, tangled embrace.

For the first time, I feel like they see me.

Not as their little girl. But as their fellow ruler.

I sniffle one more time before gently pulling back. I smooth my messy hair off my face, full of bittersweet love for my parents. Families are, well, exactly that: messy. Full of tangles and tears. But that's also part of what makes us real. I'd rather have mismatched pieces over perfection any day.

"In that case," I say softly, "the first order of business is to make sure everyone left in town is safe. Scorch, can you fly Luna to Town Hall once there's a break in the storm?"

The dragon flutters his wings. "Scorch can!"

"Good. I want the two of you to go there and wait for me. I need to stay here to pack up my spell book and some ingredients. Mom and Dad, do you still have the Mayor's hearse?"

My dad nods, resolute and crisp.

"Get in the hearse and crank the alarm. You'll be safe there—the storm can't get you indoors, and that should hold true for automobiles. Use the loudspeaker to tell everyone left in town to meet in Town Hall. We'll hunker down there together and barricade the door. The graveyard ghosts should be fine—they can stay in their coffins underground. And the Creature Under the Stairs is hibernating until summer. That leaves the residents of Recluse Woods . . ." I take a deep breath. "But I'm still banished from setting foot there. There's no road for you to drive on to warn them. I'm afraid they'll have to be on their own."

I think of Dahlia's little cottage, left abandoned. Where did she go?

I go to the window, wiping away the condensation so I can study the silhouette of my town against the night sky. Hemlock Hall rises like a gargoyle perched on a precipice over town—the electric lights are on, pulsing softly.

A hitch pulls in my throat. "Dr. Finkelstein is still here?"

"It's the travel restrictions," my mother says, holding out her hands. "As soon as they're lifted, we'll send him back to Dream Town. In the meantime, we gave him permission to use his former laboratory to work on Jewel's damage."

Something sharp stabs my stuffing, like I've swallowed a rusted nail. I hate to think about the doctor being back at his old experiments. Working on Jewel the same way he used to "fix" me. Adjusting her. Improving her. Making her his. Even if he hasn't touched my seams in years, I can still hear the distant clatter of his surgical needle.

That triggers the ghost of a memory.

Dr. Finkelstein said there had been other creations before Jewel, made from bits and bobs that Igor found in the cemetery. Now, I can almost remember the patter of small footsteps that weren't mine. Two wind-up toys left spinning on the floor beneath the lab table.

And my breath catches. Did I . . . *know* those other creations?

"We're heading out, Sally." Behind me, my parents pull rain jackets over their silk pajamas, jolting me out of my thoughts. "There's just enough of a break for Scorch to fly Luna to Town Hall. We'll get the hearse and meet you there. Stay safe."

Lightning flashes again, and my attention is pulled to the window. "You too."

Once I'm alone, I unhook a basket and start to pack herb bundles, keeping an eye on the window. To my relief, Scorch's dark silhouette lands without incident in front of Town Hall. I watch my parents dart into the Mayor's hearse and peel down the rainy street. My mother cranks the alarm to a shrill wail, and my father flashes the headlights as he barrels toward the cemetery road.

I'm about to close the curtain when a flash of movement across the town square catches my eye. Three child-sized shadows dart from behind the Undersea Gal's well to the Cobweb Café. One of the figures hefts a stone from the wall in his small hand, motioning to the others that he's going to break the front window.

I recognize the outlines of their costume masks—a devil, a witch, and a skeleton.

Lock, Shock, and Barrel are out in the storm.

"Oh no." I drop a bundle of herbs. "No, no, *no!*"

As my heartbeat kicks into a gallop, I forget about my spell book and ingredients. I grab my raincoat and slide it on as I race down the stairs and out the front door. Before I know it, my feet are splashing through deep, muddy puddles as rain pelts my hood.

"Hey!" As I draw near, I wave my hands high overhead and shout to them. "Hey, you three! Get out of the storm! Right now!"

Lock, hefting the stone, tips up his devil mask to stick out his tongue at me.

"We're only after some treats, Pumpkin Queen," he whines. "Cyclops left a tray of bat-wing cookies behind the counter, and no one's around to eat them!"

"We're *helping* him," Shock says with mock sweetness, batting her long lashes behind her witch mask. "We don't want them to *spoil*."

"I like sweets," Barrel adds offhand, patting his round tummy.

"It isn't the time for *tricks*!" I cry.

A tree is down across the square, and climbing over it slows me considerably. Lightning cracks overhead, lifting the delicate fibers on the back of my neck. A grave-dark shadow falls over me, and for a second, I'm too afraid to look up. The memory of finding Jack's lonely footprints is too raw. Of watching Zero swept away in Dorian's storm. Pearl, too.

I cry out as hard metal raindrops suddenly ping against my raincoat, bruising my fabric skin beneath, clattering to the stone courtyard like coins falling from the sky.

"Hurry!" I yell as I swing one leg over the tree. "Dorian's storm clouds are here—he'll capture you!"

Shock lifts her hand to her ear. "Can't hear you over the wind!"

The three of them snicker together as Lock aims the stone at the bakery's big picture window, painted with a smiling pumpkin spice latte.

Everything happens too fast after that. I drop down from the fallen tree, ready to grab the trick-or-treaters and drag them into the café even if I have to break the glass myself. But before I can, a cloud so heavy and black that it looms like death breaks off from the storm.

Three wisps of storm clouds siphon off, bathing the square in thick mist. Before my eyes, the wisps form into smoky creatures shaped like wolves, bounding on the wind instead of the ground, their teeth forged of sharp iron raindrops, their eyes glowing sparks of lightning.

This, I realize. *This is what Jack warned me about. Dorian's storm beasts.*

And these wolves? They must have been pulled from the Wolfman's spirit. My sweet, frightful, hairy friend would never want his essence used like this.

"Behind you!" I shout to the children. *"Run!"*

The three flying stormwolves descend on the unsuspecting trick-or-treaters, whose faces are pressed against the glass as they drool over the baked goods inside. With the rain and wind, and their masks muffling their faces, they can't hear the near-silent stormwolves approaching.

Just as the closest one opens its jaw to seize Barrel, I draw my needle-sword and thrust myself between the creatures and the trick-or-treaters.

"No more!" I yell, standing tall against the pounding iron rain. "You won't take a single person more from my town!"

Lock, Shock, and Barrel shriek as they finally notice the snarling monsters. They shrink back, their eyes oversized behind their masks' eyeholes as they press their backs against the bakery window.

I make myself as big as I can, sweeping out my arms. "Back!" I shout at Prince Dorian's minions. "Get back!"

The three stormwolves whirl around me, gliding on the wind like tufts of cotton, moving with the easy comfort of bats in the dark. The first one gives a sharp growl that sounds almost like laughter as it dives for Shock.

Gritting my teeth, I bring down my needle-sword across its back. It explodes into curling lines of mist.

The other two stormwolves retreat away from my sword, only to immediately double back for a fresh attack. One of them dives, dodging my sword, and clamps its jaw around Barrel's leg. With a powerful bound of its cloudy hind legs, it drags the poor screaming boy into the air.

"No!" I slash my sword as high as I can, but the first stormwolf is already re-forming itself, dark wisps pooling together to form the shape of a swishing gray tail.

As soon as the creature dives for me again, I raise my sword, keeping Shock safely at my back.

The third stormwolf latches its jaw around the edge of Lock's devil mask. The boy tries to pull the mask off, but the string gets stuck, and the stormwolf lifts him a few feet into the air.

I lunge and spear the creature's chest, reducing it to curls of smoke—but the first stormwolf darts forward to catch Lock by the arm, dragging him high into the clouds.

No!

My heart thrashes like a cornered animal as I grab Shock, wrapping her tightly in my arms, and squint toward the sky. The driving rain stings my eyes as I search frantically for any sign of Lock or Barrel.

But both boys are gone. Vanished into the storm like Zero.

The only silver lining is that two of the storm-wolves disappeared with them.

"Shock, Shock, are you okay?" I kneel next to the girl, shaking her gently.

Her mask falls off to clatter onto the stones, and her real face looks back at me. For as tough as she acts, she's still just a child. Alone in this world except for her two co-conspirators.

Her bottom lip wobbles precariously.

"We'll get them back, Shock," I promise, fighting tears pushing at my own eyes, pulling her in for a hug that I need just as much as she does.

Frantic honking from the alleyway announces my parents as they barrel into the town square in the Mayor's hearse. My mother throws open the backseat door, waving us in.

"Quickly, quickly!" she cries.

Glancing over my shoulder, I see the third storm-wolf beginning to form again, coming together with crackles of lightning and rumbles of thunder.

I take Shock's hand, and we tumble headfirst into the back of the hearse. Dr. Finkelstein, Jewel, and Igor are already there, wrapped in blankets, their faces wan and shell shocked.

Jewel touches a fresh bandage around her skull. She blinks at me, and I jump. She's always had matching seaweed-green eyes. Now, though, one shows a muddy brown iris. Dr. Finkelstein replaced it.

Dorian's eyes are mismatched, too. I grip the seat hard, eyes shooting to Dr. Finkelstein, a sharp question forming in the soft folds of my throat. . . .

"To Town Hall," my mother says to my father. We bolt forward at breakneck speed and screech to a hard stop in front of Town Hall.

The only safe place left.

18

"Everyone, stay away from the windows," I call out to the small group huddled in Town Hall. "Albert has hot elderflower tea and blankets if you're cold. We need anyone who can help barricade the door to meet onstage in five minutes."

After I make my announcement, I weave among the individuals gathered in the aisle, checking on everyone. It's a shock to see Town Hall this empty. Our people usually pack every seat, but today, the remaining residents—Scorch, the Clown with the Tear-Away Face, the short witch, Shock, Dr. Finkelstein, Igor, and Jewel—barely fill a bench.

Once I'm satisfied that I've tended to their immediate needs, I step back into the stage wings, where my mother is waiting with a warm mug of tea. As she hands it to me, she tucks a strand of yarn hair behind my ear, giving my cheek a tweak like I remember her doing when I was a little girl.

"You're doing a great job, Sally," she says gently, and I can hear in her voice that she's working hard not to advise me, but simply to love me.

"It isn't enough, Mom." I close my arms across my chest like a knight's armor. "It won't *be* enough until everyone is home again."

"You saw those . . . those things," she says. "Those wolves made out of Shadow Magic. Prince Dorian got that from the Wolfman. This ability of his to use people's strengths makes him the most powerful ruler anyone has faced. More than Oogie Boogie. More than the Sandman. Even with your determination and grit, it isn't going to be easy."

I slump into one of the metal folding chairs backstage, burying my head in my hands. It feels like there's a swarm of bees in my chest, buzzing and agitated. My fingers press into the soft fabric of my temples, trying to find the answer in my cotton brain, but I only come up with thin air.

I was supposed to be smarter. Stronger. Prince Dorian has beaten me at every turn in the road, and I've disappointed everyone.

"No," I admit, twisting my bone wedding finger in a slow circle. "I can't fight him alone. We don't even have enough people *left* for an army if–when–Prince Dorian's storms return." I draw in a deep breath, trying to calm the unnerving buzz. "Which is why it's so important that I solve the Night Mare's last riddle. Only the mare's Night Magic can rival Dorian's. Without his shadows and his stormwolves and whatever else he commands, we'll be on an even playing field. If he realizes he can't fight us . . . he might be willing to listen."

My mom silently takes this in. A few days ago, she would have rattled off a speech about leadership. *Her* style of leadership. Now, she simply listens. Stays with me.

It isn't much, but I need it desperately.

I slump my chin back into my hands. "Maybe it doesn't matter, anyway. How can I possibly catch a star? Luna and I have brainstormed everything. Sending fishhooks tied to a balloon into the night sky. Making a net out of chain mail and dried wither root. Training a pet bat to fly to the moon and back. All our ideas . . . they're just *fairy tales*."

My mother rubs my back, her love warming me like the steam curlicues from my dad's tea, but not even a mother's love can do the impossible.

"Ahem."

Someone clears their throat behind me. My back goes bolt straight as I quickly dry my eyes, not wanting to appear as anything but a competent leader to the people who rely on me to keep them safe.

An electric hiss comes from the backstage shadows as a wheelchair steers into the light.

Dr. Finkelstein clears his throat again. "Fairy tales, you say? I knew a girl who once believed that anything was possible in fairy tales. It's what I so admired in her. Her courage. Her creativity. It was unlike anything I'd created before."

What exactly did he create before he kidnapped me? I would ask, but I don't want to exchange one more word with my tormenter than I must.

"What do you want, Dr. Finkelstein?" I ask, keeping my voice as steady as I can.

He wheels closer, drumming one gloved hand on his lap, as he looks me up and down with a scientist's—not a father's—cold appraisal.

Still, I know that look. I know *him*. For better or worse, that look is the closest he comes to showing paternal care.

"You mentioned catching a star," he observes calmly. "I might have an idea."

"No." My voice is hard as granite as I pace in the storage room backstage, where my mother and I have retreated for a little space. "I don't want to work with him. He shouldn't even be here, anyway. Jack banished him. The second the travel restrictions are lifted, I'm sending him away."

"Dear, I understand." My mother's voice wraps around me like a warm blanket. "We will never forget what he did to you. To us. But he *is* a scientist. If he thinks he has a solution, then perhaps we should at least hear him out."

I press my back against the door, arms hugged tight, hair curtaining my face to hide my expression. *I'm scared.* That's what I don't want to say. What I don't want my mother to see.

It hurts to turn to him. To need him.

"I understand." I take a deep breath, tilting my head to get the hair out of my face. "If I do this, it's going to be on my terms, though."

I step out of the supply room to the stage wings,

where Dr. Finkelstein is studying a hefty textbook open in his lap.

With a jolt, I recognize its red leather binding: *Patterns & Paradoxes in Theoretical Physics*. How many times did I see him reading that book instead of asking me about my day? Jotting notes in the margins instead of coloring pictures with me?

I tip my chin up and say firmly, "Tell me how the science would work."

He looks up in surprise, his beady eyes blinking fast behind his dark lenses. "Science? Oh, my dear, I'm not talking about science. At least not *only* about science." He closes the book, marking his place with one of his fingers. With his other hand, he adjusts his glasses. "You see, a long time ago, I knew a little rag doll who believed in fairy tales. Or rather, dreams."

The blood drains from my face, and my stuffing feels thick and clumpy. Uncomfortable. Suddenly, I'm a child again, alone in a high tower with a barred window, gazing down at a town I'll never be a part of. Wishing on every star in the sky that I could be carving pumpkins in the square, howling up at the moon, dancing to the town band's mournful tunes.

I sink into the chair opposite the scientist, tugging

the loose string on my wrist. In a hollow voice, I say slowly, "Go on."

"You were an imaginative child. Given to stories and fancies—a holdover from where you were born, I imagine. I always tried to extract the daydreams out of you, to train your mind instead toward empirical reasoning, but it was useless. Your head was always in the clouds."

My hands curl around my fabric knees, the leaf stuffing inside itchy and stiff, sweat beading in my palms.

Not trusting my voice, I nod for him to continue.

"One day, I left for a specimen-collecting expedition only to realize I'd forgotten my collecting tweezers in my laboratory. When I returned for them, I was surprised to see all the lights on. Even the plasma coil was burning red-hot and bright. I hid in the doorway, curious to see what you were up to while you thought I was gone. You had this book open on the worktable"—he pats the experimental physics text—"and a canister of argon gas, one of the noble gases."

I blink hard, the memory he's describing not there. I've been working hard to recover my memories from those lost years, but some of them are still buried too deep.

Still, other memories slip back. Strange memories.

The small pair of footsteps on the stone stairs. The wind-up toys under the laboratory table. A darkness like being buried alive…

"It didn't work, of course." He chuckles coldly. "You had nothing to contain the gas, so when you released the valve next to the plasma coil, it caught fire and nearly singed off some of your threads! When I returned from my expedition, you were still clearing out smoke."

Self-conscious, I swipe a finger over my right brow, remembering a wisp of memory from when the threads were burned.

Then I let my hand fall. "Please get to the point—what was I trying to do?"

"Ah. That's the question, isn't it? I didn't know until I was reading through this book. To my surprise, young Sally had scribbled in the margins. See for yourself."

He opens the book and turns it toward me. My mother and I both lean in, curiosity thrumming through me like raw electricity.

The faint squiggles and jotted notes are childlike, not at all orderly like Dr. Finkelstein's careful annotations. I trace my finger over the pencil lines.

"'If I can't find a star to wish upon,'" I read my childhood handwriting aloud, "'then I'll make my own.'"

"Precisely." Dr. Finkelstein closes the book so fast that I'm hit with a blast of air. He taps the cover twice. "Back then, Jack Skellington was just a strapping young teen with a scheme to construct the world's largest jack-o'-lantern. It held a thousand candles. Burned so brightly that we couldn't see the stars at night for weeks. Well, Jack soon abandoned the idea and moved on to his next scheme. But for a time, the stars weren't visible, and you were always wishing on stars—for what, I can only imagine. I'm not prone to wishing, myself."

To belong, I think.

The answer hits me so surely and swiftly that it nearly knocks me out of the chair. I always wished to belong. To skip to town and join Jack and the others in the holiday festivities. But it was more than that, wasn't it? I wanted a family. I used to press my face to my bedroom bars and search the night sky for a star. Any star. That's all I needed, just one to pin my hopes to.

The ache I felt wasn't just loneliness—it was like I'd lost something. I've always assumed that missing puzzle piece was my parents.

But . . . was there someone else?

"I remember now," I say, my voice catching on a fold in my throat. "At least, a little. I remember that when I couldn't find any stars in the sky, I decided to make my own. I wanted to make a wish on it like they do in fairy tales. I thought if I could make a star, keep it under glass, I'd finally get my wish."

Dr. Finkelstein tuts. "A childish thought, naturally—but not an altogether *wrong* one. You see, after I discovered your failed experiment, scientific curiosity got the best of me, and I dabbled myself in how it might be possible to manufacture an artificial star."

He hands me a sheaf of papers tucked in the back of the book.

I fan through them briefly. Notations and charts, the periodic table of elements with tungsten and hydrogen circled.

"You mean to tell me that you solved it?" I blink hard, the paper crumpling as my hand tightens. "That you can create a star? That you can, essentially, 'catch' a star?"

My eyes widen, darting between the paper and his face.

"No, my dear." He folds his hands calmly on the book in his lap, eyeing me up and down in his analytical way—a scientist's unnerving stare to anyone else, but I know it's the best he can do to show affection. "I never solved it. It was impossible to achieve through science. Oh, I could form a containment vessel, add a heatproof lining, and extract and distill a hydrogen marble. That resulted in a starlike glow. But it couldn't be called a *star*. A true star requires stability. Gravity must pull particles and gas together, then pressurize it. That kind of pressure isn't possible to manufacture here on Earth."

I tap my heel anxiously on the floor, my face growing hot now with irritation and a sprinkle of dashed hopes. "So what is your point, then? Are you telling us this story just to humiliate me?"

His head cocks as he peers at me, birdlike. "You don't understand what I'm saying, my dear. I have limits within my scientific pursuits. Not every creation I've made has been a success. But you? You do not have those limits."

I hold my hands palm up in frustration. "What do you mean?"

"Magic, of course!" He throws his small hands into the air. "That's where my science ends and your talent begins. I can't create a star on my own—but with my equipment and knowledge, and your spell book, I believe we can fill in each other's missing gaps." He wheels closer, lifting his glasses to look me straight in the eyes for the first time I can remember. "*If* we work together."

19

Work together?

I pace tightly, my knees slack, like all the stuffing holding me up has suddenly turned to dust. The thought of cooperating with the scientist who erased all my childhood memories makes me want to gnash my mother-of-pearl teeth, tear down the black velvet curtains, shove the podium right off the stage.

From the benches, Luna and Scorch look to me. My townspeople, too. Waiting for orders. Trusting in me.

I turn sharply to face the cool shadows behind the backstage curtain, where I have a moment of privacy. I let my eyes sink closed. Here, I can look inward to the thoughts sewn deep in the folds of my brain, heed no one else's opinions but my own.

In the smooth fabric behind my eyelids, I see my life play out like a film on an old black-and-white projector. I remember lavender-drenched cuddles under cozy quilts, my mother's voice reading bedtime stories, dreamy gazes at the moon-kissed stars.

A tear forms at the corner of my eye as those memories are replaced by frigid stone floors, iron bars on the windows, the ever-watching lens of a microscope.

As a girl trying to create a star, I failed. I wasn't enough. And even after all I've experienced, I'm still the same rag doll, the same blue thread and stick-straight hair, the same collection of wrinkled linen and worn seams.

How could things possibly be different this time?

My dad gazes at me with a supportive nod, and my mother rests her hand on my shoulder from behind, spreading warmth through my fabric skin that reaches all the way down to my chest, unraveling some of the knots wrapped around my rib cage.

It will *be different,* I think. *It will be different because, this time, I'm not alone.*

I turn to my parents with tears caught in my fishhook lashes, wiping them away as I clasp both their hands in mine.

"Okay." My voice is firm, deep. "Let's give this a try. That's what Jack would say—nothing ventured, nothing gained."

My mother's cheek seams pull back to show her pearly smile as she wraps me in an embrace.

When we part, I look around the auditorium, blinking to clear my watery vision into pinprick focus.

"Everyone, please pay attention," I announce, stepping center stage. Worried conversations fall silent as eager, concerned faces peer at me from beneath quilts and over steaming mugs of tea. Luna climbs on Scorch's back to see better.

I continue, "We're going to set up a workshop in Hemlock Hall, in Dr. Finkelstein's former laboratory. We'll need help gathering supplies." I turn to Dr. Finkelstein, forcing myself to draw a deep, centering breath before asking him, "What do you require, Dr. Finkelstein?"

He joins me onstage, adjusting his dark eyeglasses as he peers at the auditorium's equipment. "The spotlight's bulb contains tungsten. I'll need that, as well as the Mayor's laser pointer, and the magnets from the announcement board. Oh, and a string of Christmas lights—Jack keeps them backstage."

He turns my way and, briefly, our eyes meet.

For so much of my life, my feelings for this wizened

old man were as multifaceted as a diamond, anger and longing and pity all crushed together under immense pressure. Yet when I look at him now, there's something new, too.

There's also . . . *hope*.

Wind howls at the door, making the hinges groan, as we work together to scavenge supplies from Town Hall and load them into the backstage cart. With Scorch's help, my father uses a ladder to reach the mezzanine's spotlight. My mother and Luna search through backstage trunks for Christmas lights.

Shock and I are busy collecting announcement board magnets when a blinding bolt of lightning lights up the windows. Thunder crashes a second later, and Shock shrieks and covers her head with her hands.

"It's okay, Shock." I rush to her side, adjusting her crooked witch's hat. "I promise, everything will be okay. We'll get Lock and Barrel—and everyone—back."

She nods, sniffling. I only wish I felt as confident as I sound. But my stomach balls itself up, and I slowly count on my fingers all the supplies we need, stopping when I reach my thumb.

"My spell book!" I gasp.

"What's that?" My mother sets the Christmas lights in the cart and dusts off her hands.

"Mom, I forgot about my spell book! I was packing it

and the ingredients when the stormwolves attacked the town square . . ." I feel my eyes stretch wide as I press a hand against my temple. "Oh, how could I be so thoughtless! I can't do any magic without it. It's still at home, with my herb basket."

We both turn to the window, to the dark clouds outside. The howling wind. Another flash of lightning lights up the sky.

There's no way of knowing if it's a regular storm—or *Dorian's* storm.

"I'll go." Greta's voice is decisive, though there's a tremor in her chin. "You have to work with Dr. Finkelstein to set up the experiment—I'll go to your house, get the book, and bring it to Hemlock Hall."

My fabric hands knit together. "Mom, it's dangerous."

She hesitates, then cups my cheek in the soft curve of her palm. "There's danger in every dream worth chasing, Sally—*you* told me that. All this time, I never realized that we had as much to learn from you as you did from us."

I grasp her hand, squeezing tightly, just as she used to do for me so many times when I was a little girl kept up by nightmares.

It's so hard to let her go—but I must. Just as I asked her to let go of me.

I nod, swallowing back tears.

Turning to the group, I raise my voice above the wailing wind. "It's time, everyone!"

The Clown with the Tear-Away Face unlatches the bar across the door, and cautiously, we crack it open. At first, the wind seems mild, only small gusts ruffling the hem of my dress.

I start to open the door wider, but Scorch suddenly slams it closed with a heavy paw.

"Queen Sally—look!" He jerks his chin toward the western windows, where iron pellets smash into the glass with sharp metallic rings. "Not a simple storm!"

I press my back against the front door as though I alone can hold off the Shadow Prince's darkness, my heart hammering so hard I'm surprised the whole auditorium can't hear it.

Luna pats Scorch as a reward for his swift thinking.

"We don't have a choice," Dr. Finkelstein says. "We're running out of time. The full moonrise is in three hours and twenty-one minutes; it will be a race against the clock already."

Sweat breaks out along my hairline, soaking through to the stuffing underneath, and I wish more than ever that I could stretch myself to be everything, to do everything, as easily as folding into a lemon crate.

"You heard him!" My father's rousing voice seems to shake the cobwebs out of people's ears. "We have a job to do, storm or not. Let's take a lesson from my bold, brave daughter, and *fight!*"

Scorch steps forward. "Scorch is not scared!" He shows his lopsided fang, sharp and gleaming even though it's missing its twin.

"Yeah!" Luna pumps her fist in the air. "Neither am I!"

Their enthusiasm soon spreads. The Clown with the Tear-Away Face claps his hands, pedaling back and forth like a rabid dog ready to be let off the leash.

Beside him, Igor moans eagerly as he grips the cart handles.

"Thunder roars," the short witch crows, swinging her wrinkled fist in a tight left hook in the air. "But so do we!"

Proud tears push at my eyes as I watch the townspeople that I've known my whole life step into their true, frightful roles. *If only Jack could see this.*

"Clown with the Tear-Away Face, get ready to open the door," I say. "Everyone, move fast and keep in a zigzag pattern. You can't let Dorian's wind or stormwolves sweep you up."

He honks his horn in a final rallying cry before reaching for the door latch. The wind blusters against the door now with such force that it sounds like monsters clawing on the other side. My father holds a prop sword from backstage—sharp enough to defend himself with—at the ready. The short witch raises her wand.

I move to stand in front of Shock, securing her small hand in mine with an iron grip.

"Okay," I breathe. *Now.*

The Clown with the Tear-Away Face flings the door open, and chaos erupts like a broken dam.

A blast of frigid wind throws my hair back, assailing my face with a rash of iron rain that stings my linen skin and pokes holes all the way to the stuffing. A preternatural howl rolls off the wind, sounding more like an animal than any force of nature.

From the corner of my eyes, squinted against the storm, I see wisps tear off from the black clouds, already forming into wolfish shapes.

For a moment, the townspeople stare at the mayhem with pale faces, frightened for the first time in their lives—*they're* usually the scarers.

My mother gives a soft moan as she clutches the top button of her pajamas, her eyes rimmed in fear. Luna climbs on Scorch's back, holding tight, though her eyes are wide and round.

"Everyone, hold strong!" I shout, leaning into the wind, squeezing Shock's slight hand tightly in my own. "Remember who we are: monsters and ghouls! Now, go—they can't catch all of us!" I draw my needle-sword from the twine belt around my waist. "For Halloween Town!"

Our small troupe of scarers runs out to meet the full force of the snarling storm. Immediately, the iron rain swells, pounding us with wave after wave of bullet-like drops. The three stormwolves whip around the square, their smoky black tails slicing through the air, their iron teeth bared.

"Go, Scorch! Fly!" Luna shouts. "Everyone, we'll cover you!"

Scorch thunders forward, taking wing, waving his tail fire like an anglerfish lure for one of the wolves to follow.

"Boo and brawl!" The Clown with the Tear-Away Face wheels straight up to the second stormwolf, where he pulls an absurdly large accordion fan from his pocket and waves it toward the creature, trying to waft it backward.

To my surprise, it works just enough to create an opening in the clouds for Igor, moving as swiftly as he can with his limp over the square's uneven cobblestones, to push the cart loaded with our supplies.

Dr. Finkelstein drives his wheelchair behind him, mashing the button to make the chair move at full speed. The third stormwolf is baring its teeth, ready to assail him on the next gust of wind, when the short witch thrusts her gnarled wand toward it.

"Hex power!"

A wave of warm swamp air hits the stormwolf, blasting it backward across the square to slam into the stone wall, where it bursts apart.

She cackles in delight, kicking her feet in a jig as she points her wand toward the other stormwolf. "You want a taste of what your friend got?"

Greta's bottom lip trembles, though her eyes hold nothing but courage. "I'll meet you at Hemlock Hall, Sally. Now, *go*."

She gives me a gentle shove toward the door and steps out behind me, clutching her robe tightly as she strides purposefully into the rain. Every instinct inside me screams to stop her. To keep her safe. Locked up tight where nothing can ever harm her.

But being locked up? That's no way to live.

"Hey! Scram, you oversized rain cloud!" Before

I can stop her, Shock charges toward the closest stormwolf, waving a gavel pilfered from Town Hall overhead.

"Shock, wait!" I dart out after her, pumping my arms, as iron rain falls over my bare head and arms. My heart hammers harder with every step, urging me forward like a steam engine.

I dodge around Igor pushing the cart, who is blocked ahead by the biggest, darkest stormwolf. Nearby, Clown pedals his unicycle smack into the big stormwolf, disappearing inside its smoky body. The creature gnashes its iron teeth as it writhes, but the Clown with the Tear-Away Face keeps pedaling until he pushes right through the other side, leaving a clown-shaped hole in the creature's smoky outline.

I have only a second of hesitation before I dart after him through the hole, my legs burning, smoke filling my nostrils as I come through the other side.

I pinwheel my arms to a stop, run my hands down my cotton sides to make sure I'm in one piece. I'm okay, but the two halves of the big stormwolf are already melding back together behind me.

"Shock!" I cry.

A few steps ahead, the third stormwolf snaps at Shock and catches her dress's hem in its teeth. I run forward, needle-sword raised to stab the stormwolf, but it sees me coming and shoots into the air, dragging a kicking and squealing Shock with it.

Her witch mask snaps loose and falls.

"Let her go!" I jump up onto the fountain's rim, steadying myself on the gargoyle for balance, thrusting out my sword in my other hand.

But the stormwolf flies high on an updraft, carrying Shock by the dress hem, her bare face just as pale as the mask she usually wears.

She's gone. Taken. Abducted, like all the others.

I balance precariously on the fountain rim, swaying as I stare up into the rain, the horror of what I've just seen crashing over me like cliffside waves.

Dread runs backward up my throat, thick and bitter, as I climb down from the fountain. I pick up her fallen mask and tuck it under my arm.

From the corner of my eye, I notice a stormwolf close its jaws around Jewel and drag her into the rumbling storm clouds.

"No!" I cry.

There's only one stormwolf left—the big one—and it's almost fully re-formed itself, the wisps of black clouds knitting together like wool on a spinning wheel.

"Sally, run! Get to Hemlock Hall!" My father places himself between the stormwolf and me, his chin high and the prop sword firm in his grasp.

I pause, biting my lip hard enough to nearly split the seam. I don't want to, but I know I have to let him do this. To take the risk.

"Help Igor with the cart!" Dr. Finkelstein calls to me, his face pinched, his voice snapping with urgency.

I throw Shock's mask in the cart before taking one of the handles. Igor grips the other, and together, we heave the rickety cart over the bumpy cobblestones. It's backbreaking work to push the load uphill to Hemlock Hall, but with Igor's single-minded resolve and my nimbleness, the wooden wheels roll steadily up the path.

Dr. Finkelstein follows behind us.

A sheet of rain drenches me, plastering my hair over my eyes, and I can't see what's happening in the battle back at Town Square. I can only hear the grunts of the short witch, the Clown with the Tear-Away Face, and my father as they try to hold back the stormwolves.

High overhead, Scorch's silhouette against the dark clouds darts down toward one of the wolves. His tail fire flares. I can barely make out Luna's outline on his back.

I wave to them, signaling toward Hemlock Hall.

"Keep pushing! Not much farther now!" I call to Igor, who nods resolutely despite his limp growing more pronounced. The lights of Hemlock Hall glow ahead, inviting and warm, and I double down on my speed, anxious to get inside the building's safety. I hear a toy horn honk behind me, the sound suddenly strangled halfway through, and I gasp and turn around.

"Clown with the Tear-Away Face?" I start, squinting into the darkness, alarmed by how still it is in the town square. "Witch?" My voice peaks to a higher pitch as I shout, half-panicked, *Dad?*"

Dr. Finkelstein shakes his head forcefully, herding me forward with one of his gloved hands. "Ahead, Sally. Focus only on what's ahead, not behind you."

My mouth fills with sharp-edged words, but he's right. My father knew the risks. He accepted them. Dorian's henchmen might have captured him, but it only makes me more determined than ever to get him back.

I swallow my fear and keep pushing the cart. We make our way across the narrow bridge that spans a gully, then reach the stone steps leading to Hemlock Hall's arched door, shadowed by the observatory telescope overhead.

Dr. Finkelstein zips up the entryway ramp, casting a thin-lipped grimace at the HEMLOCK HALL sign posted on what was once his house. He disappears inside the building. Igor and I are almost at the door when a dark wisp of cloud sweeps in overhead—and two hot-coal eyes blink open.

The biggest stormwolf has found us.

I reach for my needle-sword, but before I can draw it, a blur of light streaks through the storm. Scorch dives from above like a comet, wings flared, his tail fire cutting a golden gash through the gloom. Luna clings to the base of his wings, steering him.

"Hey!" she shouts at the stormwolf over the roar of wind. "Over here, you grumpy rain cloud!"

The stormwolf snarls, lightning crackling in its throat, and veers straight toward them. Scorch pivots midair at Luna's direction, leading the monster away with bursts of flame as he flies in daring loops.

For a heart-stopping moment, the sky becomes a battleground of fire against storm clouds.

Then, the fire goes out.

I stare at only dark clouds. The rain lets up slightly, giving me one last glimpse of Luna turning to look back at me before they vanish, stolen away by the clouds.

"No!" I scream into the sky.

My chest sinks like a leaden weight, threatening to pull me into some deep, dark place I'll never float up from.

I can't stand this. Losing everyone I love to the storm, one by one.

Besides Igor, Dr. Finkelstein, and me, only my mother is left. At least, I *hope* she is. My house is too far away to see anything but the spinning weather vane on the tip-top of the roof.

"Come on, Mom," I murmur. "You can do this. I can't lose you, too."

Still, Scorch and Luna's brave stunt buys us the precious few minutes it takes to maneuver the cart into Hemlock Hall. We wheel it straight to the laboratory, where Dr. Finkelstein has lit blazing lanterns and cleared off the worktable.

Bent over a collection of sparking live wires, Dr. Finkelstein peers up at us with a questioning lift of his eyebrow.

I whisper the spell to shrink my needle-sword, then tuck the spare needle in my pocket. A bitter taste fills my mouth. "The storm took all of them—my father, too."

Dr. Finkelstein blinks behind his dark lenses, his head cocked at a strange angle like I'm an equation that has stumped him for years. There was a time when I called *him* my father. I haven't forgotten it—and I can see in his beady eyes that he hasn't, either.

I'm just left wondering if anyone else has ever called him father, too.

He seems like he might speak but then thinks better of it and returns to his experiment, sorting through the live wires while mumbling softly as if to himself. "Focus on the task at hand, my dear girl. That's the surest way to be back with your father soon. And Jack. And all of them."

His gaze turns to an empty stool beside him. His companion, Jewel, was also taken, I realize. He's fighting for a loved one, too.

I take a deep breath. His tone is cold, but I'm used to coldness from him. What matters is that we're here, willing to work together. I unhook a canvas apron from the wall and tie it around my waist, taking up my lab assistant position beside him, falling into the old role like I'm easing back into last winter's coat.

His busy hands pause, the wires sparking. He asks quietly, "Your mother?"

"Fetching my spell book." My words are clipped, confident. "She'll be here in no time."

He peers at me curiously, unspoken words hinged on the tip of his tongue, but then clears his throat and points to the spotlight bulb in the cart.

"Break that light bulb, carefully," he orders. "So I can extract the tungsten coil."

In a snap, Dr. Finkelstein and I fall into a rhythm—one as familiar as it is unsettling. I move robotically, my hands knowing which switch to flip as deftly as if turning on my own bedroom light. Emotions churn inside me, a pot on the verge of boiling over, ready to spill across the floor.

But the one thing holding it all together … is hope.

We work as efficiently as we can, Dr. Finkelstein painstakingly scraping tungsten from the light bulb's core, Igor and I soldering the announcement board magnets to the rim of my old cauldron, which I've used for years as a soup kettle. As I see it, if it's tough enough to withstand acid-drop stew, then it can handle anything.

When I glance at the chrome clock attached to the telescope, an hour has already passed. A gasp slides over my lips as my gaze shifts to the high skylight window. In just two more hours, the full moon will rise.

We'll be out of time.

"Sally, coat the inside of the cauldron with this alchemical paste."

I nod as I take the glue pot and start on the task.

But as we work together, there's a difference. It's unspoken. As small as the eye of a needle, but it's there.

In his eye contact, his posture . . . it's starting to feel like he *respects* me.

Someone pounds on the front door, pulling me out of my focus. I nearly drop the paste, catching it at the last moment.

"Igor will answer the door," Igor volunteers.

He limps a few steps toward the spiral ramp, but I shake my head, set down the glue pot, and rest a hand on the uneven curve of his back.

"Stay here and help Dr. Finkelstein. I'll get it."

I break into a run, unable to wait a moment longer to throw open the door. My palm is sweaty on the brass jack-o'-lantern knob, my heart thumping like trapped bats against my ribs.

"Sally!" The person knocks again, the soft rap of cloth knuckles that I know so well. "Sally, it's me!"

"Mom! You made it!" I throw open the door, tears springing to my eyes as I throw my arms around her. She's soaked through and through, so that when I squeeze her, water drips from her fingertips.

She laughs through matching tears, wringing out her rain-logged ear with one hand while the other clutches my spell book beneath the fold of her robe to keep it dry. Her eyes are alight with the thrill of her adventure, her cheeks red and windblown.

The wind gusts up from the gully, ruffling my hem and chilling my damp ankles. I keep my smile pinned in place. I can't tell her about Dad. About Luna and Scorch and all the others. I can't tell her that *we're* all that's left—those of us in Hemlock Hall.

"Oh, Sally, it was wild!" She tucks back a wet strand of crimson hair, blinking the rain out of her eyelashes, as she takes a few steps backward onto the bridge to point in the direction of my house. "One of those terrible creatures chased me—"

In one second, she's standing on the bridge gushing about her adventure, and in the next, she's simply . . . *gone.*

It takes my mind a few beats to catch up to what happened, because it's simply too terrible to believe. I blink. Then blink again.

The bridge is empty.

In the darkness behind my eyelids, all I can see is what happened in a flash. A cloud of bat-shaped storm creatures that swept in out of nowhere, sudden and dark as night itself. Hundreds of tiny bat claws digging into my mom's midnight-blue robe. Lifting her. The shock painted over her face as my spell book fell from her hands.

"No!" I fall to my knees in the foyer, bloodless as

a corpse, every stitch of strength utterly slackened from my head to my toes as I stare at the place my mother was standing only seconds ago.

A ghostly wind blusters up from the gully, and a rash of goose bumps crops up along my arms as I feel more dark clouds closing in. The wind turns to an animalistic howl. More storm monsters are coming—I can feel their approach like electricity snapping across my skin.

Wolves conjured from the Wolfman.

Bats from my vampire friends.

What next?

Shaky, I push to my feet to retreat inside, but the next gust of wind blows open the cover of my spell book, still resting on the bridge where it fell.

My jaw snaps shut as my back goes ramrod straight.

My spell book—I have to get it!

I scour the skies, searching for more storm creatures with a looming feeling that they're lurking just behind a dark cloud, ready to pounce the moment I set foot out of Hemlock Hall.

As my pulse rattles, I dare a step forward onto the steps. Iron raindrops slam into my leg. A snarl like thunder rumbles from behind the big oak tree.

If I run out to get my spell book, I'll be captured.

But I can't complete the experiment without it.

What do I do?

Suddenly, a blaze lights up the darkness. I shade my eyes, blinking into the rain, one hand still clutching the brass doorknob in case I need to flee back inside.

A cloaked figure holding a lantern rushes toward the bridge, kneeling next to my spell book.

My muscles tense, stitches pulling so taut I'm sure they'll snap, as one hand falls on the spare needle in my pocket.

But then, the wind blows the figure's hood back, and long bluebell curls spill out. The woman gathers my spell book in the basket of her arm, moving with a nimble confidence like she knows exactly what she's dealing with.

A stormbat shoots out from behind the oak, flying menacing loops over her head, but she lifts the lantern high, and the light makes the creature hiss and retreat.

"Over here!" I cup my hands around my mouth and shout. "Hurry—bring the book!"

Princess Dahlia races across the bridge, my spell book tucked into her cloak, and bounds up the stairs just as the stormbat doubles back. Dahlia blows past me into the foyer, and I slam the door closed behind her, throwing my weight on the latch.

My breath scrapes against my lungs, straining the fabric.

Dahlia leans against the entryway, rain dripping off her cloak, as she struggles to catch her own breath.

For the first time, I can see her up close—close enough to see she, too, has mismatched eyes.

Like her brother.

Like Jewel, too.

"I swore that I'd never again set foot in this home," she says between breaths. "Never look Dr. Finkelstein in the face again. But, then, I got your letter." She pushes aside her cloak and holds out my spell book with my crumpled letter resting on top, worn at the edges as though it's been read and fretted over many times.

She looks up with trepidation at the ceiling of Hemlock Hall's cold foyer. "Do you really not remember what happened all those years ago?"

I shake my head, eager for answers but just as fearful of what those may be. "Remember what?"

"Remember that you, Dorian, and I—we all lived here together. Like siblings." She pauses. "Here, under this very roof."

20

"Siblings?" I repeat, my voice hollow as a grave.

"Not biologically," Dahlia continues breathlessly. "Only in the sense that, for a few months, we shared a parent in Dr. Finkelstein." Dahlia holds up my rain-splattered letter. "For so many years, Dorian and I thought of you as Dr. Finkelstein's devoted youngest daughter. That you only had stars in your eyes for him. It wasn't until you used that word to describe him—your *tormenter*—that I wondered if we'd overlooked something. And then I got your letter and found out about the forgetting potion. I realized we'd misunderstood everything."

I find myself leaning against the door as the wind

outside rattles it, trying to make sense of words that feel topsy-turvy and backward. The conversation is too much. Too heavy. Compared to standing up against it, the raging storm outside feels like a springtime sprinkle.

"I . . . I don't understand. We're sisters? Dorian is my . . . brother?"

Dahlia's lips tip slightly downward, sympathy softening her mismatched eyes. "You really don't remember, do you? Dorian and I . . . we were Dr. Finkelstein's first creations. He made us from the spare parts in his laboratory. Tinkered away until we breathed life. He called us his 'children,' but right away, it was clear we weren't what he wanted. Dorian had no interest in helping with his science. I refused to cook and clean. We were failures to him—and soon, he lost interest. Forgot about us. Acted like we were only *shadows* in our own hallways."

She looks away, blinking back tears, tightening her fist around her satchel's strap. "One day, he turned up with a new daughter. A dreamy little rag doll who baked him stardust cookies and giggled at Igor's antics. Dorian and I were immediately worried about how he'd gotten you. We did some digging and found out he'd taken you from Dream Town, where you had parents." She pauses to take a deep breath.

"We tried to save you—it's still hard for me to believe you don't remember. We wrapped you up in a body bag to smuggle you out the basement morgue, but you screamed and screamed for the doctor—for your *father*—to come save you."

I clasp the doorframe, afraid one wrong breath will blow me down like a dandelion puff. My heart hammers an unsteady rhythm that reverberates down to my toes. *This.* This is the memory that's been haunting me. Part of it, at least. I thought my memory of total darkness was from somehow being buried alive, trapped underground like Jack . . . *but it was the blackness inside the body bag.*

I can't ignore the way my pulse raps insistently against my veins, like a wake-up call, and I can start to see more than just the hazy edges of the memory.

"I got you and Dorian in trouble," I whisper in a daze. "When you were only trying to help me."

Dahlia wipes her face clear of rain, looking at me with pinprick attention. "Dr. Finkelstein was furious. He told us we had to leave Halloween Town. That's why, when I returned here, it had to be in secret, under a new identity, even though this was my original home."

Thunder cracks outside, and I jump. As eager as I

am to finish the experiment, I can't tear myself away from Dahlia's words. "Where did you go?"

"Once we were on our own, wandering the Hinterlands, Dorian and I found a strange hickory tree. Its roots formed an entrance to a cave. There was magic in the soil. The darkness gave us powers—to control shadows and storms. We decided to start our own realm, for everyone who had been forgotten, like us. For *shadows*."

"I didn't know." The words bubble out of me. "I—"

"I realize that now. The doctor erased your memory. Made you believe you were his daughter." She steps forward, holding out my spell book like a peace offering. "You were only trying to save yourself."

I stare at the spell book, too stunned to move. Now I understand why Dahlia and Dorian call themselves twins even though they look nothing alike. His pale purple skin, the shock of dark hair streaked with white. Her bluebell curls over warm brown skin. The only similarity is their mismatched eyes.

A trait they share with Jewel. Because they're *all his creations.*

I shake the weight off my shoulders and step forward, taking the spell book and clutching it close. Its weight and shape are so familiar, like hugging a family member. The tight stitches in my chest begin to loosen—but then a new darkness settles over my brow.

"I–I don't understand," I stammer. "If Dorian started Shadow Town with good intentions, then why is he now–"

An explosion from the laboratory rattles the rafters, and Dahlia and I both duck as a sheet of dust falls down over our shoulders.

"Sally!" Dr. Finkelstein bellows from the second floor. "We need you!"

At the doctor's thin voice, Dahlia shrinks back, suddenly transformed from a formidable hedge witch to a neglected daughter.

"You're here now." I grip Dahlia's free hand in mine, squeezing tightly. "You're *home.* This isn't Dr. Finkelstein's house anymore. It's Hemlock Hall, a place of welcome for all. I know he is the last person you want to see right now, but I'm afraid we're on the cusp of a critical experiment. I have to get back upstairs."

Her demeanor shifts. She steels her jaw and straightens the satchel over her shoulder, like a soldier preparing to go into battle. "I can help. For better or worse, I know how to use his equipment."

"Then follow me," I tell her, tugging her along with me up the spiral ramp. "Because we have a star to catch."

She blinks hard. "Catch a . . . star?"

When we spill into the laboratory, Dr. Finkelstein is bent over his worktable, prodding at the light bulb's coils with steel tweezers. When he hears two sets of footsteps—one much too heavy to belong to me or Greta—he switches off the light on his standing magnifying glass with a suspicious frown.

His cold gaze settles on Dahlia, and for a long time, he doesn't speak. "So. You're back. I can't say I am entirely surprised. When your brother first stirred up all this trouble, I knew you would be at his side."

I whip around with a sharp gasp, cheeks blazing. "You knew who Dorian was this whole time?"

"Knew? No. But I had my suspicions." Dr. Finkelstein's face remains pinched as he blinks from behind his dark spectacles, about as welcoming toward Dahlia as an ice-cold morgue.

Igor, however, shuffles forward with a pumpkin-orange towel, and Dahlia spares an affectionate smile of thanks for him.

"This is Dorian's causing, not mine," Dahlia asserts. "The Shadow Magic we unearthed deep in those caverns . . . it gave us powers, but it came with volatility. For a long time, we were happy building our new realm. But then our residents began disappearing as they were remembered in other realms, and with each one, our powers diminished."

"He didn't want to lose his power," I murmur.

"Nor his town," Dahlia says, her voice firm and unyielding. "It was *your* fault, Father. You made us only to cast us out. How could Dorian *not* turn into what he did?"

"Dahlia—" Dr. Finkelstein scoffs in a familiar, dismissive way, but then he glances sidelong at me from behind his dark spectacles. The sneer pursing his lips fades. As the silence stretches, broken by the howling storm outside, his fingers drum anxiously at his chair's armrests. Finally, he nods. "I am . . . sorry. All I can do now is attempt to make up for my past."

Dahlia's face is wide and open, awash with disbelief at the apology.

He looks away, clearing a rattle from his throat, and motions to the star-catching machine. "There will be time for restitution. At the moment, the most pressing concern is that we're severely shorthanded, and you have two. Come hold this magnifying glass steady for me."

She doesn't move an inch.

He looks down at his experiment and murmurs, "Please."

I can imagine that the last thing Dahlia wishes

is to take orders from Dr. Finkelstein, but she doesn't bat an eyelid as she strides over to the worktable and holds the heavy glass for the scientist.

I snap back into work mode myself, glancing at the laboratory clock. *One hour left.* I open my spell book and quickly thumb through the yellowed pages.

"Over the past weeks," I start to explain, "Dorian has managed to abduct everyone but the four of us. If we can catch a star, then I unlock a way to get to Shadow Town and confront him with magic stronger than his own. *This* will help us."

I find the page I'm looking for and smooth open the spell book, running my thumb along the script printed at the top to show to Dahlia.

The Balancing Act Equilibrew

It's a spell to bring balance to any endeavor; I've cast it for the Clown with the Tear-Away Face on icy days when his unicycle might slip, and for the wobbly chairs at the Cobweb Café. Dr. Finkelstein said we need magic to keep his experiment stable, and I can't see why this spell won't work for high-heat fusion just as well as uneven chairs.

"We're ready for the heat chamber," Dr. Finkelstein announces. "Get your final preparations in order.

Dahlia, wrap this string of Christmas lights around the outer portion of the cauldron's rim, here. Yes, like that—the bulbs will flicker to alert us if the experiment overheats."

While the two of them set up the scientific portion of our experiment, I work swiftly to brew the Balancing Act Equilibrew in my mixing bowl.

1. *Fill a bowl with full moon water and a dash of beetle blood (freshly squeezed).*
2. *One at a time, add in crushed dried eyebright, preserved foxglove root, a sprinkle of charcoal dust, and day-old cobwebs (to help the potion set!).*
3. *Mix vigorously while counting to ninety-nine, close eyes, then walk backward in three circles. If balance is desired for a person, ingest one spoonful. For anything else, bathe the object in the potion.*

With everything combined, it's only a matter of stirring the concoction until it thickens, like beating egg whites into stiff peaks. I drag a stool over to the laboratory table, where Dahlia is fastening the Christmas lights to the cauldron with clothespins.

Thunder crashes outside, and Dahlia flinches as she sets another clothespin.

She glances at me from behind her eyelashes

and says quietly, "I've been afraid of storms from the moment Dr. Finkelstein made me."

I touch my lips, curious. "Is that why you found an underground kingdom?"

Dahlia nods thoughtfully. "There's a strange peace down there, in the dark. Dorian liked it, too. Before the professor banished us, you told us a story that frightened Dorian. It must have been something from Dream Town—a bedtime story. It told of a cruel shadow that, day by day, swapped places with its owner. Every day, the shadow gained more and more physicality, and the boy disappeared that much more. The story terrified Dorian."

I crane my neck to look at the shadows in the rafters. "The Shadow Prince is afraid of his own shadow?"

Her face is stark and serious as she nods. "It was only a story, but yes, that's how his fear started. I think . . . I think he was afraid of *himself*. A sort of darkness inside him. A portion of our brains came from Dr. Finkelstein, you know. A madness he couldn't control any more than, well, his own shadow. In the underground, there are no shadows. Storms block out shadows, too."

She's talking about a person I should know. My brother, of sorts. A boy I shared a house with. I want to ask her a million more questions, but lightning flashes, so close that its thunderous boom echoes half a second later. The entire laboratory rattles like one of Santa Claus's shaken snow globes.

"Sally! Dahlia!" Dr. Finkelstein joins us at the cauldron. "It's time to place the hydrogen marble into the containment chamber—we must make haste, as the compound is highly unstable. Your potion?"

I test the thickness with my wooden spoon. "Ready."

He nods. "Get the thermometer—Dahlia, you'll hold it in the cauldron."

I jump up, setting my mixing bowl on my stool, and fetch the candy thermometer I used for years to make birchbark brittle.

"Goggles on, everyone," Dr. Finkelstein advises. "We must maintain safety protocol even with our enemies at the windows."

Dahlia, Igor, and I slide on rubber goggles while the storm rages harder outside. The skylight rattles, iron rain assailing it with an ear-splitting din.

Dr. Finkelstein shouts over the rain, "Now, when the light sparks, do not look at it directly! It will be too bright to safely see. As soon as I place the hydrogen marble in the cauldron, we'll be ready for the stabilization spell." He pushes his goggles up to meet my eyes directly with his small, beady black ones. "We'll have to work in unison, Sally. Like a ballet. If this step is successful, you'll need to quickly put the glass lid on the cauldron to contain the star."

Nerves skate down my body, but I ball my fists, stand tall, and think of seeing Jack again.

"I'm ready, Dr. Finkelstein."

He holds my gaze an extra beat before nodding, then unscrews a frosted glass jar in his lap. A puff of frigid air floats toward the ceiling, and the room's temperature drops. Carefully, he inserts his tongs into the jar and pulls out a frosted-over pellet that's barely larger than a pearl. It's cloudy and coated in ice, and cracks form along the surface the moment it's exposed to room-temperature air.

"Pure hydrogen!" he shouts over the rain. "Very difficult to extract from water, and nearly impossible to keep stable except in subzero temperatures. Your old deep freezer did the trick nicely, Sally." He holds the marble over the cauldron. "Ready. One, two, three . . . now!"

He releases the marble, which falls into the cauldron but is immediately suspended in the air by the magnetic field created from the announcement board magnets.

"Igor, the laser!" he cries.

Igor throws a switch on the wall beneath the skylight, activating the laser pointer he's wired into the electrical system. The thin beam shoots through the magnifying glass on the worktable, widening as it refracts before striking the floating marble.

Immediately, more cracks splinter across its surface. Wisps of blue smoke curl toward the ceiling as the marble begins to vibrate under the growing pressure.

I hold in a breath, clutching my mixing bowl tightly, when glass suddenly shatters overhead.

Before I can even gasp, shards from the skylight rain down on the doctor's worktable. Wind immediately howls its way inside.

"What's happening?" I cry. "I thought we were safe—Dorian's powers can't get inside!"

Dahlia shouts back over the storm's roar. "That's how it's been, until now! He must have taken someone whose essence allows him to break glass!"

My mind flips through all of my friends swept away by his storms. *Glass, glass* ... With a gasp, I realize glass is made from sand. And there are two people who are rulers of a kingdom full of dream sand.

"My parents—it's their essence that he's siphoning!"

A gust of powerful wind sweeps through the broken skylight, surrounding Igor with dust and scrap lab notes like a miniature tornado caught in one of Professor Cirrus's weather machines.

"Igor!" I cry.

I've taken only a single step toward him, still clutching the mixing bowl with my potion, when the air shifts. A stormwolf materializes from the clouds, its body coiling like living smoke, eyes burning with crackling yellow light.

In a flash, its jaws snap around the back of Igor's shirt, lifting him clean off the ground as if he weighs nothing. Igor kicks his legs, moaning. His hands scramble to grab something but find only air.

The stormwolf surges upward, dragging him toward the skylight. Between one blink and the next, they vanish.

I scream, wanting to toss aside my mixing bowl to scramble after him, but Dr. Finkelstein presses his hand over mine. "Focus, Sally!"

"They took Igor!"

"Focus! If this experiment fails, we'll likely burn alive in a sunburst and take all of Halloween Town with us. Now, I need a temperature reading before it overheats!"

Dahlia leans in to read the thermometer. "It's . . . it's all the way to the top. It looks like it's about to explode!"

"Sally, add your potion!" he cries, though I can barely hear his shrill voice over the howling wind. "Now is the time for magic!"

Though my pulse slams so hard I can barely think, it's my step in our delicate dance, and I carefully pour the Balancing Act Equilibrew into the cauldron. Rain torrents down from the broken skylight, and out of the corner of my eye, I can see dark storm clouds closing in from all sides.

"Dorian's found me!" Dahlia yells. "He's found all of us—he's coming!"

"Stay focused!" I call to her, but I'm not sure she can hear me. The wind blows my hair around my face like writhing snakes, but I don't dare let go of the mixing bowl. Papers swirl around us, the wind grabbing greedily at my patchwork dress. I can feel the batter of stormbat wings just overhead, but I grit my teeth and hold on to the bowl even harder.

Dahlia screams, and the next thing I know, she's gone.

Taken by stormbats.

Gasping, I grab the candy thermometer she was holding before it falls off the cauldron rim.

"Sally!" Dr. Finkelstein sounds far away, though he's just opposite me at the cauldron. "The stabilization spell is working, but it won't hold for long. You have to turn off the laser before it overheats—"

Dr. Finkelstein's instructions are cut short as he's suddenly swept in the air, wheelchair and all.

He vanishes through the broken skylight, tiny cry fading away as he's carried off into the night.

The wind claws harder at me—it's just me now.

I'm not supposed to abandon checking the candy thermometer. . . . Grimacing as my hair whips around me, I push through the wind, fighting for each step toward the switch.

The clouds press in. Stormbats' pounding wings beat against my skin. More glass shatters overhead.

Yellow eyes suddenly appear in the cloudiness, blinking awake, as a deep growl rumbles the laboratory.

A stormwolf, I think, but something about that feels wrong.

The smoke takes shape not into a wolf but into a massive winged beast with smoke jowls pulled back in a snarl. Its claws float a few inches above the ground, while its storm-cloud wings beat in warning.

"A storm . . . dragon," I breathe.

This dragon came from Scorch—I feel certain of it. When he was captured, Dorian must have siphoned off his spirit to create a mindless monster that has none of my sweet friend's kindness.

I plunge a hand in my pocket, clutching my needle, ready to draw my sword. But at the same time, I have to turn off the laser.

I can't do both.

Just as the stormdragon plunges toward me with claws bared, I lunge forward, wrapping both hands around the switch.

My fingers tremble, but I hold firm.

For everyone I love. For Halloween Town. For all of us.

With my last ounce of strength, I throw the switch.

The laser cuts off, the last of its powerful light gobbled up by the glowing hydrogen marble.

There's a terrible moment of uncertainty when the marble pulses, continuing to crack and shatter as though it might explode at any moment, as the storm monsters descend on me in unison.

A second before the stormdragon sinks its claws into my fabric skin, a burst of light tears across the laboratory. It radiates out to every nook and corner, chasing away even the wiliest shadows, bathing every inch of the sterile workspace in warm, dazzling light.

I shade my eyes, daring to peek through my fingers at the too-bright light. As the marble glows brighter and brighter, the storm clouds are pushed back. The wolfish creatures bound away through the skylight. The bats swarm to escape the brilliant twinkle.

The stormdragon falters, collapsing to the ground. There, it contorts like a serpent, trying to flee the relentless light. But the brightness is too strong for it. With one final shriek, it bursts apart.

Eventually, the wind dies down.

My eyes burn. My fabric skin feels sunbaked and raw. I'm still shaking, still braced for an attack. Yet I inch closer to the cauldron, pick up the glass lid from the floor, and manage to close it over the cauldron before I'm thrown onto my back by the sheer force of light.

By *starlight.*

We've managed not only to create a star—a real, stable star—but to catch it in my cauldron. The wonder of it dances in my chest like fireflies in a jar.

The laboratory clock dings. It's eight o'clock.

Moonrise.

I don't know how long I kneel on the laboratory floor, marveling at how such a harsh place has now been transformed by beautiful, warm starlight. At once, I'm a little girl again, so lonely that she tried to make her own star to wish upon. To have a family again. My parents. Dr. Finkelstein's first children.

Now, here it is.

My own wishing star.

My guiding light.

My way back to Jack.

The Balancing Act Equilibrew keeps the star going for several spellbinding minutes, but eventually, the reaction burns through the hydrogen marble. The light begins to dim. As the star slowly fades, its light recedes, and I can once more make out beakers and test tubes, my spell book and the ingredient jars.

With a soft, final pulse, the star collapses back into a simple pearl-sized marble, which falls with a plink into the bottom of the cauldron.

I blink, still splayed on the floor, so overwhelmed that my chest caves in on a shaky exhale.

By all appearances, the laboratory is back to normal—except for the ten-foot-tall Night Mare standing in the center of the room.

Her tangled hair is wild and billowing as she extends one front leg and lowers her head to me.

Bowing.

Acknowledging that I did the impossible three times over, all before the full moon's rise.

"Congratulations, Queen Sally of Halloween Town." The Night Mare's melodious voice floats on the air, unspoken yet perfectly audible. *"With your perseverance and ingenuity, you have achieved what few have. You flew without wings. You solved an unsolvable maze. You caught a star. As you have achieved wonders yourself, I can now grant you wonders of the night."*

I push to my feet in a daze, brushing the tangled hair out of my eyes, blinking hard against the lingering sting of burned metal in the room.

"I'd . . . I'd like to go to Shadow Town," I say in as steady a voice as I can manage, while I slip my empty satchel over my head with trembling hands. "I'd like to save my townspeople."

The Night Mare blinks, slow and calm like we're suspended in one of Father Time's hourglasses. Then, she lowers her head, giving me access to the graceful arch of her back. *As you desire. Climb on my back. I will carry you there.*

I double-check my pocket for the spare needle, then bend down to pick up Dr. Finkelstein's dark spectacles, which fell when he was captured. I rub my finger over the smudged lenses, then slide them into my satchel.

My body is worn through, my stuffing in dire need of a fluffing, but I take a long, deep breath. *I'm so close, Jack. Mom. Dad. Everyone. I'm coming.*

I drag over the laboratory stool and use it as a mounting block to climb onto the Night Mare's back.

I weave my fingers through a section of her coarse mane to steady myself. I've never ridden a horse before. Certainly not bareback. But I *have* ridden Scorch, and a horse can't be that different from a dragon, can it? I tighten my legs to hold me in place and lean forward.

"I'm ready," I say.

The Night Mare breaks into a gallop down the

spiral ramp and out the door, and tears at breakneck speed across town square toward the gates.

I can only hold on for dear life.

At first, riding the Night Mare is a pure jolt of adrenaline. My muscles tense, my fist tightens in her mane, my eyes narrow against the wind. I'm so jostled that I fully expect my heart to end up somewhere lodged around my throat.

But as she hits her stride in the fields outside of town, I'm able to take calmer breaths. I haven't fallen off—in fact, I think I might be getting the hang of horseback riding.

I open my eyes to watch the world fly by—the empty cornfields, the pumpkin patch, Recluse Woods in the distance. For the first time, I feel bigger than the town, not swallowed by it.

The wind whips my loose hair, and I feel like a comet streaking through the sky, ready to collide with my own fate as surely as if drawing a card in Chance Town. The Night Mare's muscles flex and bunch beneath me with every bound. Steam rises from her nostrils. Her hooves pound the dirt path, leaving a record of our travels.

Maybe one day, maybe even *tomorrow*, I'll show her hoofprints to Jack.

See, Jack? This is how fast I rode to reach you.

As we crest the next hill, the Hinterlands roll out beyond. The Night Mare pitches downhill, easily vaulting over fallen logs in the path, as the forest's strange light bathes us, plunging us in alternating bands of shadows and light.

We pass the grove of holiday trees. We pass the pint-sized pixie door to Tooth Town. We even pass the two crossed spruce trees that mark the end of the Hinterland Maze.

This is as far as I've ever ventured into the Hinterlands, but the Night Mare shows no sign of slowing.

By the time she does finally drop into a walk, my legs feel weak as snail slime. I've been rattled up to my molars.

"The entrance to Shadow Town is just ahead," the Night Mare's ethereal voice chimes.

I look around, confused. The trees here are tall and sickly thin, much too narrow to hold a doorway. But the horse confidently strides to a thin shagbark hickory, its bark peeling off in long strands like a child's papier-mâché project.

The Night Mare stops, and I start to swing one leg around to dismount, but she gives her head a toss. *"Stay on my back. Just wait."*

Uncertain, I settle back into place, goose bumps running over my forearms as I look around this unfamiliar section of the Hinterlands. The Night Mare lifts her hoof, then brings it down three times on the dirt ground. *Like she's knocking.*

The ground rumbles underfoot, and I sit straighter, holding more tightly to her mane.

Fallen leaves and pebbles quake underfoot. A hole near the hickory tree's roots yawns open, dirt raining down into the opening void, and dark knots of smoke rise up from the depths.

The Night Mare stomps again. The tree's roots obediently slither out of the ground, folding themselves until they've formed an archway into an underground passage. The smoke trembles and shrinks back beneath the Night Mare's dazzling glow.

"Dorian's magic blocks the door," the Night Mare explains. *"But my moonlight outshines it."*

My lips part in wonder. In a way, the underground arch reminds me of the Hinterland Maze, where the brambles had a life of their own. Yet this feels different. These roots aren't trying to trap us—they're parting to make way.

"Hold on," the Night Mare says. *"It's quite a fall."*

"A fall?" I've barely tightened my calves when she springs forward on powerful hind legs, diving into the root passageway. Wisps of misty clouds whip by on either side as we plunge headfirst into a pit that seems to stretch forever.

I dig my heels into her sides, clutching her neck so I don't fall off. The smoke thickens as we descend, but the Night Mare shines brighter, beating back the darkness, taming Dorian's magic wards.

We crash down in total darkness, and though the Night Mare gracefully lands, *my* landing involves a lot more awkward flopping. Somehow, however, I manage to stay astride her.

"It's as black as coal down here," I whisper. "I've never been to a realm this dark."

"We're hundreds of feet underground, far beyond the moon's reach."

She walks forward, hooves echoing against the earthen walls of a tunnel, and soon, clouds swirl around the next corner, looking ghostly in the Night Mare's glow.

I sit up straighter, bracing myself, sensing trouble.

When we turn the corner, the horse stops.

A golden gate, long tarnished, spans the full width of the tunnel.

Though the hinged door is wide open, thick clumps of storm clouds cluster on the ground, rippling despite the lack of wind.

CHAPTER TWENTY-ONE

Every bit as menacing as "get out" signs.

I nudge the Night Mare on, but she doesn't move. The storm clouds churn like boiling tar, then rise in a shaking plume, swelling into a dark balloon large enough to fill the tunnel.

"Another storm creature," I murmur, bracing myself.

The Night Mare shakes her head. *Not this time.*

Tendrils of smoke contort into pits that begin to take shape—cheekbones, jagged teeth, empty eye sockets—and then the whole thing *grins*. It's a ghoulish skull, easily ten feet tall, and worst of all—I recognize it.

"Jack?" I choke out, fingers knotting around the Night Mare's mane.

The smoke skull's jaw unhinges with a hissing roar like wind sweeping through a canyon, and it lunges forward as if to swallow us whole.

The Night Mare rears, hooves flashing. I barely hold on to prevent being thrown. I can't take my eyes off the smoke skull. It's . . . Jack. My husband. And there's only one way this is possible: if Prince Dorian siphoned off his essence to make this final trap. Taking the one person I love most and twisting him into a monster.

The yawning jaw tears toward us, ready to

swallow us whole, but I feel something harden in my chest.

"No," I say. "You won't ever set me against Jack."

The Night Mare comes crashing down. I jolt forward, catching myself at the last moment, then sit up straight to face the apparition.

"Only one thing chases away the dark," I mutter, and spur the Night Mare. "Use your light!"

The Night Mare stomps her massive hooves and paws the ground, steam rising from her nostrils. The tunnel reverberates, dirt raining down from the earthen ceiling. Her moonlit glow swells until it's so bright I have to shelter my eyes and peek between my fingers.

The storm skull twists to the side, contorted mouth howling as though in pain.

The Night Mare stomps another hoof, sending out another hot, bright wave of moonlight. This time, the storm skull opens its jaw wide in a silent scream.

The Night Mare stomps one more time, and with the next burst of brightness, the monstrous skull breaks apart in one loud thunderclap like a scattering cloud of bats, wisps curling in the stagnant air until they're nothing more than a candle's dying cry.

The tunnel sits open before us, empty and inviting.

I hunch forward, struggling to catch my breath, shaken to the cotton core by the lengths Prince Dorian has gone to twist everyone I love against me.

Finally, I sit straight again. Take a breath.

"Onward."

We enter.

Once we're through the tarnished gates, the air grows uncomfortably cold. After a series of switchbacks, the tunnel opens into a cavern so vast that I might as well be looking up at the dome of night. The twinkling glowworms high on the ceiling could easily be mistaken for stars.

A wave of déjà vu rises over me. *I've seen this before.*

"I saw this in the Mirror of Reverie—this exact view," I breathe, my eyes adjusting enough to pick up on the distant, faint lights of the sad little village and the castle rising high above it. "Which means Jack would be—right here!"

I twist around on the Night Mare's back, a full 180 degrees, my seams stretching as my body wrings itself out like a rag.

Set back in the cavern wall are several jail cells with straight and sturdy elm roots blocking any means of escape. I climb down from the horse and search each one, squinting into the gloomy spaces.

They're empty now—no sign of Jack—and my heart sags an inch.

But a tattered scrap of black-and-white fabric on the dirt in the last cell catches my eye. I reach through to pick it up, holding it to the Night Mare's glow.

His bat-wing bow tie.

"He *was* here," I murmur, running the fabric between my fingers, stirring his dry-bone scent back to life. "We have to find him!"

I climb back on the horse and dig in my heels, urging her on toward the shrouded village ahead. Her hooves clatter over a winding road, the cobblestones broken and uneven from disrepair, and past the first few cottages.

Most of the structures look dark and abandoned, but a few have faint candles flickering in the windows. Thin smoke rises from a few chimneys.

From the corner of my eye, I think I can make out some faces peering through curtains—but the gloom might be playing tricks on me.

I'm used to dark, tumbledown old buildings back home, but ours are *lovably, wonderfully* creaky. Here, there's a heaviness to the air, a moroseness that hangs over the few residents we pass. They peer at us with a dim flicker of curiosity that's soon snuffed out by their languor.

And yet, the closer I look as the Night Mare's glow falls over the town, the more details I pick out that make me think this place wasn't always so desolate. A handful of once-colorful crystals sit on a windowsill. A little doghouse made out of woven roots is tucked to one side, with a tarnished old bowl in front.

In the village, we find a few shops and diners, though it's hard to believe anyone still congregates here. We pass a gloomy washerwoman scrubbing laundry in an underground stream, assisted by a burrowing owl who deftly uses his beak to hang garments on a tree root to dry.

At the edge of town, a young man with bees clinging to his chin like a living beard ascends the steps to a crumbling candlemaker's shop, his wicker basket heavy with beeswax. The shopkeeper—a thin woman whose eyes glow like stars—steps out to greet him.

"They're all characters from forgotten stories," I murmur to the Night Mare. "The original Shadow Town residents from when this was a haven for their type."

"The prince has many spies," the Night Mare warns me. *"Take care with whom you speak—some here may alert him to our presence. It would be wise to make haste."*

A bell clatters outside a shop with a faded sign

reading PUSHING DAISIES FLORIST. A pair of tired-looking dodo birds carrying wrinkled paper shopping bags step out, quietly whispering to each other. One look at us and they stop in their tracks, their big bulbous beaks hanging open in shock.

I draw the Night Mare to a halt and breathlessly ask, "Excuse me. The prisoners from other realms—where are they kept?"

The dodo birds exchange puzzled looks, as if they're so unused to visitors in their town that they don't know what to make of me.

One clears the dust from his throat and squawks, "Prince Dorian moved them all to the old fairgrounds—"

"Shh, Warwick!" The other one snaps his beak, turning his head to look back at the castle perched high over the village. "Watch that beak of yours."

He hastily shuffles his friend away with a flutter of his wings, waddling as fast as his legs will carry him. Warwick spares one sympathetic look at me over his shoulder.

He tips his beak toward the end of the road before they turn the corner and vanish.

"Head in the direction he pointed," I say to the Night Mare, signaling her on, so anxious to see my loved ones that I can hardly breathe.

The mare gallops past strange roots dangling from the ceiling, and thick clusters of ferns that brush my legs as we pass. Jagged stalactites loom overhead like crooked teeth waiting to close down over us.

The path briefly disappears into another tunnel. It's narrow and mazelike, the walls slick with moss, before opening suddenly onto a rocky ledge. We pull up short, breathing hard into the still, windless underground air.

Spread out below us lies a wide barren basin. It's shrouded in darkness at first, but the Night Mare lowers her head, her mane and tail flowing in a phantom breeze, and her glow burns even brighter.

Now, I can see: In the heart of the basin stand old fairgrounds.

One glance makes it clear no rides have turned here in decades. There's a rusted carousel with chipped wooden badger, fox, and mole riding figures. A dilapidated fun house with boarded-up windows. A Ferris wheel whose enclosed cars creak and groan as they sway.

It looks less like a place of children's laughter and more like something ripped from my darkest nightmare—forgotten, cursed, and hungry.

"Enter slowly," I whisper to the mare. My eyes search everything at once, as much on the lookout for

Prince Dorian's storm beasts as for my townspeople. As the horse's hooves clatter past the dusty old ticket booth with faded posters and rusted metal bars, a hand shoots out.

"Sally?" a weak voice squeaks. "Queen Sally, is it really you?"

I whirl around, still clutching the Night Mare's mane, and squint into the faint light radiating from the horse's body. I can make out a girl's face pressed to the bars. Cheeks as rosy as candied cherries. Unruly curls falling on either side of her furry ears.

"Thorna!" I cry.

I dismount and run to the ticket booth, reaching through the bars to clutch her hands. The first time I saw the centaur girl, she was nothing but a projection. Now, she looks thin and worn and tired, but alive. *Real.*

"You really came!" she exclaims, eyes so wide they could swallow the moon.

I squeeze her hands, tears threatening to spill out of my own eyes. "I'm going to get you out of here. But first, tell me. Are my townspeople here? Jack Skellington and my parents? Luna and Scorch?"

"You have to be careful, Queen Sally." Thorna's eyes shift to the shadows lurking at the edges of the abandoned fairgrounds. Her throat bobs with a hard swallow. "Dorian's shadow beasts could be anywhere, hiding in the dark...."

A shiver creeps up my bare ankles. She's about to say more when another young voice suddenly rings out.

"It's Sally! Look, boys! I told you she would come for us!"

"Sally!"

"Goody—it really is her!"

Lock, Shock, and Barrel. I'd know their voices anywhere—squeaky, mischievous, and wonderfully familiar.

My breath catches in my throat as I give Thorna's hand one final squeeze and then stumble over muddy ground, using the Night Mare's glow to lead me toward a looming carousel.

Shock is the first I see, her pointed witch's hat falling crooked as she scrambles off the back of a chipped mole carousel figure. Chains rattle as she throws her squat arms around me, bare face buried in my patchwork skirt.

Behind her, Lock and Barrel struggle forward, each shackled by similar chains to a wooden badger figure. They trip over the chains but don't stop until they're close enough that I can see hope gleaming in their eyes.

"Of course I came." I take Shock's mask out of my satchel. Her eyes light up, and she gasps and hugs it close before sliding it down over her face.

"Thank you, M-Majesty." Her muffled voice breaks behind the papier-mâché. "I haven't at all felt like myself!"

I kneel down to pull all three trick-or-treaters into an embrace. "Halloween Town wouldn't be the same without its trio of troublemakers. You've no idea how much I've missed your mischief."

Barrel bursts into tears behind his mask, blubbering about how he wants to sleep in his tree house bed again.

"Sally?" Another voice comes from somewhere in the shadow-draped fairgrounds. "Do I hear my girl? *Sally?*"

A door rattles at the old fun house, and I jump up and sprint across the bare ground and up the rickety metal stairs to find my mother clutching the bars.

Her eyes are wide as an owl's as she calls back into the cell for my father to hurry and see. There's a groan of worn thread, then the slow shuffle of his threadbare shoes.

"Mom! Dad!" I exclaim. "You're . . . you're *okay!*"

The word catches in my throat. In the faint light, I can see they're anything but okay. Deep wrinkles sag beneath their button eyes. Their fabric skin looks faded and sallow, their stuffing in dire need of a good fluffing.

Still, worn through as she is, my mother pulls back and touches my cheek, searching for any extra rips or worn spots in my own fabric.

My father's gaze shifts behind me, and he lets out a soft gasp. "Look, Greta. It's the Night Mare. Sally completed the third riddle—our daughter did the impossible!"

"Is it true?" My mother weaves her fingers between mine. "You caught a star?"

I nod, afraid to speak, afraid sobs will spill out. I wipe my nose on my sleeve and say with a broken smile, "It was so beautiful, Mom. I wish you could have seen it."

"I've no doubt," she says, wiping away her own proud tears. "Stars are the marvel of the night sky—and tonight, one of them found its match in you."

I smile so hard that my cheeks ache, but if I could, I'd stretch them even farther.

My mother wrings her hands, glancing in the direction of Shadow Town, where the castle's uppermost spire is visible over the hills. "So, what does this mean?"

Before I can answer, more shouts come from the

crumbling carnival grounds, along with the urgent rattle of bars and scrape of chains. Familiar faces—too many of them to take in at once—press against the makeshift cells, lit up by the Night Mare's glow.

"Sally!" Luna's weak arm reaches out from beneath a roller coaster track, its broken rails now twisted into bars. Her voice is weak and wispy as cotton candy. Behind her, Scorch shuffles forward and pushes his head through the bars to give me a feeble missing-tooth grin.

"Luna! Scorch!" I grip the closest metal bar, tugging with all my strength, but it doesn't budge. "I'll get you out of here, I promise."

Nearby, the short witch tugs at the bars of a Ferris wheel car suspended in midair, her green finger trembling as she points at me. "It's her! It's Sally!"

The tall witch peers out of the car above, gray hair tangled like spiderwebs.

I tumble from one makeshift cell to the next, gripping my friends' hands, checking on their bruises and aches, hugging anyone I can get to.

The Undersea Gal slithers up from the murky waters of an old dunking booth, secured now with a heavy padlock, and presses her wide eyes against the dirty glass. The Clown with the Tear-Away Face is crammed inside a prize booth with wooden boards nailed crudely across the front, honking his horn with delight. "You came!"

Jewel and Igor are shackled to opposite sides of a rusty old concession stand, and a chain connects Dr. Finkelstein's wheelchair to the remnants of an old balloon cart, the ground littered with muddy, broken balloon carcasses.

"Long live the Pumpkin Queen!" the Wolfman howls.

"It's Sally, our dear Sally!" the Mayor warbles.

"She fought her way past Dorian's magic!" Corpse Mom cheers.

Laughter bubbles up on my lips, mixing with the salty tears streaming down my cheeks, and I'm grinning from seam to seam. "Oh, Wolfman. I've missed you. And Undersea Gal! And the Corpse family! And Melting Man and your dear turtle!"

Murmurs ripple through the fairgrounds, muffled by iron bars and rusted chains. I give a soft gasp when I spot a tiny pair of fists pumping defiantly through the slats of a birdcage.

Pearl.

Beside her floats another tooth pixie, a bit older—he must be her brother, Cusp. *This is where she ended up after being swept away in Chance Town.*

I crook a finger at her in a pixie-sized wave, a swell

of emotion stirring up my stuffing, chasing away the last scraps of doubt that I'll do whatever it takes to protect those I care about.

To my surprise, I recognize more faces among the cages.

Locked in a ring toss booth are a few leprechauns in their green felt hats. A handful of Easter Town bunnies are closed in a cotton candy cabinet. A few Time Keepers are trapped in a photo booth. Amore Buttercup is here, too, with her ruby-red sequined gown and gold-dusted hair, bound by rope to the mast of a pirate ship ride.

As bittersweet as it feels to see everyone again, there's still one knot pulling tight in the back of my head. My eyes keep darting between old rides and game booths, waiting for a skeleton to call out my name in his deep, resonant voice.

But the Night Mare's light only extends so far, and I can't make out anything beyond the soft glow of her orbit.

A bark suddenly comes from the shadowed edge of the carnival grounds.

"Zero!" I gasp.

The ghost dog, too immaterial for chains, swoops out of the darkness with his glowing pumpkin nose, weaving between my legs in excitement.

"Oh, Zero, I missed you, too! Where is—"

He barks again, zipping forward and looking back for me to follow him. My feet lurch on their own, as desperate as every other part of me to see Jack. The need to be with him overwhelms every lingering fear. I race after Zero, heart hammering in my threadbare chest, lungs so taut with hope that they forget how to fill.

An oversized puppet theater looms from the shadows, crumbling and overtaken by tree roots. Puppet strings hang down in loops and tangles like a giant spiderweb.

And trapped inside them is Jack.

He doesn't see me. He doesn't seem to see anything. He's slumped center stage, tangled in the strings like a marionette abandoned by a careless hand. His eyes are empty, his bone shine dulled.

Zero whines, then barks again.

Jack stirs. His skull lifts with effort, bones creaking in their joints. When he sees me in the hazy moonlight, the strangest look crosses his face, his eye sockets widening with disbelief.

"S-Sally?" His voice rasps, dry and brittle.

"Jack." My knees give out. I sink down, reaching for him, trying to untangle the strings—but it's useless. "I'm here."

He sits up, more joints creaking, embers now stoking deep in his eyes. "How in the world did you—"

"I have so much to tell you—"

"Are you—"

"Are *you*—"

We both stop, breathless as we gaze into each other's eyes, hands clasped tightly like otters, lest we float apart in our sleep. *Oh, Jack. My dear, dear Jack.* He looks even gaunter than usual, his bones shrunken and hunched.

Yet the spark still shines in his eyes.

"Sally." Choked up, he touches a spindly hand to his chest, puppet strings pulling as far as they'll go. "Your parents told me about the impossible tasks—I told them nothing was impossible for my beautiful wife. And sure enough, here you are, like a fairy tale knight."

Tears spill from my lash line as I lean my forehead against his, breathing in his clean, dry-bone scent, knitting my fingers in his striped suit lapels. "It was awful, Jack. Having everyone torn away, one by one. Losing *you.*"

"Shh." The puppet strings protest as he strains to run his hand down my crimson hair. "I'm here now. We're together. Remember? *Nothing's ever lost if it has an echo—you just have to close your eyes and listen."*

I do. I close my eyes and listen to the wind weaving through his bones.

I've been so swept up reuniting with Jack that it takes me a moment to realize the fairground prison has fallen silent. Not merely hushed. Not subdued. But eerily, fearfully silent.

My heartbeat kicks up with a warning beat, a hiss of premonition in my veins.

I spin back around.

The Night Mare stands where I left her, by the ticket booth, her moonlit glow softening the harsh angles of the old rides.

The carnival gates slowly groan open, their rusted hinges shrieking like something being torn apart.

And then, he appears.

Prince Dorian rides in on the stormdragon I saw at Hemlock Hall, re-formed now out of wine-dark clouds. Lightning cracks deep within its billows, bleeding out a fierce wind in the otherwise still air.

The Night Mare's moonlight pulses, and Dorian's eyes dart to the ground and widen for a flash before returning to me with a sneer.

What was that momentary flicker of fear?

I study how the mist rolls off the bottom of his cloak, obscuring his shadow. Is *that* what he was looking for on the ground? Is he *truly* afraid of his own shadow?

Princess Dahlia rides behind him, hands clasped so tightly they tremble. She isn't chained like the others, but she still bows her head like a prisoner, as though she would rather be anywhere but here.

A knot pulls tight in my chest—anger, yes, but wrapped around something else. Curiosity. Pity. A quiet, aching grief.

These are Dr. Finkelstein's first creations. My childhood companions for a time. My siblings, of sorts. In another life, I could imagine us as a happy family, playing chase in the graveyard, riding the wild skeleton reindeer in the woods.

But the spike of cruelty in Dorian's eyes tells me that future is a lost dream.

"Pumpkin Queen," he announces in his hollow, echoing voice. "What a heartwarming family reunion. It's ironic, you know. This is exactly where I wanted you. You could have saved yourself so much effort if you'd simply let yourself be captured through the mirror portal."

"F-family?" Jack coughs, confused. He tries to rest

a protective hand on my shoulder, but the puppet strings hold him back.

"They're from Halloween Town, Jack. They're Dr. Finkelstein's original children." I gently touch Jack's forearm, silently urging him to trust me, then turn to face Dorian with one hand in my dress pocket, wrapped around my spare needle.

"You ruined everything, Sally," Dorian says. "Because of you, we were cast out of our old home, left lost and forgotten. Now, you're hell-bent on destroying our new one." Dorian spurs his stormdragon's flanks, stoking crackling lightning within the beast. "I won't *let* you, this time."

Pure rot burns in his eyes. There's no reasoning with a madman. No falling back on mistakes and misunderstandings.

This is the moment when I prove I am the Pumpkin Queen—or am swallowed by the dark, my people lost, my holiday *forgotten*.

The enlargement spell hovers on the tip of my tongue when, suddenly, Scorch lets out an earthshaking dragon roar. Dirt rains down from the cavern ceiling high overhead. Luckily, my townspeople are sheltered within their cages.

Dorian lifts his cloak to protect himself.

"Dragonkin." Scorch speaks directly to the storm

beast in a clear rumble, his head thrust proudly through his cell's bars. "Listen to Scorch, because you come from Scorch. Dragons belong to no one. Dragons obey only themselves. Dragons are not villains—if they choose not to be."

The cavern falls so silent I can hear the broken flutter of my pulse. For a heavy second, no one moves, shocked by Scorch's speech.

Until the stormdragon twists its head backward, blinking its cloud-wisp eyelids at the prince on its back. For a moment, it does nothing.

Then, it bares a row of sharp teeth formed from iron rain drops.

"Do not listen to that creature!" Prince Dorian digs his heels into the dragon's sides with a painful kick. "He's a failed dragon, shunned by his own kind for his weak-hearted nature. So meek that tricking him into doing my bidding couldn't have been simpler."

Scorch keeps his square chin steady as he continues to address the other dragon. "Once, the prince twisted Scorch's mind. Scorch hurt the ones he loves. Do not make the same mistake as Scorch. Hero or villain—each dragon gets to decide. A dragon's fate is not sealed by its nature. Even if it is made of storms."

The stormdragon swings its massive head

between Scorch and Prince Dorian. Except for the crackle of lightning deep within its coiled body, the air is perfectly quiet.

I squeeze my needle tight, ready to speak the enlargement spell and fight at a moment's notice. My heart hammers.

But I wait.

A sound like cracking ice breaks the silence. A rush of wind follows. My hair blows back over my eyes, Jack's weakened bones tremble on his puppet strings, and Zero is catapulted back toward the shadows.

When the wind's roar settles, I straighten.

Just like that, the stormdragon is gone. Dispersed into thin air. The last crackle of thunder echoes on the distant cavern walls.

Without the dragon supporting them, both twins fall. Dahlia crashes to her hands and knees, splayed in the muddy fairgrounds. Dorian stumbles but catches himself.

He's hunched, breath rasping, *glaring*. Not at Scorch.

At me.

"I'm sorry about what happened when we were children," I say steadily. "I can understand why you felt I betrayed you. But no amount of anger justifies what you're doing to my people."

He scoffs, but I notice how his left hand falls to his side, where a dark crystal-hewn sword hangs from his chain mail belt. *Carbonado*, I think. Black diamond. According to my spell book, it's one of the toughest minerals, found only in the deepest underground caverns.

"It doesn't have to be like this," I plead, one final attempt to reason with him.

"It was never about when we were children," he snarls. "Everything changed when you were crowned Pumpkin Queen. Your initiatives meant the spread of visitors, but even more troublesome, of *ideas*. Rumors even reached us down here, in this protected underground realm, of other worlds and other ways of life. My people—who Dahlia and I worked so hard to create this haven for—became curious. They wished to leave. To explore. Perhaps even to see if they could revive their forgotten realms without influence from other worlds. They wanted to remember *themselves*."

I look around the fairgrounds and catch sight of Thorna locked in the ticket booth, the rest of her herd corralled by a fence of turnstiles, and all I can think is how much some child would love reading her story. *Remembering* her.

"It was wrong for you to stop them from try-ing," I say. "To lock up your own people. Dahlia knew it—but your mind was too twisted by the dark to see it clearly."

A tickle drips down my spine seam, and I realize with a strange flutter in my stomach that I'm doing my old nervous habit, tugging on the loose thread at my wrist. *Trying to hold on as tightly as I can, too. Just as Dorian has done.*

I let the thread go slack.

Dorian whirls around to face his sister. "You went back to our father. To our sister. You betrayed me worse than *she* ever could."

My own worries fall away as I jerk backward as if hit by a gust of winter wind. "Leave Dahlia alone. She was trying to help your people."

"And where would that have left Shadow Town, if she'd succeeded?" Threads of anger pull tighter in his voice. "A ghost town!"

A bolt of lightning sparks from the storm clouds at his feet, hitting the top of the Ferris wheel, showering the fairgrounds with sparks. A mother from Fourth of July Town in a star-spangled dress cries out as she scrambles to protect herself and her daughter behind their cell bars.

I take out my spare needle, working the smooth metal between my fingers. *Dahlia was right.* For as cold and stone-faced as Prince Dorian presents himself, there's a storm of fear simmering just under his lavender skin.

"I'd be alone," Prince Dorian growls. "My town destroyed. I'd lose my home again. So I had no choice but to destroy yours first!"

His storm clouds swell in size, wisps breaking off to spin themselves into his stormbats, which immediately circle around the Night Mare and me. More lightning sparks from the clouds at Dorian's feet, flashing in the twilight darkness. A clap of thunder shakes the ceiling as more dirt and debris rain down. A rock smashes into an abandoned bumper car ride, and the imprisoned people inside shrink away from the bars.

To my surprise, I recognize tufts of white hair amid the prisoners. It's Professor Cirrus from Weather Town. He's with two women with windmill emblems on their overalls and a man tightly clasping an umbrella.

I pull in a sharp breath.

Beside me, Jack works one arm free from the marionette strings and snatches up a wooden baton, brandishing it like a club. That dark, determined gleam that I know so well shines in his hollow eyes, and I know that my brave husband will move entire worlds to fight by my side.

And yet, I also see how Jack's rib cage, tangled in

strings, wheezes with every breath. How his bones are dry and dusty—they've lost their luster. Even if I cut him completely free, he's weak as autumn leaves.

"Jack, I can do this," I call to him. "You don't have the strength."

His browbones shoot up in surprise, the ferocious spark softening in his eyes. He opens his suit jacket and, for what seems like the first time, peers down at his shrunken rib cage, taking full stock of his weakened state, and the tips of his eye hollows tilt downward.

"But . . . I'm with you, Sally."

His browbone furrows, his hands curling at his sides like he still wants to fight, to stand beside me—but he isn't strong enough for battle. Not like this.

He glances at me, torn, but then gives a nod.

I exhale sharply, steadying myself, and take one look at the haunted faces around me—my friends, my family—before signaling to the Night Mare.

"Now!"

The Night Mare strides into the crowd, hooves clomping over broken cobblestones, and I swing up onto her back as if onto a carousel horse—only this one is bound by no wooden poles. In fact, she's bound by nothing.

Least of all Shadow Magic.

"You used Scorch," I say to Dorian. "You tried to

use Dahlia. Let's see how powerful you are when you aren't hiding behind someone else."

"Yes. Let us *see*, sister." Prince Dorian surges forward on his storm cloud cape, circling the Night Mare with a hooded expression. "Do you think I fear a rag doll, made to comfort children?"

The Night Mare rears, hooves pawing in the air, and the crowd gasps. Her glow intensifies—first moonlit gold, then white, then *blinding*. Dorian's storm clouds coil tight, like a snake sensing fire.

She turns in a slow, deliberate circle, casting off waves of light. Her brightness surges outward, stinging every scrap of darkness. The stormbats shriek as the light cuts right through them, their smoky forms bursting apart into ribbons of air. The rest of Dorian's stormy cloak frays away until the magical hem is simply . . . fabric.

The whole thing happens fast enough to leave the crowd stunned.

No one, though, is as stunned as Dorian himself.

He's as pale as if one of my rag doll hands popped off and slapped him across the cheek. His jaw hangs slack as he shakes his cloak, trying to revive his magic. Only a few specks of dust float off.

As his shock fades, he draws his carbonado sword. "So, moonlight can banish my Shadow Magic? Well,

I'd like to see it try to stop black diamond—pure, natural, mined from the bones of the earth."

He lunges at us.

"Expandere!" I yell, and thrust my needle out as it extends into a gleaming weapon that deflects his blade with a shower of sparks.

The Night Mare steps back, and I breathe hard, holding my needle-sword at the ready.

A gust of wind kicks up, blowing a ring of old carnival tickets around us like a makeshift fighting ring.

"A needle?" Dorian drawls with the hint of a smirk. "Are you going to darn me, Rag Queen?"

I focus on his sunken eyes, my sword lifted high as Jack taught me in our sparring sessions. "We don't need to fight, Dorian. Don't make me leave you in need of stitches."

Dorian lunges again, this time slashing diagonally with a calculated strike. The Night Mare sidesteps gracefully, but not quick enough—I have to roll off her back before his sword hits my cotton leg.

I land softly on both feet as he strikes again, but I flick my needle-sword just in time to block his blade. He presses forward without pause, slashing again, trying to overpower me with sheer strength and momentum.

And if it were a test of strength between me and him, he'd win—but it's not.

I fold in half, tucking myself in a ball as only a boneless rag doll can do, and roll right between his legs. I pop up behind him, smashing the blunt end of my needle-sword against the back of his head.

"Surrender," I say. "We can talk and find another way."

Dorian growls and swings again, but I dodge backward, hopping onto a tree root for height. With a forward lunge, I flick my sword's tip at his cloak's hem, hooking a stitch and tearing the thread loose. As he whips around, the whole thing begins to unravel.

"Looks like you're coming apart at the seams, Highness," Jack coughs wryly.

Angry, Dorian unpins the cloak from around his neck, tossing it to the ground, and then readjusts his grip on his carbonado sword. He swings at me in a downward strike, but I raise my sword perpendicular to block it. Our swords collide with a deafening squeal of metal on diamond. I tilt my needle-sword so the blade of his slides down mine, and then, with a flick of my wrist, slip the end of his blade through the eye of my enormous needle—trapping it.

He tries to pull his sword back, but a bright dot of

light suddenly dances right in his vision, temporarily blinding him. I follow its source and find Jack clutching his mirror shard, angling it to catch the Night Mare's glow.

My heart swells with love.

I use the split-second distraction to yank the sword out of Dorian's grasp. It falls to the ground, where I kick it to Jack, who manages to pick it up and toss it to the Harlequin Demon, who swallows it in one satisfying gulp—followed up with an earthshaking belch.

My own breath saws in and out of my lungs, my arms trembling from the effort of our fight. Jack and I never practiced sword fighting like this: desperate, wild, and *real.* My palms are soaked in sweat, making it hard to grip the needle-sword, and every stitch in my body screams.

But the fight isn't over—not yet.

Then, I see Dahlia.

She's quietly waving her hand, trying to get my attention. She has stealthily moved to the abandoned Ferris wheel and now holds open an empty car's door. She closes her hands just like one of the animal traps littered through Recluse Woods. *She's trying to tell me something.*

Inspired by Jack's trick with the mirror shard, an idea sparks in my mind, bright and alive.

"Mom, Dad," I yell. "Tilt the fun house mirrors!"

I lift my needle-sword so it catches the Night Mare's glow. Understanding crosses both their faces as they hustle around their fun house prison, yanking and twisting the distorting mirrors into place. The warped glass catches the horse's light, bouncing it from mirror to mirror, the reflections stacking and multiplying until they form a blinding ring of brightness.

The light hits Dorian like a comet.

With the bright light, his shadow stretches beneath him, grotesque and twisted by the warped angles of the fun house mirrors.

A look of terror crosses his face.

A weak cry snakes out of his throat as he turns and, stumbling over his own boots, barrels his way past his startled prisoners. No matter where Dorian runs, his shadow clings to his heels, mirroring every frantic step.

Running in blind terror from his pursuing shadow, Dorian tumbles straight into the old Ferris wheel car.

Dahlia slams the door shut, holding it closed with all her strength, and then slides her wand into the latch to lock it.

Dorian rattles the bars, howling. *Trapped.*

In the end, Prince Dorian is defeated by his own shadow.

23

Slowly, the onlookers dare to edge closer to their cell bars, their anxious murmurs shifting to hopeful exclamations as they see that Prince Dorian is well and truly trapped. Dahlia reaches into Dorian's pocket and snatches his key ring. She begins unlocking cells, freeing the prisoners.

Luna and Scorch.

The Mayor.

A family of leprechauns.

Professor Cirrus and his weather forecasters.

My *parents*.

One by one, the freed townspeople rush into the moonlit glow cast by the Night Mare, embracing one another among relieved sobs and cries. Luna immediately runs to Jack and uses the sharp mirror shard to cut through his bindings.

The needle-sword hangs limp in my hand as I stagger forward over the crumpled carnival tickets. Freed of the strings, Jack rushes in to meet me, catching me just as the stuffing in my legs gives out, holding me up with his everlasting love.

"My brave wife." A cough rattles out of him, but his eyes hold nothing but bright pride. "Look at what you've done—the impossible, once more. Is there anything you can't do?"

"Yes," I murmur, resting my head on the sharp angle of his shoulder. "I can't think of anything more perfect than this moment with you."

He chuckles as he combs the tangles out of my hair, his nimble fingers knowing every smooth lock by heart. Footsteps pad toward us, and I look up to see my parents with gleaming tears of relief in their button eyes.

"Sweetheart." My mother wraps me in a warm hug, while my father wipes the tears from his eyes. "All these years away from Dream Town's sewing school, and you're still top-notch with a needle."

A laugh rumbles in my chest, my stuffing settling in its rightful place. As soon as my parents step aside, a long line of freed prisoners files in to shake my hand, outpouring tearful thanks, marveling over my majestic entrance on the back of the Night Mare.

Once I've managed to extricate myself from my friends and neighbors, who all chatter among themselves about returning to their home realms, I shrink my needle-sword back into a regular sewing needle and secure it in my pocket, patting it twice with a soft smile, knowing that it will always be there for me— for mending my body *or* mending tears in the world.

I stroke the Night Mare's neck, her midnight hair soft as forget-me-not blooms beneath my palm. Her bottomless black eyes meet mine. *"Our trade is complete now, Pumpkin Queen."*

I smile brightly but then grow serious. "Thank you. Truly. I couldn't have saved my friends without you."

"No need to thank me. I am merely a force of nature. I am the night. And the night does not grant favors—it trades magic for magic. You were the one who completed the three tasks to earn my aid. However, I will give the people here a parting gift. Free of charge this time."

I swear that she winks at me.

She raises her front hoof and brings it down three more times. The earthen walls tremble, and a tremor spreads up through my toes all the way to my knees as the cavern's ceiling rumbles open. Instead of a shower of rocks, though, only a gentle dusting of dirt wafts down.

A ray of sunlight shines like a soft spotlight over Shadow Town.

Bathed in the beam of sunlight, I press my forehead against hers, letting my eyes shutter closed, breathing in her fresh straw scent. For the first time in what feels like forever, I let go of the fear, the doubt, the endless weight of waiting.

The sunlight is real. The open sky, too.

And so is Night Magic.

When I open my eyes, I step backward, touching my hand to my patchwork dress in a final gesture of gratitude. The Night Mare tosses her mane once more before rearing up just like her statue in Villain Village, then galloping toward the golden gates. Gates, I'm certain, that will firmly remain open from now on.

Jack comes to my side, already looking healthier now that sunlight has kissed the round dome of his skull. But with his newfound vitality comes a devilish twinkle in his eye.

"You know, I have a few ideas what we can do with the Shadow Prince." He rubs his dry palms together, the bones squeaking. His jaw curves in a wicked grin.

"I say that we get that Ferris wheel going, keep him spinning in circles for the rest of his cursed life."

"Tempting, but no." My hand drifts to the loose thread on my wrist, toying with it lightly. It would be so easy to let the desire for control take over. To hold on so tightly to everything I have that I squeeze the life right out of it.

"Dorian." I look at Shadow Town's ruler through the metal bars. "You spent so long running from your shadow—from your fears—that you never saw where you were going."

He wraps his long fingers around the bars, glaring at me as I stand in the spotlight of filtered sunlight. "And where is that?"

I absently pat my pocket, where the luck drop's cellophane wrapper rustles, as I think back on Fortuna Luckwell and the heady, sweet taste of pure luck.

"Where all leaders go if they do not have guidance. If they cut themselves off from their community and lose sight of what matters. You're so concerned with protecting people who have been forgotten by the world, which is a noble goal. Yet in the process, you, too, forgot something essential."

I look at Dahlia, who rests her hand on the Ferris wheel car door, still looking tenderly at her twin brother even after all the pain he brought her.

I clear my throat. "I'd like to tell you a story."

Surprised, Dorian draws himself up to his full height so fast that his head hits the top of the car. He rubs his scalp, wincing.

"You aren't the only family that I forgot," I start, touching the seam at my breastbone. "When Dr. Finkelstein abducted me, he erased all my childhood memories of who I was and where I came from, and raised me in a place I didn't belong. I felt unmoored from my own past. I didn't even know that I had parents who missed me dearly and had never forgotten me for a single day."

A tear rolls down the hill of my cheek as I look at my parents with a loving smile.

"One day," I continue, turning back to the prince, "I was reunited with them. I found myself back in Dream Town, amid the lavender fields and Lullaby Library, with sonnet singers reciting half-remembered tales from my childhood. I slept in my own bed, beneath the quilt my mother had sewn for me out of generations of hand-me-down pajamas. For the first time in my life, I felt what it meant to have a home. Until then, I'd lived in Halloween Town, and even though I made friends there and built a whole life for myself, I wasn't *remembered* there. Once I learned about my past in Dream Town, once I was remembered by others, and once I remembered them as well, I went from a lost girl to a daughter to a queen." This time, I squeeze Jack's hand. "That's what each of your people deserves, too. Maybe you've tried to give them a good life here in Shadow Town. But they'll never truly belong here—at least not *only* here. They all come from somewhere else. And if they are remembered, and their home realms revived, then they should be free to return. To step out of the shadows, just as I did."

My parents look at me with joy shining in their button eyes. For now, Jack is quiet, content to simply listen.

"That's what *you* deserve, too," I add. "You deserve to be allowed back into your hometown. You deserve to have a family. You deserve to be remembered— *I* want to remember you. In time, maybe I can be a part of your family."

He scoffs and looks away, but I can see the deep shift in his eyes.

Dahlia blinks away a tear, gripping one of the Ferris wheel car bars. "Dorian," she chokes. "Every-thing Queen Sally says is true. We might be from Halloween Town, but this is our home, and I love it as fiercely as you do. Nothing would please me more than returning here to run the kingdom again at your side. But we cannot force the remembered townspeople to stay."

"And if they all leave?" he scoffs, fear snapping in the high notes of his voice. "If every single townsperson is remembered, and it's only you and me at the end?"

"It won't be," says Dahlia. "As the world changes, characters will rise and fall out of favor. Stories will be forgotten. Holidays will fall by the wayside. Animals will go extinct. All those forgotten creatures will need a place to go—they'll need the haven we first envisioned."

Scorch clears his throat, a tuft of smoke slipping from his nostrils. "For a long time, Scorch felt lost. Like Scorch didn't belong anywhere, even in his own town. Scorch could have used a place like Shadow Town."

Dahlia pats him fondly on his horn nubs, then turns back to her brother with tears glistening in her eyes. "Do you hear that? This place could be a refuge for anyone in their time of need, whether they've been forgotten or not. You've harmed people, but this could mend the past. In time, people will understand and forgive you. Please, brother. Let's rule this town together as we did in the old days."

For the span of a few heartbeats, I wait. I study

every detail of Dorian's face, looking for tiny cracks in his cold exterior, where his love and dedication for his people can shine through. His mismatched eyes waver; his long throat tightens with a swallow.

An image hits me. *Sitting cross-legged under the laboratory table, Dorian showing me how to wind up the spinning toy, a rare laugh on his lips.*

I don't know if it's a true memory. Maybe it's just my imagination. But I like to believe it's true.

The Clown with the Tear-Away Face accidentally knocks into one of the mirrors, and it angles the beam of sunlight directly into Dorian's face.

He scowls and shades his eyes. "I'd dig my own grave before I tore down the golden gate. Shadow Town residents belong in *Shadow Town*."

Dahlia's shoulders slump, her chin falling to her chest. Her hand trembles on the bar, and I can feel the words on the tip of her tongue—the urge to continue trying to convince her brother—but she, too, swallows.

"He's more like our father than he'd like to admit," she says softly, turning to Jack and me. "Dr. Finkelstein wanted to control us. Abuse like that doesn't just fade. It festers. I managed to follow a different path, but Dorian inherited the worst of the doctor."

"Give it time," Jack says, which surprises me so

much that I look him up and down, wondering if my headstrong husband has switched places with someone else. "One thing I've learned is that people change. *I've* changed—especially when I met Sally. She might have been made of cloth, but she showed me that patience is strength."

I smile up at him with love bright in my eyes. "I agree. The world is changing, and some of us will adapt faster than others. As rulers, we need to show compassion."

I turn to my parents with a soft nod. They've always had so much to say about what I should do and who I should be. How to lead, how to love, how to forgive. I might not agree with every word they've ever spoken, but that's the beauty of being my own person—with my own kingdom.

Compassion. That was their refrain, and now, it's mine, too.

They wrap their arms around each other, all tender smiles.

"And now, as princess, the fate of this town falls to me," says Dahlia, stroking her chin. Her eyes slowly light up. "There's a portion of All Souls Castle we can close off, where Dorian can roam somewhat freely and care for himself without risk of escape. Perhaps in a hundred years, he will learn what it truly means to be forgotten, and he'll be ready then to rule as a true leader should." She motions to two jackrabbits in guard uniforms, signaling for them to stand guard at his Ferris wheel cage. "Now, Sally, Jack, let me escort you—all of you—back to the gates so you can finally go home."

Two badgers tromp in carrying a litter decorated with gauzy silver fabric that makes it look swaddled in shadows. They lower it to the ground, and a third badger holds out a hand to help Dahlia climb into the chair. They lift it on the count of three and march along the path back to Shadow Town's center, followed by Thorna's herd of centaurs and the motley collection of Shadow Town residents.

But Thorna glances back at me, grins, and comes over to give me a hug. Her tawny curls tickle my cheeks.

I pull back, gently ruffling her curls. "Where will you and your herd go now? Will you stay in Shadow Town?"

"We'll have to see what hand fate deals us," she says, eyes big and determined, ready for whatever may come. "If people remember us, then maybe we'll be able to return to our home. Our realm. But if they don't . . ." She turns back toward her herd, where her parents patiently wait for her before following the others. "If they don't, then we'll stay here. Same goes for the other Shadow Town residents. Anyone who stays behind will reshape this place, under Princess Dahlia's guidance. Into a *new* home."

The note of hope in her voice warms me, and I give her another hug.

Once she's returned to her herd, Jack and I join the procession, hand in hand. My parents, all of Halloween Town's residents, and the townspeople from other realms fall in line, too, all taking up a melody led by the members of Halloween Town's band.

When we reach the center of town, Dahlia climbs down from the litter with grace—no longer the reclusive observer she's been for years, but someone who's ready to claim her place as a ruler. After a slow, deliberate breath, shadows surge to her fingertips as she sets Dorian's key ring on a block of carbonado. She summons powers she's kept buried for too long. Powers far greater than a humble hedge witch's.

Powers of a Shadow Princess.

With one whispered word on her lips, the shadows harden around the key ring.

"Now," she says to the crowd, "no one locks that gate again—and the keys stay here, encased, to remind us of it."

For a beat, silence hangs heavy—then the crowd

erupts in cheers as Shadow Town's trapped souls finally embrace their newfound freedom.

The residents from different towns break off, each passing through the golden gates on their way back to Tooth Town, Weather Town, Christmas Town, or wherever their paths lead. We say our tearful good-byes to my parents as they return to Dream Town, and then Jack and I turn to face our own townspeople.

There are the witches, spiderwebs clustered in their mossy hair. Lock, Shock, and Barrel, their pockets stuffed with crystals pilfered from the caverns. Dr. Finkelstein, holding Jewel's hand. And all the rest of our friends who look to us to lead them home.

So we step through the golden gates and don't look back.

EPILOGUE

Halloween Night

"Oh, Jack, what a night!" I tumble out of the zombie-horse-drawn carriage that carried us for our holiday travels, the taste of candy corn still coating the tip of my tongue. I feel utterly alive from my head to the stitches holding on my toes—light as a crow feather from the success of another Halloween night.

"Exceptionally frightful, indeed!" Jack steps down from the carriage, grinning like a madman, giddy from the evening's escapades. For this year's costume, he wears his usual Pumpkin King attire, regal as always.

I laugh, even as the first ruffles of unease curl in my chest.

Because truth be told . . . the holiday wasn't frightful. Not really.

Not the way it used to be.

But tonight is a celebration, regardless. We've saved our town. We've triumphed over shadows. We *need* this. The rest of the Halloween Town scarers follow us through the gates in their own carriages and wagons, cackling loud enough to spook the bats that roost in the cornfield. The bats take off across the full harvest moon.

Jack pulls me into a waltz across the town square, singing *da-da-da-dum* as I hold up the hem of my gray chiffon-and-gauze gown. I wore it as part of a vampire bride costume, complete with a spiderweb veil that I lost somewhere during our journey, but as he spins me in front of the reflective window on the Cobweb Café, I can't help a jolt at how much it looks like I'm floating on a cluster of dark gray storm clouds.

I pause, memories flooding back of shadows in the dark, dark deep.

But then one of the vampires pops a bottle of blood-red punch with a bang, and I flinch.

Around me, everyone laughs and sings and clinks

glasses. The scars of what we survived–Prince Dorian, and everyone's imprisonment in Shadow Town–are fading.

And maybe that's precisely the problem.

Many months have passed since Prince Dorian stole everyone I love away to Shadow Town. Dahlia and I have grown close in that time, bound by our past, slowly reviving memories of our childhood together. We most like to stroll through Recluse Woods to visit old Abner and Lewin, to dust their creaky bones and laugh at their groan-worthy jokes.

Dr. Finkelstein traveled back to Dream Town to finish out the rest of his community service. Once, we ran into him while I was showing Dahlia the Lullaby Library. After some awkward greetings, he suggested we check out a book on the astrophysics of wishing stars, and it opened the door for us to swap book recommendations. I suspect Dahlia may never call him father again, but at least she seems at peace.

We've even tried to rehabilitate Dorian while he's imprisoned in the east wing of All Souls Castle. He is my brother, after all. And I continue to learn a thing or two about compassion. I have my parents to thank for that–because for all our ups and downs, we're growing, and at least we grow *together*.

Once a month, a different realm's ruler travels to

Shadow Town to share a meal with Dorian and discuss what it means to lead. Dorian flatly refused to meet with the first visitor, Dream Town's Governor—my mother.

By the second month, however, he was so stir-crazy that he grumbled his way through a meal with Father Time. I invited Lady Lore for the third month, suspecting the two ever-serious leaders would connect over the role of stories in their realms, and indeed, Dorian warmed up to her sentiments on aging fairy tale characters.

Since then, he's had productive conversations with Santa Claus and Queen Ruby Valentino about what real leadership looks like.

And another silver lining? A tourist from Chance Town brought a newspaper with the headline FORTUNA LUCKWELL STRIPPED OF MAYORAL TITLE AFTER CHEATING SCANDAL UNCOVERED. Beneath the headline is a black-and-white photograph of the couple whom I slipped Fortuna's duplicate entry forms to as I was fleeing town.

So I guess, in the end, Fortuna learned the same lesson as Oogie Boogie. *Cheating never pays.*

Even with this newfound peace and safety, I can't shake the bone-deep worry that Halloween's spine is softening, weakening. *Being slowly forgotten.*

"Scorch! Luna! You made it!" A grin stretches across my face as I spot Luna riding atop the dragon's back, disguised as a cowgirl and her horse. Like last year, they stayed behind in Halloween Town to take care of the youngest monsters—including a roly-poly new undead baby born to the Mummy family.

Luna's yarn eyebrows shoot up to her hairline. "How was it?"

I pin on a wide smile and don't tell her my fears. "The Wolfman growled loud enough to spook an entire movie theater into spilling their popcorn!"

"Excellent," Luna says with a sly sparkle in her eyes. "I'm glad it went well, because this isn't just any after-party. I have a gift for you. Well, not just me— all of your friends and fellow rulers contributed to get it, to commemorate your victory over the Shadow Prince. We've been working on it for some time."

I tilt my head, long eyelashes clinking together. "A gift?" A sly look cuts across my face as I turn to Jack. "Were *you* behind this?"

He holds up his bone hands with a perfectly inno- cent shake of his head, but I know my husband well enough to recognize the guilty twinkle in his eye hollows.

"This way!" Still riding Scorch, Luna grabs my wrist and nearly pulls me clean off the ground as she leads me to the center of the square. Before we left for Halloween, we stacked all the empty pumpkin crates here and covered them with a canvas tarp. Now that I peer closer, however, the shape beneath the tarp has changed.

Less boxy and more . . . lumpy.

Luna hops off Scorch's back to grab one corner of the tarp. Jack grips the other, unable to hide his corn-kernel grin. The town band quiets their music, and the rest of the Halloween Town revelers crowd in close.

"One," Luna says.

"Two," Jack counts.

"Three!" everyone shouts together.

They tug off the canvas, which flutters to the ground, revealing a majestic statue. It rises ten feet tall, carved of polished black obsidian and almost identical to the Villain Village statue of the rearing Night Mare—except in this version, I'm riding on the mare's back, one hand high in the air, clutching my needle-sword.

I press a soft linen hand to my mouth to hold in my gasp. A shiver of awe comes over me, tightening each of my stitches as I step forward to gently touch the statue with my fingertips.

"A beautiful nightmare," I say. "Terrifying in the best way."

I look around at the statue, at my monstrous friends, and a stitch pulls tight in my chest. *If only the world could see what I see, they'd never forget the true spirit of Halloween.*

The band starts up again, and the nearby doorways burst open. My mother and father spill out of Town Hall, followed by Ruby Valentino and Amore Buttercup, holding cups of chocolate champagne to toast me. From the Haunted Bed and Breakfast come elves and leprechauns and star-spangled patriots waving Fourth of July sparklers. Pearl and Cusp fly down from where they were hiding behind Town Hall's chimney, throwing armfuls of pearly white confetti over me—confetti that feels suspiciously hard, like some small creature's incisors. Soon, friends from across the holiday and ancient realms all gather around the statue, voices raised in a cheer.

"Long live the Pumpkin Queen!"

The words ring out, the night hums with magic, and I can feel Halloween Town alive around me— electric, mysterious, *mine.*

And maybe . . . just maybe . . . I know how to share this feeling with the world after all.

When Jack and I are finally able to step away from the party, my limbs are worn as a ragged old puppet's, but I still have stars dancing in my eyes. It's so late that morning light is breaking on the eastern horizon, but when we reach the fork in the path that leads home, my feet drift to a stop.

"Do you mind if we keep walking?" I ask Jack. "I'm not quite ready for bed."

"As you wish, my beautiful vampire bride." He brushes his thumb bone over the ruby-red paint across my neck, and I give a soft giggle.

We stroll, hand in hand, along the cemetery path. Like the soaring bats overhead, memories of the evening's adventures flit through my head. Beneath all the marvelous scares, something still unsettles me.

This year's Halloween was fun—maybe too fun. Everywhere I looked, there were glittering fairy costumes, superheroes with silly padded muscles, newborns dressed up like baby chicks. It was adorable. It was charming. It was . . . seriously concerning.

"Something on your mind, Sally?" Jack asks, looking at me askance.

I squeeze his hand. "I've been thinking about the

committee meeting we held back in the winter, back before everything went haywire. The Mayor's concern that everyone is forgetting Halloween's true purpose. That it's meant to be *scary*."

He nods, stroking his jawbone in quiet contemplation. There was a time when my over-excitable husband would have been bouncing off the stone walls, chasing one harebrained idea after another—and honestly, I adore his enthusiasm.

But tonight, he's more subdued, strolling at an easy pace as he gives a heavy sigh. "With all the trouble from Shadow Town, we had bigger priorities this year."

"That's just it," I say. "Halloween is meant to haunt people. To linger in their bones. To live in nightmares three hundred sixty-four days a year, until the next Halloween. I'm afraid if we let it drift too far into whimsy, people will forget its terrifying *heart*. We'll end up forgotten. We'll end up *just like* those lost souls in Shadow Town."

He stops. "But how do we guide the world back to us?"

There's a scuffle in the abandoned building to our right, and I turn to face it just as an owl family flies out the broken upper window. It's the former hospital—the one that housed so many of the ghosts who moved to Recluse Woods. Moonlight glows in the windows from the caved-in roof.

I rest a hand on Jack's chest, my first two fingers stained from the black paint on his wrist. "You said there was once a portal in the old hospital. What if we restored it?"

I gaze up at the ruined building with dreamy eyes, already imagining what it could be. "Let people from other worlds come here—into the heart of Halloween. Just once a year, on Halloween night, we'll open the portal. Visitors will stumble into our world without warning. And we'll give them a Halloween they'll *never* forget. The kind that rattles their souls all year long. The kind that makes them run home to their beds, recount tales at campfires, spread our lore far and wide."

Jack's grin is slow, wicked. "You mean . . . *really* scare them?"

I nod. "So they never forget. So *we* never forget."

He's quiet for a moment, fingers drumming against the rusted railing. "Sally," he murmurs, eyes aglow, "that might be the most ghoulishly brilliant idea I've ever heard. An idea only the Pumpkin Queen could come up with."

The idea buzzes through my head like a hundred

fireflies, and I can barely stay still, my fingers twitching, mind racing.

"The only problem is reopening the portal," Jack points out. "When it collapsed, no amount of hammers and nails could fix it. Time and space themselves broke. That kind of rupture needs more than tools. It needs someone who understands the very fabric of reality."

Gripping the iron railing around the abandoned site, I hesitate, eyeing the crumbling walls, the ruined roof, the broken windows. "Dr. Finkelstein. He's the only one who could do it."

Jack's mouth goes flat, his disdain for the scientist as evident as a cat's for a cold bath. "Do you really want to work with that madman again? He not only wronged you, he wronged Dahlia and Dorian. You could have grown up with siblings. Not . . . alone."

"He's the only one with enough scientific knowledge to open the portal," I say. "I'm not saying I'll ever forgive the doctor for what he did. He stole me from my home, kept me under lock and key, prevented me from getting to know Dorian and Dahlia. He doesn't get to erase that. But . . ." I glance up at the empty hospital. "He didn't have to help me create the star, Jack. He could have left me to fail. But he didn't. He chose to help. Not for himself—he didn't stand to gain much, given he'll spend the next ninety-eight years in Dream Town—but because he knew we were strongest together. As a team. As a *town*."

"What are you suggesting?"

I look up at the early morning stars. "What if we speak to my parents about transferring his Dream Town community service years into time working here in Halloween Town, instead?"

Jack's breath hitches.

I let out my own breath, slow and steady. "I don't want to carry Dr. Finkelstein like a ghost anymore. I've spent too long letting him be the shadows I'm afraid to look at. I know better now." I turn to the old hospital. "Halloween is changing, Jack. We have to fight for it. If we want Halloween to be scary, we need to get past our *own* fears. Use every resource—every person, even an awful old scientist—that we can."

Jack's eyes tip downward as he folds his hands over my arms, giving me his silent strength. "Oh, Sally."

"He'll never be family," I continue. "He'll never be a friend. But maybe he can be . . . well, maybe he can just be what we need. And maybe, after everything, that's enough."

"I have every confidence in you, my clever bride." Jack's voice is soft as moonlight, deep as the darkest cavern. He tips up my chin, getting black paint all over the both of us, but I couldn't possibly care less. "You know, with you in this costume, you might be in danger of making me fall in love with you all over again."

Our lips come together, slow and sweet, like we've captured the spark of a star between us. His hands cradle my face. For a moment, the wind in the trees and the owls overhead fall quiet—it's just us and our love knitted over time.

"Would you marry me all over again?" he asks, one corner of his mouth tipped in a playful grin.

"I would," I whisper. "I *do*."

He touches his forehead to mine. "I do," he echoes. "Now and forever."

ACKNOWLEDGMENTS

I have so many people to thank for their commitment to bringing more of Sally's adventures into the world.

The entire Disney and Penguin Random House team might as well have been sent from Dream Town: my editor, Hali Baumstein, who helped stitch every disjointed piece of this story together; designer and cover illustrator Gegham Vardanyan; design directors Kurt Hartman and Scott Piehl; illustration manager Jeff Clark; managing editor Rodger Weinfeld; copy editors Jennifer Black, Rachel Rivera, and Megan Speer-Levi; studio franchise reviewer Aileen O'Brien; Tim Burton Productions reviewers

Sadie Doherty, Brogan Porter, and Leah Gruber; and the global marketing and creative operations teams.

A huge thanks as well to the whole team at PRH: Britt Rubiano, Chris Angelilli, Wendy Loggia, Elizabeth Cervantes, Cindy Johnson, Bess Schelper, Colleen Fellingham, Tanya Mauler, Mike Meskin, Christine Kell, Troy Wallace, Patty Collins, Kerri Benvenuto, Jena DeBois, Mariana Batista, Elizabeth Ward, Meredith Wagner, Katie Halata, Madison Furr, Katherine Robertson, and Noreen Herits.

My gratitude as well goes to my fantastic literary agent, Barbara Poelle, who deserves a shiny crown herself.

Life is so much more interesting because of my husband, who hums the film's soundtrack while cooking, and my children, who shriek with glee whenever they see a Sally key chain or mug out in the wild and proudly tell everyone that it's "Mama's character."

And of course, my gratitude goes to Sally's true maker, the master of fright himself, Tim Burton.